CARNIVAL OF SINS

ALEXA O'BRIEN HUNTRESS BOOK 15

TRINA M. LEE

CARNIVAL OF SINS
Copyright 2019 by Trina M. Lee

All rights reserved. No part of this publication may be reproduced, stored in a retrieval system, or transmitted in any form or by any means, electronic, mechanical, recording or otherwise, without the prior written permission of the author.
Published in Canada

Editor
B. Leigh Hogan

Cover Artist
Marvin Lee Cover Design

Published by
Trina M. Lee

This is a work of fiction. The characters, incidents and dialogues in this book are of the author's imagination and are not to be construed as real. Any resemblance to actual events or persons, living or dead, is completely coincidental.

CHAPTER ONE

"Relax, Lex. I've got it. I'll watch this place like a hawk." Sipping from a blood-red cocktail, Jez settled in against the squishy scarlet couch. "Damn this is a sweet couch. Probably don't want to bring a black light anywhere near it though."

I rolled my eyes at her remark but didn't argue because she was probably right. "I don't want anyone to know I'm gone if possible. I'm hoping to be back before word gets out. Three nights. That's what I told Arys. Then we're out and it's Jenner's problem."

Leaving made me anxious. Three nights in Las Vegas was already too many. I hoped it would be a quick visit. Just long enough for Arys to lay the smackdown on this Loric guy, so we could get back home.

A pissed off demon queen had escaped her prison. For now Lilah was God only knew where, but eventually she'd be here. For me. I couldn't stand the thought of her showing up when I was away, finding those I loved instead. Left behind. Unprotected.

"We'll be fine here. All of us. We're not entirely defenseless. It's cool." With a shrug that was as chill as the easy vibe she exuded, Jez slapped my knee. "Seriously. Vegas is important too. It's good to form a stronghold there. Help Jenner get his playground back, and we'll hold down the fort here."

Letting my gaze stray around the interior of my nightclub, I eyed the many patrons and gave a tight nod. "I know. Falon can be here in a heartbeat if you need him."

"We won't need him," Jez scoffed. Pursing her painted red lips, she sneered at the bar where the fallen angel in question did shots with a few frat guys. "Come on, Lex. Smudge and me, we've got this. Keep Falon busy with you. We could use a break. He's a domineering asshole."

Laughter spilled from my lips. When tasked with Circle of the Veil business, Falon was an especially giant pain in the ass. In all honesty, he went a little darker than I usually saw him. Serious to the point of vicious. Although, I suspected he knew more about the price of failure than I did. I hoped to keep it that way.

Though I'd never say so to him, Falon's promise to go between cities and maintain a presence in both was the only reason I'd agreed to go on this trip. As long as Lilah and Salem were out there, no time would be a safe time to leave my city.

I was all packed and ready to go, my bags already in the car. Our flight left just after midnight, giving us enough time to land and get to our hotel before sunrise. But first, a brief meeting with my progeny, Agent Thomas Briggs. Who was late.

If he didn't arrive soon, he'd miss my window of opportunity, and I'd be pissed. I'd agreed to give him blood before I left, to ease his sick craving for me. Only because he was still seeing my sister and I didn't want her on the receiving end if he lost control. Unfortunately, their relationship was the main reason I couldn't erase the mistake that was Briggs from this city. This country. This planet.

"All right." I nodded, eyeing Falon. Studying his profile as he laughed and tossed back a shot, I tore my gaze away before he could feel it. "I'll keep him busy. But if anything happens here at all, the second it does, you call and I send him. Promise me."

Falon had been sticking closer than I liked him to be. He claimed it was his job as my partner, that The Circle of the Veil expected it due to the danger of Lilah and Salem being MIA. But I knew it was far more about Bane for him than it was about the immortal twins.

My fallen lover's past spewed a terrifying foe into my present. I still wasn't sure who I should fear more, Lilah or Bane. However, I'd faced Lilah before. I understood her power.

But Bane? Everything about him felt wrong.

"I promise," Jez repeated, telling me what I wanted to hear. "Everything will be fine. I won't even have a party while you're gone. Don't want to trash the place like Kale."

We shared a bittersweet laugh. We'd always miss him, but we knew he'd found the peace that had eluded him for many long centuries.

"I still don't know everything that went on here while we were in Vegas the first time," I laughed, finding comfort in the memory now.

"I'm kind of bummed that I'm not coming this time." Jez tucked a golden curl behind an ear and pouted. "Don't have too much fun without me."

"Never," I swore, crossing my heart. "It's going to be a total sausage fest. And as much as that appeals to the vampy, succubus part of me, it's going to suck without you."

She leaned forward to set her empty glass on the coffee table. "Damn right it will. As much as I'm going to miss the fun though, I'd rather stay here with Smudge anyway." She giggled and blushed, twisting a lock of hair around a finger.

Jez and Smudge had made their relationship official not so long ago, as in, they were now sleeping together. They'd held off. After playing the field for so long, Jez wanted to make sure there was more to their relationship than just sex.

So far they seemed like a perfect match. The serious, dark-haired vampire balanced out the feisty, golden-haired necromantic shifter. I'd seen Jez in love before, but I'd never seen her glow like this.

"Yeah, I'll bet," I teased. "Just don't let all the sex keep you from playing watchdog."

"Says the succubus who can't go a night without getting plowed," she snickered, raising a hand for another when a waiter passed by.

A familiar vibe stiffened my spine. Briggs. I glanced up to find him striding through the front entry with a scowl.

"Hey, I don't get plowed every night," I admonished with a finger wag. "And don't say plowed. That's so unsexy."

Jez pretended to seriously consider my request. "Is banged better? How about humped? That's always a good one."

"Not hump. Never that." Her laughter rang out as I made a face of disgust. I shoved to my feet. "Now that you've put that in my head, I need to go have a little one on one with Briggs. If I'm not back in five minutes, come find me. Seriously."

I caught Briggs's eye and jerked my head toward the back, expecting him to follow. He did. As I weaved through patrons to the back hall where the private rooms were, I didn't look back to see how close he'd drawn. I felt Falon's gaze upon me as I went.

My office sat at the end of the long hall, so I passed many rooms to get there. Tendrils of sex-charged energy and vampire power drifted lazily about, visible only to the supernatural eye. Like vines they grew and writhed, outlining doors and snaking down the hall. Passing through created a rush all its own.

Arys and Shaz were taking care of a few things at Doghead before heading to the airport. Jenner and Willow already waited there. I had no idea where Gabriel was, but since he'd begged to come, I figured he'd be ready to board with the rest of us.

Needing to take care of one specific thing before heading out, I was here, luring the vampire I'd made into my office. I entered the room and sat on the edge of my desk, legs swinging. A moment later Briggs entered, purposely leaving the door open.

It was a nice effort, but ultimately it wouldn't do shit to stop us if things spiraled out of control. So far they never had and I doubted they ever would. Sharing a lover with my sister was pretty much at the top of my 'Fuck That Shit' list.

"Where's Juliet?" I asked, skipping any bullshit small talk. "Does she know you're here?"

I didn't need her bursting in on us. She'd shown nothing but discomfort regarding Briggs's tie to Arys's bloodline through me. Except for when his fangs were buried in her flesh. My little sister had become a bite junkie. Thanks to Arys.

"She's at my place planning a romantic evening. She thinks I'm on a wine and snack run. For her, obviously." Standing stiffly in the center of the room, Briggs folded his arms across his wide chest. "So let's make this fast."

He'd been in my presence for seconds, and I already wanted to send him packing with my foot in his ass. Eyes narrowed, I growled, "I took time to be here tonight too. If you'd prefer to be on your way, by all means leave, and take your attitude with you. But if you lose it on my sister, I'll watch you burn in the morning sun."

His jaw twitched and he rocked on his heels. I got the feeling he struggled to withhold his true response. Somehow he choked it down and through clenched teeth said, "Got it, O'Brien. Can we proceed?"

Briggs was antsy, like he couldn't stand completely still. There was a spike to his energy. High strung. Stretched to a dangerous limit.

Shit. I'd have to start giving him blood more often than I had been. Making him wait longer stretches than the others was torment that he deserved and I enjoyed dishing out. However, with Juliet's safety on the line now, I'd have to rein in my torment.

"Yeah. Here." I thrust my wrist out. "But there's a few things we're going to discuss before either of us leave here."

His gaze fell to my wrist, to the pulse pumping there. As he reacted to my mere presence, the frequency surrounding him grew to a high-pitched whine. Briggs was hard up for my blood, hurting for it more than he wanted to reveal. He couldn't hide that from me.

When he reached for my wrist, I jerked it back out of reach. "Just one thing, Briggs. Going forward, if this shit gets to be more than you can handle, tell me. Immediately. I won't do anything to put Juliet's safety in jeopardy."

After he met my gaze and nodded, I let him take my wrist. It wasn't what he wanted. It never was for any of them. They craved closeness. Going for the jugular while they pressed their hard on inside me, that's what my vampires hungered for. Even Briggs.

If possible, he hated it more than I did. Holding my wrist tight, he closed his eyes and breathed in the scent of me. A slight tremor racked his body. A battle went on inside him. What I wouldn't have given to get a glimpse inside his mind right then.

Dressed all in black, hair short and face clean shaven, everything about Briggs's appearance screamed federal agent. Even his damn shoes were squeaky clean enough to see my reflection. But when he bared his fangs and those brown eyes snapped open, he was something else entirely.

And I kind of loved it. Because I had made it.

With a small and, I grudgingly admit, sexy snarl, Briggs bit deep. Sharp and fast, causing me to suck in a breath between my teeth. I bit back any gasp or noise, fighting to stay silent. Any and all reactions were going to feed the swelling charge.

It wasn't easy. Not with the burn of fangs buried in my vein or the sudden rise of heat between us. I swallowed around the knot forming in my throat as I watched his mouth move on my skin. I was both disgusted and mildly aroused.

Guilt slithered through me. It wasn't the incubus charge that I enjoyed but having Briggs at my mercy. Wrong. It was so damn wrong. I knew that. Part of me just didn't care.

His hold on me tightened painfully. Like he knew what I felt and hoped to punish me for it. When the tip of his tongue flicked sensually over the wound, I tensed. Before I could pull away, he released me.

Pupils a yawning abyss of black, Briggs licked the blood from his lips. Already his energy had changed, humming steady without that frantic, frazzled buzz of needing a hit of hybrid blood.

"How long?" I asked, giving my bitten wrist a cursory once over. His technique had improved. "How long before it starts to get bad?"

Raging with lust and a power surge, Briggs paced out into the hallway for a moment. He rubbed both hands over his face.

I waited right where I sat, perched atop my desk. This part was always awkward. Now he'd go home amped up on me and do my sister.

How did it even get to this level of fucked up?

Briggs strode back into the room pretending like he wasn't inwardly trying to talk his boner down. "About a week or two, give or take. It varies."

Nodding, I considered this information. It fit with what I knew from the others. I'd forced Briggs to go longer than that. Hell, I'd done it to Jenner and Kale too.

Feeling uneasy, I forced myself to hold his gaze. "I want some things to change between us. We're never going to see eye to eye, but we both love the same person. Not only that, but I want to do right by all of you. I don't want a reputation as some mad queen tormenting my own people. Because you are my people now, Briggs. And as long as Juliet loves you, you get to live."

"So if she comes to her senses and drops me," he dared to ask, his expression hard as steel, "you kill me?"

"We'll cross that bridge if we come to it. In the meantime, I need your word that if anything goes down while I'm gone, you'll protect Juliet. Above anything else." I searched his hard face, taut jaw, and the deep lines of a man who frowned a lot etched between his eyes. He loved her. I knew that.

"Without question." Briggs eyed me suspiciously. "Is there something going on that perhaps she and I should know about?"

They'd been told as much as they needed to know. Everyone tied to me in any way knew about Salem and Lilah. Some of the details were kept private, such as the fact that the Shya stone was back in my possession. Technically. It had been hidden on hallowed ground. They also didn't know about Bane, nor did they need to.

"You know all you need to know. I won't be gone long if I can help it. Just a few days." An uneasy tension rolled through me. That was the plan, but when had my plans ever worked out?

Briggs turned to leave, like he couldn't stand to be in the same room as me a moment longer. "Anything else?"

"Actually, yes." I hopped off the desk but didn't approach him. I didn't need to. "Just remember, Briggs. My safety is your safety. There's nothing but me standing between you and a demon queen intent on reclaiming her empire in this city. An empire that dwells within the FPA property."

I paused, needing this all to sink in. With a grave nod, Briggs asked, "What do you want from me, O'Brien?"

"Keep the city safe. Work with The Circle of the Veil rather than against it. We all have the same goal." Hesitating, I gnawed my lip for a moment, weighing my next words. "If anything happens to Juliet, anything at all, it's over for you."

Briggs's jaw twitched. Anger flowed freely from him. Turning on a well-polished heel, he stalked from the room. "Have a nice trip."

CHAPTER TWO

A brilliant mess of color lit the Vegas skyline. Flashing neon signs adorned the Strip from ground level to the top of the many hotels. It was the calling card of a city that thrived on those seeking a good time.

As we shoved through the glass doors into the main lobby of Caesars Palace, a sense of nostalgia hit me. It left me momentarily disoriented until I realized it was Arys's emotion, not mine. His tie to this city ran far deeper than mine.

A glance at him revealed a perfect poker face. It had been born and perfected here. I glanced down at our clasped hands, revelling in our renewed connection. Power crackled along our entwined fingers. Solid and strong. Unbreakable.

After so much unrest between us, I didn't think I'd ever get used to this. Feeling whole. Complete. It was surreal.

Arys reluctantly released me and approached the front desk to check-in under whatever fake name he'd used to book our suite. The rest of us hung back near the fountain with the Three Graces statue.

At this time of night, the lobby was empty. Electronic bells and buzzers carried from the casino around the corner. The three am crowd had hit the slots. Of course, they'd probably started as the dinner time crowd. Possibly even the breakfast crowd.

Jenner paced a circle around the fountain while the rest of us stood there checking our phones and taking in the massive lobby. On his fourth time around, I stuck out a foot to stop him, smirking when he stumbled over it.

"Chill out, Jenner," I said when he shot me a glower upon catching himself. "I get that you're nervous, but you're starting to make my skin prickle."

"This is my city, Alexa," he snapped. "Don't tell me how to feel."

I held up both hands in surrender and made an exaggerated face of shock. "Whoa. No need to be so testy."

"Tell me that again after you meet Loric." Jenner could barely say the guy's name without shuddering in displeasure. Who was this vampire that had run Jenner out of his own nightclub? I probably shouldn't make light of this situation.

His anxiety continued to pick at me. The heavy infectious vibe tormented me in the worst of ways. I had enough of my own problems back home without the weight of Jenner's added on. Until I met Loric for myself, I couldn't let the unknown vampire get to me. He hadn't earned it.

Extending a hand to Jenner, I beckoned him with a head tilt. He eyed my hand with suspicion. Pain in the ass vampire. If I let a slip of allure flow freely, every vampire in Vegas would react. This was just for Jenner.

After wiggling my fingers in his face, he snatched my hand in irritation. The strength of his fear and worry slammed into me, and I gasped. With some focus it eased off, and I soon pushed it back. "You've got to get out of your head." I pulled Jenner closer, into my personal space. Taking command of his energy, I aligned it with my own and drenched him in a relaxing, albeit sensual, calm. "Relax a little. It's almost sunrise. There's nothing we can do until dark anyway."

"This is manipulation." Jenner stated the obvious, but his eyes glassed over and his tone lacked contempt.

"Yeah, well you're starting to make my skin crawl. If things are about to get as bad as you think, then you might as well enjoy the calm while you can." Another erotically charged push and I had him.

Jenner's ice blue gaze fell to my lips.

A second before he kissed me, I stopped him with a hand on his chest. I was very much aware of Gabriel's intense stare and Willow's sudden need to check out a piece of hideous art down the hall, as far as he could get from us without disappearing entirely. Shaz ambled over to where Arys stood at the front desk.

I caught Jenner's face with a hand and forced him to meet my eyes. "Everything will be okay. We're here with you. We won't leave until you're ready for us to. All right?"

I still planned to be out of Sin City within three days. Hopefully Loric wouldn't botch that up, but I intended to keep that promise to Jenner. He'd been there for Arys and me, despite their rocky relationship. Sure, he wasn't my favorite person. Not even close. But he was one of mine, and as his queen, I owed him comfort and protection.

I owed it to all of them.

He blinked slowly, heavily under my spell. Drawing me into his arms, Jenner buried his face in my hair and breathed in my scent. "What if I can't stay here? What if I'm stuck living in your god-awful city?"

It didn't take long for Jenner to remind me why he wasn't my favorite person. He sought out my neck, his mouth on my skin. I shoved him away before he could make a stupid move in public. He wasn't in his right mind.

"There's a whole world out there. Go wherever the hell you want." Easing off on the manipulative touch, I put space between us.

Arys was still at the desk. I grew impatient, wanting to get into the safety of our suite.

Stuffing his hands into his jeans pockets, Jenner shivered as my touch fell away. "You made sure I can't be more than a short plane ride away from you for long. Traveling the world isn't really an option anymore, is it?"

"Guess you got me there. But that's still a lot of ground." I bent down to fetch my shoulder bag where I'd set it down by the fountain with the rest of our luggage. "I'm here, Jenner. Arys and I, we both are. So give us credit for that much at least."

He looked like he wanted to say something more but decided against it, as he scrubbed a hand through his bleached-blond hair.

Arys and Shaz came back with room keys, saving us from the awkwardness that had settled. It took greater effort to connect with Jenner than any other man in my inner circle. I didn't know how to change that.

Jenner grabbed his bags and stalked on ahead without waiting for us. He needed our help and he hated it.

"I haven't seen him this tightly wound in decades," Arys remarked, watching him go. "Probably since that whole marrying his fiancée fiasco."

With an eyeroll, I grabbed the handle of my suitcase and followed Jenner, rolling the case along behind me. "Can we not rehash that little incident again? I'm so over it."

Carnival of Sins

Arys grinned, revealing fangs. "You and me both."

Listening to this, Shaz tried and failed to stifle a laugh. He slung his large duffel bag onto his back and nudged Arys with an elbow. "A Vegas vampire wedding that ended in chaos? You don't say. Must be a rite of passage or something in this city."

"You have no idea, pup."

After a short ride in the elevator, we arrived at our suite. Because we didn't know what we were dealing with and there was safety in numbers, we were all rooming together. We stepped into a living room with an attached dining area and a bedroom off to each side. The master had a king-sized bed, and the second room had two double beds, each complete with a lavish bathroom. A tacky chandelier hung above the table, and a matching sofa and chairs had been arranged in front of the television. Stock artwork adorned the walls. Typical hotel suite. Nice but impersonal and humming with the residual energy of the group who'd stayed there before us.

Pretty similar to the suite we'd occupied during our last stay in Sin City, I decided.

I wasn't a fan of hotels. Too soulless and a little dirty. I mean, could they ever be really clean?

Jenner dropped his bags in the middle of the living room and went to gaze out the floor-to-ceiling window at the Las Vegas Strip below. Willow and Gabriel checked out the second bedroom. Shaz dragged my bags along with his to our room, leaving me to follow Jenner's gaze out the window. For just a moment we were alone together in the living room. The Eiffel Tower across the street at Paris stood against the sky in our direct view. Paired with the Bellagio fountain, it was the perfect Strip view.

Jenner had likely seen this city from every angle. It was nothing new to him. Brow furrowed, he gnawed his bottom lip and stared down the street.

I approached with a hand slightly raised as I considered touching his heavily tattooed arm. "Jenner? We've got this. You know that, right?"

Without turning to look at me, he flung up a hand to ward me off. "I need some distance, Alexa. Being in here with you is killing me already. I can smell that bite."

Jerking to a stop, I covered Briggs's bite on my wrist with my other hand as if that would make a difference. Okay, so maybe I hadn't fully thought this whole rooming together thing through. If everyone was hurting for a taste of me, they wouldn't be at the top of their game. I'd have to fix that.

"Sorry. I'm not going to leave you hanging, all right? But I need to ask you something." Keeping my distance, I waited for him to meet my gaze before continuing. I wanted to search those frosty blues. "How long after you take my blood before it starts to get bad? I mean, really bad."

Jenner's stare was cold as ice as it slid over me, hovering between my neck and my cleavage before returning to my eyes. "There's never a time when I don't want you. I'd say I can push it a few weeks or so before it really starts to eat at me. Although fucking you didn't help."

Someone was bitter.

I didn't know if I should feel insulted. "Is that something we should take off the table then? It doesn't have to happen again. Maybe it's better if it doesn't. Tell me what you want, Jenner."

A noise from the bedroom drew his gaze over my shoulder. When nobody appeared he softly muttered, "Since when do you care what I want?"

His attitude was understandable. Arys and me, we'd made Jenner's life hell in the last year. Some of it he'd deserved. Not all of it though. I felt bad about how much torment I'd put him through. An apology wouldn't be enough, but maybe my presence here would be. For now.

"I know I'm not your favorite person." I kept my voice low as well. There were keen ears all over the suite. "But I'm trying here. We're all tightly bound, whether we like it or not, so we can make the best of it or forever fight amongst ourselves."

He eyed me with thinly veiled skepticism. Jerking a thumb toward the master bedroom, Jenner shook his blond head. "It doesn't matter what I want. Arys would never be cool with it."

"This isn't about him. This is me asking what you want from this. From me. When you're ready to share whatever that is, I'm all ears." A few slow steps backward carried me away from him. As I turned to leave the room, his hand landed on my shoulder.

"I want my city back." A gentle squeeze of my shoulder turned into Jenner trailing a hand down my arm to seize my wrist. Tugging it close, he sniffed at what remained of the small bite.

"And the part Arys would never be cool with?" I prodded, trying to ignore the tingle when he pressed his mouth to my skin.

Jenner's eyes closed as he savored the many sensations awakened within him. We had mere seconds before someone interrupted. Still, he took a few moments before admitting, "I wouldn't say no to a little more one-on-one time with you. If you want to, of course." A shred of doubt filled his voice.

His eyes snapped open. He pulled away as Arys and Shaz entered the room. I suspected Jenner's worry about his city was to blame for his pissy mood the last several days. Weeks even. If I could take the edge off for him, I'd be happy to do so, but was that all he really wanted?

One thing I'd learned recently was that though several of the men linked to me would never love me, nor did I seek that from them, they still had the same needs that I had. Needs that, as their queen, I felt responsible to meet because I'd forced those twisted desires upon them. Seeing as I gained from my connection to each of them, it just made sense that they should gain something too.

Arys eyed Jenner for a moment, sensing the mood in the room. "Everything okay?"

"Sure." Jenner shrugged and returned his cold stare to the street beyond the window. "Just taking a look at my city before Loric runs me out of it for good. God forbid I have to go back to that cold-ass fucking city you now call home."

To be fair, it was only cold during the winter. We had beautiful summers. Although I supposed that meant nothing to the desert-dwelling vampire.

Another wave of nostalgia hit me when Arys joined Jenner at the window. They had deep ties to this place. Ties I could only understand through my affinity to my own home town. Vegas and I had a love-hate relationship. I tried to love it, for Arys, but it just fucking hated me regardless.

"Loric is not taking over this city," Arys admonished, watching the endless stream of traffic down below. "Whatever he's up to, we'll shut it down."

Without a word, Jenner disappeared into the second bedroom, taking his dropped things with him.

Watching him go, Shaz gave his platinum head a shake. "Why do I feel like there's too much about this Loric guy that we don't know? Care to enlighten us, Arys? Who the hell is this guy really?"

Arms crossed, Arys tore his focus from the window's view and considered the request. Head tilted to one side, he studied our white wolf with blatant hunger. Despite our rebalance holding the worst of his nature in check, Arys was never sated for long. Especially when it came to Shaz or me.

Regardless, he and Jenner were obviously antsy about being in Vegas now. Because they knew something we didn't?

Arys caved under the pressure of our scrutiny. "Let me put it this way, if Hurst is the Adam of our bloodline, then Loric and Harley were his Cain and Abel."

"Not off to the best start but continue." I perched on the arm of the couch. "Wait a minute. Hurst told me our bloodline didn't start with him. How can he be the Adam?"

When Willow and Gabriel joined us in the living room, Arys waited until we were all settled to continue. "Nobody knows who Hurst's sire is. Or was. It's a secret not even Harley knew, and he was Hurst's favorite. So much so that Loric tried to kill him. Several times."

Shaz and I exchanged a look as an ominous feeling crept in. "But they started the blood ring together back in the day, right?"

"At Hurst's insistence. It was a nonstop battle for control between Loric and Harley. Only when it got so bad that Loric tried and failed to lock Harley on a rooftop to fry in the morning sun did Hurst step in." Arys paused, his gaze straying to the tiny hallway Jenner had disappeared down. "Hurst forced Loric out of the country. Off the continent, last I heard."

"Now Harley is dead, and Loric is back to claim what's his," I stated the obvious, mulling this over. "How bad can it be? He's just one vampire, right?"

"How bad can it be?" Arys repeated, a shoulder lifted in a lazy half shrug. "I guess we'll soon find out."

CHAPTER THREE

A few hours before the desert sun would set, I lounged in the king-sized bed with Shaz stretched out beside me. He'd been dozing on and off throughout the day. I'd tried, but other than a small catnap, sleep had eluded me.

With the heavy curtains drawn closed, the room was dark aside from the glow of a bedside lamp and the television quietly playing *The Hangover*. Because it was never not on somewhere in this hotel. I secretly thought it was hilarious though and giggled in spite of myself at Stu and his over the top dramatics.

At my insistence everyone had spent the day inside the suite. Vampires didn't need as much sleep as humans, and I knew there were far more entertaining ways to spend the day downstairs in the casino than up here locked away in the suite.

But it was safer this way. Loric likely had eyes on the airport. He might know we were here. Either way, we needed time to reach out to Roscoe, Jenner's right hand here in Vegas, and figure out our next move.

The door opened and closed softly as Arys entered from the fancy bathroom across the hall from our room. A towel slung around his hips, black hair damp, he graced me with that sexy smile.

"You and this movie, Alexa," he laughed. Tugging the towel free, he used it to give his hair a rub, leaving me with a hell of a view.

"Movie?" I sat up straighter in the bed, using the padded headboard to support me as I ogled Arys's tight body. "What movie?"

The towel landed over the back of a chair in the small seating area near the window. Riveted, I studied my dark vampire. From the mess of wet raven-black hair to the firm planes of his chest, down his taut abs to the smattering of hair that beckoned me to seek the treasure below.

I was pretty sure an incubus vampire was always half erect at the very least. He allowed me a moment to enjoy the visual before quirking a brow, mischief in his deep blues. "I love it when you look at me like that."

"Like what?" I coaxed, running my tongue suggestively over my lower lip.

"Like you'll never be able to get enough of me." Watching the delicate motion of my tongue, Arys edged toward the bed. "Like I feel every damn time I look at you."

The smoldering blue fire in his eyes nailed me right between the legs, but the genuine emotion in his words dove deeper. To my most sacred heart of hearts. The place I shared only with my dark flame.

Arys was my everything. He was my other half, a vital piece of me. Together we were something else entirely. We'd gone to hell and back for each other. I strongly suspected we would again.

"Pretty sure there's no such thing as enough as far as you're concerned," I said appreciatively.

Each step Arys took was perfectly placed and timed. Each one meant to drive me a little crazy for him. It worked. I threw back the blanket to invite him into the bed.

Shaz stirred beside me and mumbled into his pillow, "Pretty sure I'd have to agree with that."

I scooted closer to him so Arys could slip in beside me. His energy hummed with contentment as he eyed Shaz and I in turn, deciding who he wanted to start with. "Can't help but notice the two of you are in various states of dress while I am not."

Arys was all kinds of naked next to my t-shirt and panty clad self. On my other side our white wolf wore only a pair of low-slung boxer shorts. He stretched until something popped, then groaned in satisfaction.

"Not a good idea, Arys." My protests were weak as he brushed my hair aside and leaned in to kiss my neck. "Not until I give the others blood."

They were much too close. Any power Arys and I called would ripple through them, driving their hunger.

His lips found the silver feather etched onto my neck, and I tensed when he nipped at my skin. Though he hadn't said much in the weeks since Falon had marked me, I knew Arys wasn't thrilled with it.

"So get them in here," Arys murmured against my ear. "We'll make a party of it."

Shaz scoffed, propping himself up so he could fluff his pillow. "I think you mean orgy. I don't know about you two, but I don't think we have time for that."

Interest piqued, Arys lifted his head in order to pin the wolf with a sly grin. "So if we had the time, you'd be game?"

Shaking my head so that my blonde locks bounced, I shut that plan down. "Yeah, that's not happening. We'd probably blow the roof off the building, and I want to get home before anyone realizes we're gone."

I couldn't pretend Arys's naughty suggestions didn't appeal to me. His darkness lived inside me, a vibrant and volatile flame. Taking my entire harem of lovers to bed in one event would pose a challenge for sure, one I did not feel especially confident I could manage.

However, one of my lovers wasn't present and one of the vampires who was present wasn't a lover. Willow needed to keep calm and stay in control. We couldn't do anything to screw that up.

"So it is about the time," Arys mused, rubbing his chin as he playfully pondered the dilemma.

"Cut it out." I gave him a shove and he chuckled wickedly. "No sexy times or bloodshed in this room until every vampire here is at their strongest."

Lifting his chin in exaggerated disappointment, Arys sighed. "Fine. Then switch places with Shaz. If I have you rubbing against me, it's gonna happen."

"I'm not taking the middle unless you put underwear on," Shaz said, unphased by the vampire's open leer. "Not too keen on waking up with your dick on my leg or something."

A throaty laugh accompanied Shaz's teasing. He'd been flirty with Arys in recent weeks, something I'd never seen before. It left me both enamored and turned on.

Arys loved it. He never said so, but I saw it in the way his eyes lit up every time he looked at Shaz. Kind of the way he looked at him right then. "So where would you like it then, pup? Happy to accommodate any preference you may have."

A slight blush colored Shaz's cheeks. The sudden increase in his heart rate betrayed the cool, calm expression he forced. Without missing a beat, he quipped, "Once I've decided, you'll be the first to know."

Their relationship had undergone many changes over the last several months. Having come to his own understanding about the role he played with Arys and I, Shaz had warmed up to the intense vampire. More than I'd ever expected him to.

When Shaz had asked me how I'd feel if he wanted to pursue a more physical relationship with Arys, he had blown my mind. How ready Shaz was for that, I still didn't know. He was figuring it out, and I was more than happy to let him do that in his own time.

Arys too was content to allow Shaz to come to terms with his feelings and desires. So he ambled over to the suitcase he'd left open in the corner behind the couch and came back wearing silky black boxer shorts.

As promised, Shaz switched places with me in the bed, putting him in the middle. The fires of desire always burned hot between my dark vampire and me. We couldn't help it. Kind of came with the whole incubus and succubus territory. Keeping our hands off each other could be tough but not impossible. Although I suspected putting Shaz between us would just slow the inevitable.

The three of us formed a spoon chain, all facing the same direction, our bodies aligned. I couldn't see how close Arys lay to Shaz, and it stoked my curiosity. My white wolf pressed pretty damn close to me, his groin nestled against my ass, his face in my hair.

In just a few hours we'd be on our way out, straight to Sin City's version of The Wicked Kiss. The very first of its kind. I'd hated the place when Jenner ran it. I shuddered to think of what we might be walking into now. Because try as I might to imagine, there was just no assuming in a place like this. They didn't call it Sin City for nothing.

Shaz drew in a sudden breath inches from my ear, and the arm he'd wrapped around my waist tensed. The influx of sex-charged wolf pheromones hit like a sucker punch. Momentarily disorienting. Arys was definitely touching him. He hadn't wasted a moment.

"I thought switching places with Lex was supposed to keep the power level low in here." Voice husky with arousal, Shaz pressed his growing erection tighter against me.

After a brief but agonizing pause, Arys offered a lazy reply. "It was supposed to keep me from fucking and bleeding her. Doesn't mean I can't enjoy you a little, pup. And you can enjoy her."

"No blood, Arys." There was no mistaking the warning in my tone for anything but dead serious. I knew how fast things could spiral into the carnal pleasure zone of giving no fucks about anything but enjoying each other.

"No blood," came his sexy whisper from the other side of the bed. He'd play within the rules, but he'd push the boundaries the whole way.

Because I had to know, I reached a hand up behind me, sliding it into Shaz's hair. My fingers touched Arys's as I discovered he already fisted a handful of platinum. Trailing my hand back further, I found my vampire's strong jawline.

His mouth was on the back of Shaz's neck. Which explained the desperate hard on digging into my ass. Unable to resist, I wriggled against my wolf, pleased when he moaned close to my ear.

A sudden knock on the door was followed by Jenner's irritated, "Sorry to interrupt the lovefest, but I just spoke with Roscoe. It's bad, Arys. We need to be prepared for what we're walking into. All of us."

"Sorry my ass," Arys muttered.

I sat up, threw the blanket back, and called, "We'll be right out." Then I raised a hand to silence Arys's next snide remark.

Rolling his eyes in Jenner's direction, Arys pressed his face into white-blond hair and breathed deep. "Remind me again why I don't just kill that guy."

"If you insist." I just barely escaped the bed before Arys reached over Shaz to make a grab for me. "Because he's the closest thing to a brother you have. Jenner has taken a lot of shit from you, Arys, and he still shows up when you need him most. Now it's your turn to do the same for him."

Leaving my two loves in the bed without me took a stupid amount of effort. If I didn't get dressed and go talk to Jenner, I'd give in to the temptation. Just looking at them threatened my resolve.

Shaz rolled onto his back, allowing Arys to trail his tongue over the pack tattoo on the side of his neck. After letting himself enjoy it for a few seconds, he gave the vampire a playful shove. "Lex is right, man. You owe him one, at the very least."

A sexy-as-sin grin spread across Arys's handsome face as he caught Shaz's jaw in a strong hand. Brushing his lips lightly over the wolf's, he said, "Pretty sure I owe you a few as well. Jenner can wait."

Shaz nipped playfully at Arys before kissing him. A kiss that commanded the room, captivating both Arys and me. Then he broke it off as fast as it had started. Rolling away with a smirk, Shaz left the bed and the pleasantly surprised vampire in it.

Watching them weakened the strongest parts of me. A year ago I'd never have believed it would reach this point. Not only were they lovers, they were in love, and I so enjoyed seeing the evolution of their bond.

"You're a goddamn tease, Shaz." Sitting up straight in the bed, Arys shook his head, darkness moving through his eyes as he watched our wolf stride away. "Now you owe me one."

Pulling on a pair of jeans from his suitcase, Shaz slid me a mischievous look before nailing Arys with the same wicked gaze. "I'll see what I can do."

The reaction my vampire had to Shaz, I felt both inside and out. It hung heavy in the atmosphere. Primal. Hungry. Possessive. Unbearably turned on by the same werewolf who so many times had punched him in the face and threatened to kill him.

Funny how things change.

We emerged a few minutes later to find Jenner pacing the small living room. Shoulders hunched and brow furrowed, he regarded us with drowning black pupils. A sure sign of his control being tested. The man was severely wound up.

"It would really help if the three of you could keep it in your pants for a few nights," Jenner snapped, inked arms folded over his chest as he glared daggers at me. "Especially you." Anxiety wrapped itself around him, giving his energy a bitter vibe.

I'd never seen him so irate. He believed everything was about to be taken from him. Of course he was desperate and lashing out.

Willow lounged on the couch, channel surfing. Guess he didn't want to watch *The Hangover*. Across from him, Gabriel sat on an easy chair, scrolling on his phone.

"What did Roscoe say?" I got right to the point, refusing to let Jenner's crap mood affect me. I had my own share of crap moods they had to put up with.

I hopped up on the dining room table, feet swinging. Shaz grabbed a beer from the minibar and plopped down on the couch while Arys stood in the middle of the room with shoulders tensed, watching Jenner with a hawk-like stare.

But he gazed off toward the curtained window, as if he could still see the Strip beyond. The sun was low in the sky now but not yet low enough. Soon.

"Roscoe skipped town. He's not even here anymore. He said Loric has taken it too far. There's demon activity at The Wicked Kiss." Jenner seemed so calm and detached.

Arys shrugged, unmoved. "This is Sin City. There's always been demon activity here. The place is built on it."

"Not in my club," Jenner snapped, firing a scowl at Arys that caused the tension in the room to rise. "My club was about vampires and enjoying every fucking second of being one. Now Loric has made it a place to worship demons with sacrifices and rituals. He's making a play for control of the city, and he's not above making deals with demons to do it."

My leg swinging stopped. More demon bullshit? On top of the current steaming pile?

"What kind of demons are we talking?" Everyone looked at Willow who had the ability to diffuse rising conflict by simply reminding us that he was there.

Gabriel too was interested in this information. Sitting up straighter, he abandoned his phone and observed everyone in the room slowly, one at a time. Even though he'd promised me that he hadn't seen any visions regarding our trip, I wondered.

Fisting a handful of his hair, Jenner resumed pacing beside the sofa. "Roscoe said Loric started using the club to celebrate the Seven Deadly Sins. Once that began, Roscoe walked, cutting ties with Loric and the club. Loric threatened him, so he left town."

Naturally I looked to the two demon experts among us for a reaction. They glanced at each other.

"Got any experience with Seven Deadly Sins demons, Gabriel?" Willow asked, a glint of excitement in his eyes.

Excitement? Where the mention of demons brought me nothing but dread, it brought Willow the opposite entirely. It awakened a calling as old as time. Within him still dwelled the angel warrior, the spirit created to kick demon ass.

Gabriel nodded his dark head, long hair spilling over the shoulders of his jacket. "A little. Nothing compared to you and Falon though."

Willow gazed around at the rest of us, his pretty greens pausing on me. "Speaking of Falon, you're going to want him there, Alexa. If anyone tries to challenge that mark, he has to back it up."

"Challenge the mark?" I repeated, gripping the edge of the table under a sudden spike of anxiety.

"By marking you, he more or less slapped a 'Property of' tag on you. Most demons will know better than to challenge an angel, even a fallen one. Although there will always be those who see it as an opportunity." While his tone lacked judgment, I knew how Willow felt about the mark. He thought I made a stupid mistake to allow it in the first place. He wasn't the only one.

Right on cue Arys hissed, "Make him get rid of it. The damn thing isn't worth the risk."

Inwardly, I groaned. Outwardly, I shook my head. "We've been over this. It serves a purpose. When I have reason to believe it's more harm than good, then I'll have him remove it."

My hand strayed to the silver feather adorning the side of my neck. Falon had given me the mark during an emotional exchange. All fired up after a visit from Bane, he'd claimed me as his among immortals, needing not only Bane to know it but me as well. Naturally, the fallen angel didn't give a crap what Arys thought.

Stalking over to the table where I sat perched, Arys brushed my hair back to reveal the feather to the room. A subtle tremor shook me when he grazed it with a finger. "I swear that if a demon even looks at you wrong because of this mark I'll—"

"You'll let me handle it because it's my choice and my body." I shut Arys up with a finger over his lips and a slip of a smile on my face. No need to let this issue blow up into an argument. As much as I enjoyed the heat of my dark flame's temper, we needed to stay focused.

"We'll see about that." Like the wicked man that he was, Arys caught my finger and sucked the tip into his mouth.

Carnival of Sins

This annoyed the already much too tense Jenner who crackled with hyped-up, jittery energy. "Can you please stop thinking with your cock for two minutes, Arys? Maybe you have something to go back to, but this is it for me. It would be nice if you could take this seriously."

I tugged my hand away and gave Arys a gentle push. His mere proximity set off sparks between us. Relenting, he drew away but fixed Jenner with an unhappy sneer.

"I'm here, aren't I?" Arys snapped, adding to the thickening tension. "Leaving my own city vulnerable. If that's not serious enough for you, Jenner, then I'm not sure what it takes to please you. Perhaps another roll in the sack with my wolf? Yeah, I see the way you look at her."

My brows shot up and my jaw dropped open. These two would forever have this sibling rivalry bullshit. It didn't mean they had to drag me into it.

Jenner bristled, icy-blue light dancing over his clenched fists. "You know what? Fuck you, Arys." He stormed for the door, ignoring my call for him to stop.

Even though he couldn't leave the hotel until sunset, there were three hundred thousand square feet of hotel and casino to lose himself in. It was too early for us to be separated. Someone had to go after him.

I hopped off the table and hurried to catch Jenner before he could grab an elevator and lose me in the casino below. Before anyone could join me, I raised a hand to keep them in place. "Stay here. All of you."

On my way out, I heard Shaz chastising Arys for his inability to leave well enough alone. My socked feet made not a sound as I sprinted down the hall toward the elevators. I turned the corner right as Jenner was about to step into one that already held a few people smelling of cocktails and money.

I caught his arm and dragged him out of the elevator, flashing those inside a smile as the door slid shut. "Why do you make it so easy for him get to you like that? You know he's looking for a reaction."

"Why do you shrug off his shitty behavior?" Jenner retorted, jerking his arm from mine. "You enable him."

I choked on a laugh as I tried and failed to stifle it. "You and I both know that's not true. And we both know he cares. He just doesn't know how to show it. You guys have some seriously twisted history."

"That's putting it lightly. I don't know how it is that we haven't killed each other yet." Jenner paced around in front of the elevators, trailing high-strung energy behind him. It made my skin itch if I thought about it.

Maybe steering him onto a new subject would help. "Come back to the suite. We need to make a plan for sunset." Although nothing short of feeding and fucking it out of his system would purge all that tension.

The elevator opened, and a room service guy with a rolling metal food tray stepped out. He gave us a polite nod and rolled off down the hall. Jenner waited until he'd gotten out of earshot to say, "What Arys said about the way I look at you, that's bullshit. He's digging."

"Digging for what?" Leaning against the wall where I could see up and down the hall on either side, I watched Jenner do all he could to keep from meeting my inquisitive stare.

Quiet stretched for a moment, then giggles floated down the hall as a cork popped in someone's room.

A bitter laugh fell from Jenner's lips. "For any sign that there might be more between us than one vengeance fuck in the heat of the moment."

Arys did have a tendency to be possessive and at times a downright jealous bastard. However, I didn't think he had any reason to suspect there were any feelings between Jenner and me. Unless… there were?

"We both know there isn't." I felt my way along this conversation like it was a skinny ledge on a mountain face. "It's blood, power, and sometimes a little more. Nothing wrong with that."

When that cold gaze landed on me, a heat burned within it, slowly melting the frost. "See now it's that little bit more that's a problem."

I wanted to press him on that but refrained, afraid to go down a rabbit hole. "It doesn't have to be."

"You claimed me, Alexa. I get that I'm nothing more than another powerful vamp to call on when needed, but I have the same needs you do." Shoving away from the closed elevators, Jenner prowled toward me.

I couldn't help but flashback to our one and only time together. It had been wild and impulsive. A quick and dirty fuck that had given me exactly what I'd needed at the time. Jenner knew his way around a woman. No doubt about that.

"I know you do." My pulse ticked up a notch as I watched him advance on me. "I care about that. Really I do. I want to do right by you. All of you. This doesn't have to be a bad thing. We can all get something out of it."

Jenner put a hand on the wall above my head and leaned in close. I tipped my face up to find him peering at me with keen interest. The tiny hairs on my arms stood on end as goosebumps broke out on my skin. His energy was rife with want and resentment.

"You think we can all be your happy little harem, Alexa?" Close enough for me to feel his breath on my face, Jenner never touched me. Still he managed to make me want him to. "Think you can handle that? Honestly, I can't see Arys being cool with making me a regular playmate."

"Is that what you want?" It was near impossible not to fall into those arctic eyes. So chilling yet so inviting. "To be a regular in my bed?"

Lips pressed together, Jenner seemed to consider this. Really consider it. A slow, sultry heat rose between us. He was just so damn close. Mere inches. His inked arm stretched above me, muscles hard and tense. I didn't dare move and risk making physical contact.

"What I want is to get a hit of you when I need it and then get back to my own life until the next hit. That's it." He studied my lips, lost in his own temptation. The steady hum of his longing was near audible.

Jenner wasn't asking for a lot. It wasn't something that I couldn't give him. Maybe we could find a happy medium after all.

"Fine," I said, unable to resist dragging my tongue over the edge of my upper lip. "Consider it done. I'll handle Arys. He's not as uptight about it as you think. He's been focused on other, more important things."

"Like fucking your white wolf?" Jenner smirked. "Yeah, he's been pretty obvious. Whatever keeps him off my back."

Arys had a way of oozing desire in a manner that drew the attention of everyone around him. Naturally they'd all have noticed the changes between Shaz and him. As I searched Jenner, I thought for just a moment I caught a glimpse of longing. Not for me. For Arys.

Had Arys and Jenner ever shared more than a lover or a victim? I suspected that they had although Arys had claimed they'd never been lovers. Either way, they had a vast well of feelings for one another. As much as they resented each other, there was a deep loyalty there. One I suspected would be to the death.

"You know he loves you in his own way." The words tumbled out, driven by a memory that wasn't mine. The briefest flash. Arys watching Jenner work his seductive magic on a couple, waiting for the right moment to join. He admired Jenner. Watching him in action was a thrill.

"He needs me. And that's not the same thing as love." Jenner scoffed and shoved away, finding enough strength to resist the need I'd planted within him. "Let's go back inside. We need a plan."

Before I could reply, he stalked away, back toward our suite. I watched him go, taking a second to myself before returning to the testosterone overload.

Arys and I, we hadn't been fair to Jenner. Although I couldn't easily access the many details of their years together, I knew Jenner had gotten the shit end of the stick.

He deserved better. A coldhearted queen wasn't who I wanted to be. Somehow I would make this right.

CHAPTER FOUR

With a nervous hand, I applied stay-put red lipstick. Not knowing what to expect made me uneasy. This wasn't my city and had never been my home. I didn't have the same sense of familiarity with it that Jenner and Arys had.

Our last visit hadn't exactly gone off without a hitch. I knew better than to expect anything pleasant from Vegas. The city writhed with darkness and unrest. I had the sinking sensation that our previous blood ring encounter would pale in comparison to what we would find here now.

The tentative plan we'd agreed on so far was that Arys, Jenner, Gabriel, and I would go together to The Wicked Kiss to see Loric under the guise of a friendly visit.

Would he buy it? Well, I wouldn't if I were him. But I didn't know this guy, and Arys could be quite the charmer. Of course, in order to be convincing, we might all have to play a role, one that I didn't want to play.

Arys and Jenner had both agreed that coming in on friendly terms to scope out the situation was the safest plan. They were right. We couldn't walk in on the offensive until we knew what we faced.

Still, as I smoothed away a slight smudge from the black cat's-eye liner framing my currently blue eyes, I let out a slow breath in an effort to find my inner calm.

It wasn't that I had no confidence in myself or the now renewed bond I had with Arys. It was that I didn't want anyone I cared about to get caught in the crossfire when the battle inevitably went down.

I stood back to assess my appearance. Makeup done. Ash blonde locks tumbled in soft curls down my back, the one black chunk on the left side standing out in startling contrast.

Because I wanted to be dressed to kill, literally if necessary, I wore a one strap black cocktail dress that fell to my ankles with a slit up one side. Hey, it was Las Vegas after all. A pair of dressy yet tough boots adorned my feet, a small dagger tucked into one of them. Just in case. The rest of my arsenal was already on me.

"Absolutely gorgeous." Shaz's voice came from behind me seconds before his reflection appeared in the mirror. "Like always. I still like you best in sweats with a messy bun though." His arms wrapped around me.

I leaned into his embrace. "There's not a single part of this that I'm looking forward to. Call Jez and check in with her for me, will you? Make sure everything is all good at home."

"For sure. I still think we should all go together. I don't want to be here without you two, wondering what the hell is going on." I watched him in the mirror as he buried his face in my tresses and hugged me close. So much did I love him that not for a second did I consider compromising on this. Not after last time.

"Sorry, babe." I lifted a hand to stroke his faintly stubbled cheek. "I have no desire to see you in another cage fight in this lifetime. Besides, if anything comes up at home, someone needs to be able to get there fast."

Shaz pulled back and turned me to face him. "I'm not going home without you. No matter what happens."

"Come on, Shaz. I need you with me on this." I flung a hand toward the door and the voices of the men beyond. "They're all unpredictable. I can't rely on a single one of them the way I can rely on you. It's a wolf thing. If anything happens, either here or back home, I need you away from the center of the chaos. To come to the rescue at the right time."

I wanted both Shaz and Willow away from the heart of the mess. Safe from The Wicked Kiss Las Vegas until we knew what dwelled inside. Shaz would be mistaken for prey in that place, and keeping Willow out of the line of demon fire as long as possible was the least I could do after all he'd done for me.

Shaz nodded, pressing his forehead to mine. One hand curved around my waist while the other slid up the back of my neck into my hair. "I'll stay here tonight and wait for you to check Loric out. Don't make me promise anything else. It's too soon."

"I can live with that." I'd have to. Stifling a guy like Shaz was a mistake. An Alpha wolf, he could hold his own. He'd proven himself during our last visit and several times since. I couldn't project my own insecurities onto him.

After stealing a few kisses, we emerged to find the others gathered in the living room. Arys and Jenner were fashionably casual in dark slacks and shirts, showing an enticing sliver of chest at their open collars. Jenner's sleeves were rolled up to expose his tattooed forearms. The two of them stood close, head to head, as they spoke in low tones. Most likely about Loric.

A few filthy thoughts flitted through my mind. Smirking to myself, I shoved them aside.

But the men standing near the window drew my attention. Falon and Willow. The former with hands shoved in the pockets of his trendy trench coat, looking down his nose at the latter, who snarled something beneath his breath.

Falon would be joining us as well. However, he'd be remaining out of sight unless absolutely necessary. Walking in with an immortal in tow could be taken for a threat.

Feeling the weight of my gaze, Falon cut Willow off with a snarky, "Pretty sure Alexa can decide what's best for herself. I get it. You're having a hard time adjusting to the new order of things. You're not her guardian anymore, not that it would change a damn thing."

"I do so love it when you two manage to get along." Dripping sarcasm, I turned a pointed glower on Falon who remained unmoved. "Keep it civil or keep your mouth shut."

"Nice to see you too, wolf." Injecting a healthy dose of revulsion into that one word, Falon couldn't keep himself from ogling my attire. From my pushed-up cleavage to the tantalizing glimpse of thigh peeking through the slit in my dress, he drank in the sight of me. Catching himself, he tried and failed to avert his gaze. "Might be seeing a bit too much of you."

I flashed him a teasing grin, sensing the uptick in his pulse. "You prefer the bathrobe look, I know. It just doesn't send the message I'm going for tonight."

"And what message might that be?" Falon countered without missing a beat. "Succubus queen on the prowl for another vampire to add to your harem?"

"Hardly. I've got all the vampires I can handle." I enjoyed the distracted way he appraised me and the discomfort that wormed its way onto his perfect face. He still hated the way he reacted to me, and I still loved that. "And no worries, Falon. There's only room in this harem for one fallen pain in my ass. Your position is secure."

Nothing tripped the fallen angel up for long. With his cocky mask of arrogance back in place, he quipped, "Which position is that? From behind I presume. I mean, it is your best angle."

Our banter became too much for Willow who muttered something clearly derogatory in the language of the immortals. He only succeeded in making Falon erupt with boisterous laughter.

"Okay, guys. Let's play nice." I shot Falon a deathly warning glare before turning an apologetic smile on Willow.

Although they'd maintained a semblance of civility around one another in recent weeks, Willow would never let go of the grudge he held. He hated that Falon had not only become one of my lovers but one of those closest to me as well. Close enough to put his mark on me.

"Can I talk to you for a sec?" Inclining my head, I motioned for Willow to follow me around the corner into the small hallway outside the second bedroom. When we were alone, I asked in a hushed voice, "How are you? Do you need anything from me before I go?"

His gaze darted about my face, and he scrubbed a hand over his jaw. "No, I'm good. Just be careful. Reach out if you need me, and I'll come."

Despite the tiny corner we were crammed into, Willow managed to keep what he deemed to be a safe distance. Still, he was not so far away that I couldn't feel the fragmented energy feeding his aura.

"It's been a week, Willow." A week since he last took my blood. With him I preferred to give it every few nights. Whatever it took to keep the hunger from snowballing into the lust-crazed need the others felt. I never wanted Willow to suffer that way.

The yellow light in the hall bounced off his dirty blond hair, spattering it with gold tones. Shoving his hands into the pockets of his blue jeans, he forced a relaxed posture that didn't match the intensity of his intriguing hybrid vibes. The scent of wolf drifted from him to taunt me.

"I'm fine, Lex." He met and held my gaze, sincerity shining in the depths of those pretty gold-flecked orbs. "You shouldn't walk in there with fresh wounds anyway. Might not be the best first impression."

He had a point. But I couldn't shake the feeling that he was trying to avoid the inevitable. When his gaze wavered and slipped to my throat before drifting to the swell of my cleavage, I saw more than mere bloodlust in his predatory expression.

"When I get back then," I said, going on as if I couldn't sense his struggle. Taking my blood alone simply wasn't enough for Willow anymore. And he was too damn much of a gentleman to say so.

"Right. Sure." Letting out a held breath, he turned, ready to flee me if necessary. "Remember, don't hesitate to reach out if you need to."

The benefit of being bonded to Willow as his maker, well one of them, was my ability to call on him telepathically. A connection shared between sire and progeny, Arys shared the same link with Gabriel.

"Of course," I mumbled, but he'd already put several feet between us. If anyone else noticed the way Willow fled me like a victim running from the killer in a slasher film, they didn't let on.

"We should go," Jenner announced, nervously eyeing the time on his phone before stuffing it into a pocket.

A little jittery with nervous tension but otherwise calm and steady, he was the first one out of the suite. Tucking my phone and wallet into a small black purse, I slung it over my shoulder and let Arys usher me along, blowing a kiss to Shaz as the door closed behind us.

While waiting for an elevator, I took the opportunity to remind Falon to stay out of sight. He rolled his eyes and cast judgment over us vampy types. "How in the world did I end up the glorified backup for a bunch of sex-charged vampires?"

Arys snickered, flashing a fangy grin. "You know the answer to that."

Sighing like a den mother with a brood of naughty children, Falon pursed his lips. "Unfortunately. Try not to do anything too stupid. If we're walking into a demon nest and shit goes down, I can't protect all of you, and only one of you keeps my dick warm."

Gone. With those parting words the bastard vanished. He'd go on ahead to scope out the situation. Regardless of what was going on at Jenner's club, we needed to see it for ourselves. We'd left our mark on this city. Claimed it as our own. What kind of message would it send if we let Loric have the place uncontested?

"He could warm his dick in any number of places," Jenner muttered, standing back when the elevator dinged. "His infatuation is painfully obvious. I'm starting to think it might be bordering on obsession."

A wave of heat rushed to my face. What kind of trouble was this vamp trying to stir up for me? I couldn't tell whether it was Arys or me that Jenner wanted a reaction from.

The elevator door opened fully, and an elderly couple clutching shopping bags exited. Once the four of us piled in and the door shut, Arys eased in close to Jenner, jostling him with an arm. "And I'm starting to think you might have a little obsession of your own." My dark half snarled, low and wolfish. "If I were you, I wouldn't worry about the angel. I'll always be the one that stands in your way."

It was as if all the air had suddenly been sucked from the tiny metal chamber. The only sound was that of the small screen mounted in one corner playing ads for various performers and casinos around the city. I could have choked both of them right then.

The moment the door opened, I all but burst out in an effort to escape the suffocating confines of the elevator. Being trapped in such a small place with so much power left me momentarily dizzy and a little aroused. Based on how quickly we all spread apart, I wasn't the only one.

Outside the spring desert air greeted us. It was warmer than back home. The streets were just as busy as the last time we'd come. Jenner surged ahead to cut a path through the crowded sidewalk. We followed him across the street and down the Strip.

Gabriel tried to take in the Eiffel Tower at Paris and the fountains leaping into the sky over at the Bellagio. The rest of us stared straight ahead. Focused.

"Remember, love." Clasping my hand in his, Arys pulled me closer to him on the sidewalk. "Loric hated Harley. He'll love that you killed him. But we may have to go pretty far to convince him we're here for a nice, friendly visit."

I swallowed around the lump forming in my throat. "Yeah, I know. If it goes too far, I'm pulling the plug on the whole thing."

"Define too far." Arys wiggled a brow in a teasing gesture, but the request was serious.

Because I didn't want to even entertain the difference between my idea of too far and his, I just said, "I'll keep you posted."

We passed by one guy dressed as a Transformer and three others in various states of Elvis on our way inside the hotel. What was the plural form of Elvis when you had several? Elvises? Elvi? Fuck, I felt nervous.

Las Vegas was rife with madness and chaos. I could feel it in my bones, smell it on the air, and see it in the eyes of those I passed. Strangers drunk on the city and the glamour it cast over all who walked where the lights shone bright.

In my time among the shadows, I'd learned that the darkest dark often lay a hair's breadth beyond the glow. Just beyond the place where light and dark touched. So near it lurked, swallowing all who ventured too close.

Were we venturing too close?

Las Vegas was but one of many cities throughout the world where darkness ran rampant. It was everywhere of course. However, some places were worse than others. With the unrest I felt in the atmosphere, a swell of growing evil, I worried that perhaps we wouldn't succeed in helping Jenner.

I'd do everything I could, but if it meant sacrificing myself while my own city sat vulnerable, waiting for the inevitable return of its demon queen, we'd have to walk away. There were people coming for me, and I had to be there when they arrived.

"Stop thinking so far ahead." Sliding his hand across my lower back, Arys pressed close, his voice a sexy murmur against my ear. "You're a fucking powerhouse, my feisty, capable wolf. Loric won't know what hit him."

"Stay out of my head," I muttered without any real contempt.

Jenner slammed a fist into the side of a bus bench as he passed, ignoring the woman sitting there who told him off. "That fucking asshole will never trust me. I left on bad terms."

"Not to mention the fact that we're all Harley's vampires," I supplied as the worry gnawing at me bit a little harder.

Arys didn't share the concern Jenner and I had. With a sweep of his hands he ushered us along. "Harley is dead. If anything, Loric will thank us. We play his game until the right time, and then we let him have it. You as well, Jenner. Don't blow this."

Jenner's lips moved as he uttered something to himself. An angry storm cloud surrounded him, pulsing with the heat of his steadily growing fury. It tested me. The light flame within me wanted to comfort him and promise that we'd figure this out. The dark flame wanted to devour him. To throw him down and climb all over him, basking in the heady charge of his lust and rage.

The Wicked Kiss Las Vegas waited just off the Strip, a short walk from our location. We arrived there in no time. From the outside, nothing had changed. A mirrored exterior hid the inside from view.

It still gave me the creeps.

Sleeves rolled up to expose his tattooed forearms, Jenner strode for the door, a vampire on a mission if I'd ever seen one. He was far too emotional for this encounter.

"That son of a bitch is going to get himself killed." Arys went after him. Grabbing his shoulder none too gently, he whirled Jenner around.

As expected, Jenner's fists came up. To his credit, Arys backed off. Nothing he said or did was going to diffuse the situation. I rushed to put myself in front of Jenner before he could storm the doors.

"Hey, listen to me." Placing both hands on either side of his face, I forced him to focus only on me. "You're the most calm, self-controlled vampire I've ever known. It's one of the things I admire most about you. Please don't lose your grip now. This is when you need it the most."

His frazzled energy leapt to me, coursing through my fingers and down my arms. With the right intent I grasped that force and twisted it into something else. Something calming, comfortable, and a little erotic. Letting instinct guide me, I brushed my lips against his in a not so subtle invitation. Which he accepted. Jenner let me guide the kiss as I explored his mouth with my tongue. Through the intimate connection, I pushed that sensual calm from me to him.

When I drew back, he blinked heavy-lidded, slightly dopey eyes at me. A little buzzed but much calmer, he frowned less severely. "You don't play fair, Alexa. Not cool."

I gave him a playful slap on the cheek while stifling the urge to eat him up. "Yeah, well, whatever keeps us all alive."

Arys stopped me when I tried to take the lead. Because I wasn't content to fall behind, I kept pace right beside him as we stepped into the lobby. I half expected security to stop us, but the vampire working the door knew Jenner and stepped aside to let us pass.

The main floor of the lavish nightclub looked exactly as I remembered it. Sprawling red carpet stretched wall to wall. A ridiculously huge and tacky chandelier hung from the ceiling, lighting the place in a soft yellow glow bright enough to see by while leaving enough room for the shadows to play. Music spilled from the stage at the far end of the building, which was several times the size of my own nightclub back home.

Vampires worked the human crowd, both on the stage and the floor. The predators moved among their prey, seeking willing victims among the humans here to drink, gamble and bleed.

A spiral staircase near the stage led to the upper floor, where an array of swanky sex rooms awaited those who dared to tread so far. The real party I knew, however, happened below. The underground floor was private, special access only.

During Jenner's rule it had housed a werewolf fight ring and a small, personal theatre where he performed a full victim seduction and everything that entailed for a live audience. He'd told stories about the changes Loric had made even before the Seven Deadly Sins.

We waited inside while Jenner paused to speak with the doorman. Right away we began to draw the attention of the closest vampires and several humans as well. We put out a heady come-hither vibe whether we intended to or not, some of us more than others. Even holding our power tightly reined, we set off a ripple effect of sensual, hungry energy. A formidable force that commanded attention, I'd learned fast that that wasn't necessarily a good thing.

"Loric has been expecting us." Jenner returned in a huff, a hand jerking roughly through his tousled blond hair. "We've been given the all clear to go to the VIP poker room."

He glanced at Arys, awaiting his feedback. Not one to disappoint, Arys nodded toward the VIP poker lounge tucked in behind the staircase. "Then I guess we shouldn't keep him waiting. Let's have a little fun with this, shall we?"

Moving through the crowd with ease, Arys headed straight for the exclusive area. Jenner and I exchanged an alarmed look before hurrying after him. If Shaz had been there, he'd have been the one to keep Arys from taking things too far. Had we made a mistake leaving him back at the hotel?

No. We couldn't all come here at once. I'd made the best choice in leaving Shaz and Willow in the safe zone. They would serve us better there than here if shit went down.

"Arys, hey." I grabbed his arm, gasping at the sudden shock of power between us. The strength of our renewed balance still surprised me at times. "Don't go in there all halfcocked and ready to rumble. Remember, we play the game until we can't play it anymore. Right?"

Catching my hand, he pulled me along close beside him, pausing when we reached the poker room in question. Turning to me with a naughty light dancing in his midnight eyes, Arys said, "I assure you it's more than half. I'm content to let you decide when enough is enough, my queen, no matter what happens. I must remind you that playing along might mean going to places you never thought you'd go."

With a pang of guilt, I glanced at Jenner who waited impatiently, his face a mask of annoyance. What happened with him here last time could never happen again. I'd kill Loric before I'd bind him to me.

Besides, if we were walking into something we couldn't handle, Falon would have stopped us from getting this far. At least, I'd like to think so.

"Let's just play it by ear and see what happens." I addressed all three vampires, making eye contact with each of them, ensuring we were all on the same page. "We play it cool until we can't, and nobody flies off the handle."

Between Arys and Jenner, I couldn't be sure who I thought was most likely to do that. But I had full confidence that Gabriel would follow my lead to the letter. He stood there calm but ready, poised with confidence in his power and his knowledge of how to use it.

My trust in Gabriel had grown. He'd gone over and above to prove his loyalty when he'd hidden the Shya stone. He'd downright saved my ass when he confided in Falon that he'd seen me die a second death and believed it to be the way I would restore the twin flame balance.

And still I had not yet given him all that he wanted from me. I had yet to take him to my bed. It wasn't that I didn't want to, because I couldn't deny that I did. I'd laid my claim on him already. It just hadn't felt like the right time yet. There had to be more to it than a fuck.

I trusted him though, and I hoped he knew it. He wouldn't be here otherwise.

As we were about to enter the poker lounge, Falon stepped out from around a bank of slot machines. He caught my hand and pulled me in close.

"What's going on?" Panic leaped in my throat when Falon's hand went to the silver feather on my neck.

"How much does this shithole really mean to you?" he asked, directing the question to Arys as well. "Because I don't think it's worth it."

"Fuck you," Jenner snarled.

The touch of Falon's fingers sparked the first embers of the wildfire that burned in my darkest heart for him. They glided over my skin, drawing or writing. "This Sevens Sins shit is a fool's game. If I were you, I'd walk out that door right now and go home. You have enough problems of your own without pissing off a bunch of Sins demons who don't even know you exist. Why change that?"

"What are you doing?" I jerked from his touch.

He held me in place. "Adding a little something to my mark. If anything demonic even breathes in your direction, I want to know it. Seeing as you're probably stupid enough to go down there anyway." Another few swirls of his fingers and Falon drew back.

His fierce expression dared me to say something, anything, about what he'd done. As did the gesture he'd just made, in front of Arys no less. I knew better than that. Instead, I would wait and throw it in his face when we were alone together.

"Touching," Arys remarked, his tone icy but smooth. "Let's get to the point. What's going on downstairs? Can we handle it? More specifically, can Alexa?"

The fallen angel regarded him with open disdain. "She handled you, didn't she? I've never known this woman to shy away from a challenge. I doubt this will be any different."

A muscle in Arys's jaw twitched. "You didn't exactly answer the question."

Keeping myself between them, I gave Falon a little slap of power. Just enough to snap his gaze from the vampire to me. "What's going on down there? We haven't been admitted. They want us up here in the private lounge. Talk fast before someone comes to see what's holding us up."

Although Falon's expression remained unchanged, I felt the sudden shift in his personal vibe. Just the slightest pulse and his libido jumped. I'd so hear about this later.

"Loric has given this place over to the Seven Deadly Sins. Altars dedicated to celebrating each of them with people lined up to participate. And they didn't all look willing to me. What exactly Loric is hoping to gain by all this, I'm not sure. Probably the same thing any idiot making deals with demons wants. Personal gain."

"Then we find out." Done with waiting, Jenner entered the poker lounge.

Not one to walk away without even looking the enemy in the eye, Arys followed. Gabriel, however, glanced at me, awaiting my choice. I didn't have to think about it long.

Ignoring Falon's exasperated sigh, I nodded to Gabriel. "We've come this far already. Let's find out what's going on here."

CHAPTER FIVE

Soft, warm lighting encouraged a relaxed atmosphere. A leather sofa sat at the back of the near-empty poker lounge in front of a fireplace, along with a matching loveseat and double armchair set. It would have been inviting had it not been for the vampire with the smug smile lounging in the center of the sofa.

Loric sat poised for his guests. From the precise way he sat on the center cushion of the fancy couch, legs crossed, reclining casually with arms spread over the back, to the haughty yet curious expression on his strangely handsome but youthful face, everything about Loric appeared planned. Including the two burly, armed vampires standing off to either side.

He was draped in a black Armani suit. His deep-red shirt lay wide open to expose far too much of his chest. Dipping his head in a nod, Loric greeted us with a vicious smile. "Jenner. I'm surprised to see you back here after the way you left with your tail between your legs."

And the gauntlet had been thrown. Antagonistic right from the start, Loric was feeling us out. If Jenner blew this the second we walked in here, I'd have him for breakfast.

Before he could get the chance, Arys swept forward, all but elbowing Jenner aside. "Loric, it's been what? Several decades since you've come back this way? Europe must have treated you well. It's great to see you again."

Was he laying it on a bit thick or just making nice? I couldn't be sure, but I feared Loric would see right through us. I kept reminding myself that we all had to play a role here, and it damn well better be convincing.

"Is it?" Loric countered, causing a knot to tighten in my chest. "Last I heard you laid claim to this city and had Jenner acting as your right hand." He leaned forward so the glow of the fire lit up one half of his face.

Just how old was he when turned? Not much older than Gabriel if I had to guess. Soft blond waves, long enough to curl about his ears, added to Loric's youthful appearance. Baby-blue eyes hardened with centuries as a vampire gleamed as he took us all in.

Skipping over Jenner with disinterest, he studied Gabriel before finding me. I held Loric's penetrating gaze as he debated on whether or not to poke and prod me metaphysically. With a raised brow, I silently dared him. Surely he'd heard about Arys and me.

From where I stood I could feel what he was made of. A vibe similar to Harley's surrounded him, but it was subdued. Weaker. He could never take us in a power struggle, and he knew it, which was where the demons came into play. Their presence alone gave him power.

"I took it over because Harley was dead and someone had to do it. Things were going to hell around here." So easy and smooth Arys delivered the lie, as if he didn't really give a damn about this nightclub.

"Speaking of Harley, I hear that your other half killed him." Extending a hand, Loric gestured for us to take a seat. To me directly, he asked, "Is it true?"

Arys and I sat together on the loveseat across from Loric, leaving Gabriel and Jenner to sit in the adjacent armchairs. Beneath the weight of Loric's inquisitive gaze, I perched demurely on the edge of the loveseat, crossing my legs so the slit in my dress revealed a substantial amount of thigh.

"It most certainly is," I purred, pleased when Loric ogled the near glimpse of my ass. Might as well nail it right from the get go. "He had it coming. I'd already given him the chance to walk away. He made his choice."

To my own ears I sounded cold as ice. If it bothered Arys, he didn't let on. I didn't dare check for Jenner's reaction. The man better have his poker face on.

Loric's cat-like grin widened and he nodded in approval. "You did many people a great favor, Alexa. I only wish I'd been there to see it myself."

So I needed no introduction. Of course not. If he knew all about Arys and me, then he knew that there was no vampire more powerful in our bloodline than either of us. From the steady, relaxed hum of his energy, he didn't see us as a threat. Yet. He genuinely wanted to know what we were doing here.

Tossing a gold lock out of his eyes, Loric continued. "Let's cut to the chase. Is this visit business, pleasure, or neither of the two?"

"Maybe a little of both," Arys answered coolly, the power hovering about him blatant and undeniable. "I thought I'd return to my old stomping grounds to see what you've done with the place. I imagine it's better than anything Jenner had going on."

Inwardly, I winced as if that barb had been for me. Keeping up a front was vital, but Jenner was taking a lot of hits here. In my peripheral view, I watched him sit there perfectly still, like a statue. A lot had to be going on beneath the surface.

If he snapped and went for Loric, could I grab him in time?

"So to clarify, you have little interest in this nightclub or this city?" Loric uncrossed his legs and leaned forward. "Because as the one who helped Harley open this place back in the day, I can't help but feel that I have more claim to it than either of you do."

The guy was an unapologetic asshole. But so was Arys. The two of them stared at each other. Two predators trying to determine what the other wanted and how far they were willing to go to get it.

"No argument here." Rolling with the punches, Arys played along. "My interests are currently occupied with my own city. Like I said, I felt it my duty to ensure this place didn't fall into the wrong hands. We're here to check in on the club and enjoy some party favors while doing so."

Loric didn't buy it. I was sure of that. Although he smiled and nodded as if he did, then threw us a curveball. "I would be happy to have you as my guest, Arys. There's just one issue. Jenner. I'm not sure he's capable of accepting the new order around here. He made it clear when he left that he wouldn't give the club up without a fight.

It took great effort not to squirm in my seat. I was far more comfortable with raging into a place ready to throw down and kick some ass. This playing nice and faking friends shit didn't jive with me. Everything about this discussion caused my inner dread to grow.

A sexy chuckle spilled from Arys. With an elbow propped on the arm of the loveseat, he slid a glance in Jenner's direction. "Jenner is my right hand. Where I go, he goes. He will be returning to my city with me. He's hardly any concern of yours."

Loric and Jenner locked eyes then, and the air in the room thickened. Venom filled Jenner's frozen stare, and I willed him to keep his cool. Loric settled back against the couch, his face suddenly void of expression and impossible to read.

"How do I know I can trust him? How do I know I can trust any of you?" Spreading his hands imploringly, the vampire played us right back. "Perhaps an act of good will."

A chill tickled the back of my neck. Yeah, he was definitely onto us. Maybe we'd end up fighting our way out of here after all.

"An act of good will?" Arys repeated, maintaining his calm and breezy exterior.

More curls fell across Loric's forehead, adding to his youthful boyishness. So deceptive it was. "Yes. From one man fucked over by Harley Kayson to another. We have an opportunity to build a bridge here, Arys. I ask just one thing."

"And what might that be?" Next to me, my dark vampire felt solid. Composed. If it was an act, it was a damn good one.

The evil that danced across Loric's face socked me in the gut seconds before his request did. A request he delivered with vicious ease. "Kill Jenner."

Some part of me had expected him to say that. Still it surprised me that he had the audacity to ask for such a thing, like we owed him.

Jenner himself laughed bitterly and muttered, "Piece of shit."

"I hardly think that's necessary," I said, slowly uncrossing my legs. "Jenner is mine. We've told you that he's not a problem, and he won't be. That will have to be good enough for you, Loric."

Power flowed through me despite my attempt to clamp it down. It rippled through the room, touching every man present. Loric's pupils dilated, the only visible reaction he had.

"The queen of the bloodline," he remarked, unaffected by my wolf peering out at him. "They say that any vampire who tastes your blood becomes enslaved to you. Hopelessly addicted."

"Do they now?" Raising a brow, I gave a halfhearted shrug.

Loric chuckled, eyeing me like a piece of the biggest, brightest candy in the candy store. "Show me. Prove to me that Jenner is fully under your influence. Then I'll be able to accept your claim that he won't be any trouble."

Oh, he won't be any trouble, but I'm going to kick your slimy ass all over this city. Instead of giving voice to that thought, I merely smiled. A tight smile that somehow managed to hold in the many obscenities I wanted to spew.

I didn't dare look at Jenner. Not yet. It would convey weakness. "If you'd like a demonstration of my power, I'd be happy to show you. One on one, of course."

A sweetly spoken threat. Not that I'd ever claim this prissy jerk. I would gladly kill him though.

'When the time is right,' came Arys's voice in my head. 'There are demons below this room. Play along. Be the queen I know you are.'

"Funny." With a flirtatious wink, Loric too kept up the fake friends charade we'd started. Behind his fang-baring grin lurked a monster who wanted nothing more than to kill me. Because he couldn't, we were forced to endure such shenanigans. "It's a small gesture though, isn't it? One that would allow us to move forward with a semblance of trust and good will."

Seriously? Fuck this guy.

"I'm not sure I understand what exactly you have in mind." I allowed myself a glance at Jenner. The briefest moment where I willed him to trust me. But he stared at the thick red carpet, fists clenched in his lap.

Loric twirled a finger in the air, like a bored child trying to speed things along. "Show me what makes you the queen and him the submissive. Let's see what all the talk is about."

Every second that this smug bastard all but gloated at me fed my rage. No, I couldn't deal with this shit. Demons be damned.

Again Arys's calm voice in my head. 'You bear an immortal mark, my love. Drawing demon attention the moment we arrive isn't the best way to get us safely out of here before dawn.'

'You've got to be kidding me? You want me to roll Jenner right here for this creep to watch?' Naturally I swung frantic and aghast while my dark half remained seemingly unaffected.

'I do, and as much as I hate to admit it, I feel it may be the easiest part of this evening.'

Leave it to vampires to concoct such twisted methods of testing one another. I wasn't an exhibitionist nor was I into unfairly tormenting my lovers. Despite Arys's encouragement, I made one last attempt at getting out of this.

"I've gotta tell you, Loric, that Jenner himself made a similar demand of me once. That's why he's mine now." A wicked twist of my lips formed something sinister that belonged on Arys, not me. "Is that a risk you're willing to take?"

With a loud thump Loric plunked his feet on top of the coffee table in the center of the furniture arrangement. "I doubt it will come to that. Once we get this little formality out of the way, we can really start enjoying ourselves. I don't know about you all, but I'm beginning to get hungry."

There wasn't a single thing about this guy that didn't bring out every murderous urge I possessed. He was banking on his demons to keep him safe from me. For now, he could be right.

Every vampire present waited for me to make the next move. Though perhaps none with as much trepidation as Jenner. In a way it felt like we'd come full circle, he and I. Still I'd have done anything to change what I was about to do.

As I rose from my place next to Arys, I thanked my past self for keeping Shaz and Willow away from this place. Neither of them should see this.

In front of the gas fireplace stretched a dark fur rug. Real. There was no time to feel sorry for the bear whose hide decorated the floor. My sympathy was all for Jenner as I made my way around the furniture to stand before the fire.

Every vampire in the room angled themselves to get the best view. Loric watched like a kid waiting for a peek at Santa. He needed to see it to believe it. So be it.

"Jenner." With a finger I beckoned him to me while also slipping him a small pulse of warm, suggestive power. "Join me, won't you?"

For that tiny moment when he decided whether or not to fight this, both Arys and I tensed. Then he got to his feet and prowled toward me. There was a swagger in his step and a defiant lift to his chin. He would do this, but he wouldn't be happy about it.

That made two of us.

The firelight flickered in Jenner's eyes, a strange but beautiful mix of fire and ice. He hated me right then, and he would hate me more as each moment passed. I flashed back to our talk in the hallway and his claim that he had needs too. And after claiming to care about that, I was about to exploit those needs.

Once we were face to face, I faltered. I couldn't do this. It was too fucked up.

Arys cleared his throat. "I must warn you, Loric, everyone in here will fall under her spell. Some perhaps far worse than others."

My dark flame bought me a few more precious seconds to get my head in the game. I stood there frozen, unable to act.

Loric waved a hand to dismiss the two vampires flanking him, telling them to wait just outside the door and keep anyone from entering. He was a confident motherfucker, that's for sure.

Seeing my distress, Jenner gave the slightest nod and mouthed, "Just do it."

My hands shook, and I clenched them tight into fists, willing myself to stay calm. Forcing Jenner to submit to me to satisfy Loric's twisted demand felt wrong. I felt ill. Because I knew once I started this, there would be no stopping, and that no matter how bad it felt now, I would enjoy it.

The weight of so many hungry vampire stares killed me. My anxiety grew in leaps and bounds until, to make it all stop, I closed the distance between us. Pressing myself against Jenner, I ran both hands over his chest and brushed my lips against his, just barely murmuring, "I'm sorry."

Then I rolled him hard and fast. With control as solid as his, I held nothing back. I let the power flow between us, guiding it with precision. The swell of darkness and lust rose up like a tsunami rising from the ocean only to crash down over Jenner with enough force to pull him deep under.

Unfortunately, I got hit with the splash back. It was impossible to summon that much power that fast and not fall victim to my own spell.

Harder I kissed Jenner, slipping my arms around his neck so I could press tight against his inviting body. His hands gripped my ass, and without hesitation he kissed me back. The primal force of his desire sprang free. Crushing his lips to mine, Jenner devoured my mouth.

I wanted to throw him on the floor in front of the fire and mount him. I didn't care who watched. A dark flame of lust burned inside me, brighter and hotter than the fire in the hearth.

It was Arys's smooth as sin voice in my head that broke through the lust haze. 'Easy now, my love. The goal isn't to fuck Jenner. It's to make him want it so bad he'd do anything for you. Even beg.'

The realization of what he expected doused me like a splash of cold water in the face. 'I have to make him beg?'

'On his knees, preferably.'

I shoved Arys out of my head. Nobody liked a backseat driver.

A tight squeeze of my ass coaxed a small squeak from me. Lost in my thrall, Jenner shoved his hard on into my abdomen. I pulled back to look at him and froze. My two sides were caught in a tug of war.

Doing this to him was so fucking wrong, and yet, I wanted to do it. I wanted to see him on his knees begging to please me. Light and dark went to war inside me, and this time they were evenly matched. No winner. I had to choose which side would dominate right now.

My mind was such a jumbled mess of random thoughts that I wondered if maybe Arys and I had gotten more than we bargained for when we balanced our flames. Because it had never been done before, we were guinea pigs of a sort. It hadn't occurred to me that perhaps there would be a downside.

Jenner blinked glassy eyes at me, awaiting my next move. They all did.

So I embraced the darkness. I let it take me. And it didn't need to be told twice.

I grabbed Jenner by the throat and leaned in to drag my tongue over his jugular. A sharp graze of my fangs followed, just enough to hurt without piercing flesh. His ragged gasp brought deliciously cruel intentions to mind.

Holding tight to his jaw, I pressed a dirty, demanding kiss to his lips and purred, "Tell me what you want, Jenner."

He fixated on me with the intensely intoxicated focus of one under the thrall. If he was still aware of those in the room with us, their presence wasn't enough to break my hold. With Jenner's keen control in mind, I kept the power flowing, steady and strong, giving him no chance.

A hand moved from my ass to my face. His thumb was rough, dragging along my red painted lips. "I want you to know what you're missing. I want you to see what I can offer you."

Son of a bitch. Jenner was so far under he was spilling the truth like a sobbing drunk. Maybe I went too hard too fast. Wary of Loric's heavy attention, I reminded myself that this was as much about manipulating him as it was Jenner.

Loric wanted to see Jenner humiliated and submissive. I suspected Arys wanted that too on some level. But I called the shots here. Not them. I wasn't taking it any farther than I had to.

Retaining a level head for myself proved vital. Now was not the time to give in to every urge, despite how bad I wanted to challenge him to prove his words.

I caught Jenner's hands and held them, denying the touch he so hungrily sought. "What am I to you?"

The simplest of questions. It could be answered in an endless number of ways. This might be where he blew the whole thing.

Without hesitation Jenner said, "My queen."

Searching his heavily dilated eyes, I found only truth. Even though I'd forced the answer out of him, he meant it. Since it came as a bit of a surprise, I couldn't help but feel guilty. I kind of hoped that Falon wasn't watching this, but I knew that he most certainly was.

I released Jenner with a small push. "Show me."

Lust rolled off him in waves. Each one hit me, and I basked in the heady rush. When he slowly went to his knees before me, the wetness grew between my legs.

The tips of his fingers were cool on the back of my leg, a sign that he needed to feed soon. Taking advantage of the slit in my skirt, Jenner grasped my calf and peered up at me, something imploring in his tortured expression. Like he warred with himself for allowing this to happen.

"Let me serve you." On his knees, Jenner pressed his mouth to my leg, midthigh. "Let me show you."

My stomach clenched and my groin tightened. I very much wanted him to show me. Vaguely I was aware of Arys saying to Loric, "Have you seen enough yet?"

"I don't know," Loric said, amusement in his voice. "I'm pretty sure I could get off from the residual high alone. Impressive. Still, this doesn't prove Jenner won't be a problem."

"Yes, it does," Arys countered, steel creeping into his tone. "He belongs to Alexa. He'll do anything she says. Would he get on his knees for her here in front of you otherwise?"

Jenner's hand snaked a path up my leg. A giddy, exhilarated sensation shook me. Biting down on my lip, I watched the vampire at my feet worship me. I couldn't find a better word to describe the way he dragged fingers up my inner thigh or the touch of his tongue as it followed.

"What's wrong, Arys?" Loric asked. "Don't you enjoy showing her off? I'd think you would. I sure as hell would if I were you."

Even in a swelling haze of vampire lust, I knew when someone was being a disrespectful asshole. So badly I wanted to snap my fingers and fling a psi ball in Loric's face. Patience was not my strong suit.

"Certainly," Arys agreed with a razor-edge to his voice. "What I don't enjoy is having her ogled like a carnival act for your entertainment. Jenner is ours. You can see that. And if you have reason to be concerned with anyone, I promise you, it's not Jenner."

The energy in the room shifted. Menace crept in to taint the raw desire. Several moments of strained silence descended. I tore my gaze from Jenner to find Loric and Arys engaged in a stare down that only one of them would win.

Gabriel watched them too, ready to have Arys's back.

Then much to my utter shock, Loric laughed. A good natured, just fooling around kind of laugh. "I'd like to show you around." Loric stood suddenly and swept a hand in the direction of the door. "You might like some of the changes I'm making. Come back tomorrow night. As my special guests, of course."

Just like that he'd decided that we'd proven ourselves and were worthy guests? But he wouldn't let us see what was down there right now? My ass. This stank of suspicious.

The spell now broken, the lusty haze ebbed, allowing both Jenner and I to think clearly again, albeit with some warm, cozy feelings still going on between the legs.

Jenner pulled away, almost tripping in his haste. Anguish darted over his face as he drew himself up and tried to shake off the remnants of my thrall. Not so easily done. The glare he shot me burned with anger and… pain? I had to question what I'd seen because he turned and stormed from the room without a word, ahead of everyone else.

Needing to compose myself, I ran my hands through my hair, smoothing it back from my face. I couldn't shake the feeling that we never should have come back to Vegas.

CHAPTER SIX

We'd left without pushing the issue, although I could tell that Arys wanted to. Playing along and making nice with our vampire kin meant letting him kick us out of his nightclub without so much as a peek down below. Loric had been playing it safe tonight, but he was definitely up to something.

"That was the longest forty-five minutes I've ever had to endure," Falon muttered, stepping from the shadows as we emerged back onto the busy Strip.

I jumped and threw a punch out of instinct, which he just barely dodged. "Was it really only that long? God that was painful."

"Tell me about it. Having to watch you play vampire queen turns my stomach. Although probably not as much as it did to poor Jenner there." Falon pointed after the vampire who stormed down the street a full block ahead.

"The only reason you're even here is because I'm the vampire queen," I scoffed, sidestepping a group of drunk twentysomethings laughing their way down the sidewalk. "Don't be too quick to pity those who get on their knees, Falon."

He bristled from the much-deserved jibe. Because he'd gotten on his knees for me of his own free will.

From just a few steps behind us, Arys piped up, "What's this I'm hearing? You've knelt before your queen and begged, Falon? Now that I would pay a hefty price to see."

Falon glanced back and scowled. "The only begging I've done is for Alexa to shut the hell up so I can fuck her without that godawful voice making me go soft."

I bit back a laugh. For a man who went on about how annoying my voice was, it took only a seductive whisper to make him come once he was inside me. Maybe Falon thought he had me fooled, but I knew the truth.

"Fair enough," Arys snickered, seeing Falon's insult as the lie it was. Then he threw one more jab. "As long as you're giving as good as you're getting."

Falon, however, knew better than to give Arys the satisfaction he sought. With a snide smile he said, "Trust me, I do my share of giving. In fact, I give it to her until she screams, and then I give it to her some more. Is that kind of what you were looking for?"

Arys's laugh poured out like venom. "I do so love to hear about her time with you. I've tasted you on her, you know, Falon. Licked your sweat off her skin, among other things."

Oh boy. I tried to muster shock at their behavior, but I just couldn't. Neither of them surprised me anymore. Gabriel stifled a laugh, breaking the stoic, silent front he'd put up all night.

"You guys make me crazy," I muttered, speed walking ahead of both of them.

I was ready to go home. Since I couldn't do that yet, I planned to retreat to our hotel room and mull over our next move. Some of us might also have a few itches to scratch. I couldn't say that I didn't have one gnawing a hole in me.

Walking in and out of a place like The Wicked Kiss Las Vegas without taking a nip of someone, or more than a nip, left one feeling rather ravenous. Especially after what happened with Jenner. I began to eye the throat of everyone we passed.

By the time we reached our suite, I was beside myself with the urge to sink my teeth into someone's soft, smooth neck. I slid my keycard into the slot and all but threw the door open. The living room was empty. Willow and Shaz must have gone downstairs to the casino. An angry door slam came from the room Jenner shared with the others. The sound of the shower followed. A cold shower?

Falon appeared in the middle of the living room and immediately began to appraise the place with open disdain. "You're really clutching the purse strings with this one. I didn't take you for the type to cheap out."

There was absolutely nothing wrong with our suite. It was far from cheap as well. Perching on the edge of the couch, I proceeded to pry my boots off.

"Well, I fuck you, don't I?" With a wiggle of my brows, I gave him the sassy reaction he'd been seeking.

Brow furrowed, Falon crossed his arms and, after a long drawn out minute of silent judgment, shook his head. "I don't like you in this city. It's all wrong. You don't belong here."

Overhearing this as he entered the suite, Arys quipped, "Neither do you. Don't you have some business back home? The Circle must be keeping you busy enough."

"Not nearly as busy as your wolf keeps me," Falon retorted without missing a beat.

Arys had a point though. Keeping tabs on the activity back home was vital. I tried and failed to pin the fallen angel with a grave stare. All I could think about was the pulse beating in his jugular.

"Yes, Falon, you should, um, check up on things back home." My tongue glided over my lips, and I blinked a few times before forcing my eyes to his. "Swing by my nightclub. Make sure people see you so they think I'm around."

A protest formed on his face but never made it out of his mouth. Something in my hungry gaze, or perhaps it was Arys's, changed his mind. "I don't like that look in your eyes, wolf. Take care of your twisted urges, will you? We can't have you running amok in the city like last time."

"Hey, that wasn't my fault," I objected, hands raised. "I was drugged."

Falon didn't hang around long enough to hear my defense. With a ruffle of feathers, he vanished. Just as well. I wasn't up for playing referee between Arys and him.

Gabriel wasted no time trying to make his exit as well. "I think I'm going to head downstairs. Take a little tour of the casino."

Scope out a victim and lure her in for a covert nip. That's what he really meant. I flopped back on the couch and stretched out. "No public feeding. And don't kill anyone."

Gabriel furrowed his brow and rolled his eyes. "I think you severely overestimate how many people I've killed."

"I'll head down with you," Arys said, pausing near the mirror behind the table to run fingers through his hair. Turning to me, he added, "I'm going to sniff out Shaz and see where he's gotten to. Care to come with?"

Nothing about the idea of wading through gamblers and party goers appealed to me right then. There were other matters that needed my attention. "No, you guys go ahead. I'm going to stay here and talk to Jenner."

If Arys disliked my plan, he kept it to himself. Bending down over the couch, he lifted my chin with a finger and kissed me. "I won't be far and I won't be long."

After the sound of their muffled voices disappeared down the hall, I stood up and smoothed down my dress. I paused outside the closed door to Jenner's room. A hand raised to knock, I couldn't bring myself to do it. I was probably the last person he wanted to see.

I sensed movement on the other side seconds before he jerked the door open. My hand dropped as I took in the sight of Jenner fresh from a fast shower, wearing nothing but a towel and a scowl.

"What now, Alexa? Have I not endured enough of you for one night?" Beads of water dripped from his hair to run down his bare chest. With an arm stretched above his head, Jenner leaned on the door frame, giving me a sweet view of the moisture that clung to his skin.

"I'm not here to take," I said, putting my own spin on Arys's earlier words. "Just to give. Can I come in?"

Jenner's lips pursed. He studied me with something I could only describe as suspicious hostility. Instead of closing the door in my face, he stepped aside for me to enter.

A desk with a TV mounted above it occupied the wall to the right. To the left were two double beds side by side. Across from the beds sat a couch and coffee table. The contents of Gabriel's bag were strewn about the couch where he'd made up a bed for himself.

The open curtains revealed the city in a dazzling display of lights. I paused in the center of the room, not entirely sure how to begin. Jenner closed the door and turned to face me, his face expectant and hard.

"I'm sorry," I blurted, needing to just say it. "That was a shitty demand for Loric to make… and it was shittier of me to give in to it."

Crossing his arms over his damp chest, Jenner shrugged the whole thing off. Like his personal discomfort for the joy of others was par for the course around here. I guess it was, but it didn't have to be.

"I told you to do it, Alexa. You did. Nothing wrong with that. Now the fact that you loved it, that ticks me off a little." A subtle tremor wracked Jenner's body. Red hot anger trickled from him to prod me. "I asked for it though, didn't I? All but begged you to come here. And it's not like I haven't done the same to someone else and fucking loved it."

Jenner worked hard to keep his gaze a frozen tundra that revealed nothing. When was the last time this man had allowed himself to feel a genuine emotion?

"It doesn't have to always be this way." I gestured to the space between us. "The underlying tension and bitterness. You and Arys like to rip on each other, but I know there's love there. Otherwise you never would have come to be with us when Arys killed me and he wouldn't be here now. Being bound to each other doesn't have to be a bad thing."

Not so much as a muscle twitch indicated what, if anything, Jenner felt about my statement. I'd come to mend fences. The bonds I had to the men currently in my life affected all of us. We had to find a way to make it work, or we would be condemned to resent one another. I didn't want that.

"It isn't a good thing," Jenner snarled, the tempo of his anger increasing now. "Did you come here to kiss and make up because you actually give a shit or because having your flame restored makes you feel guiltier than you're used to?"

"Well, that was a well-aimed arrow, wasn't it?" I quipped, encouraged by the enticing vibes he gave off. "I came here because there's enough stacked against all of us without being divided amongst ourselves. And because I owe you one."

No incubus vampire could hear such words and not immediately perk up. "Owe me one? Okay, you've got my attention."

Curiosity stalled Jenner's temper, but it didn't dull the icy spark in his fathomless eyes. Proving that I meant what I said might force me to put my own comfort on the line. I had to ask myself, how far was I willing to go? I was about to find out.

I could only offer him one thing. Something I didn't offer lightly. Submission.

I went to him where he still stood near the door. Holding his gaze, I trailed a hand over his aura, so close to touching him without making contact. Try as he might, he couldn't keep from trembling. "Tell me what you desire from me, Jenner. Have me any way you want me."

His pupils dilated and he searched me, like maybe this was a cruel trick. I waited for him to find the truth. I watched the incubus hunger take him as he accepted that this was indeed real.

With a monster's darkness lurking behind his keen stare, Jenner gruffly said, "Get on your knees."

His command sent a sudden shockwave of excitement through me. A lump formed in my throat, and I struggled to swallow around it. Yeah, I should've seen that one coming.

Without breaking eye contact, I slowly sank to my knees. The carpet was soft enough, though my focus was on other sensations. Such as the scent of raw, hot desire that made Jenner's aura hum with a dizzying frequency.

Jenner watched me with disbelief as he swept a lock of hair back from my face. "I want to watch that gorgeous mouth devour my cock."

It wasn't that I didn't enjoy being submissive with the right man at the right time. More that I was usually the dominant with my vampires, Arys aside of course. That tended to be a constant tug of war. So getting on my knees for Jenner and claiming my role here proved more difficult to swallow than I'd anticipated.

But what kind of queen would I be if I expected only to be served and to never serve those so tightly bound to me?

I grabbed a corner of his towel and tugged. It fell away easily, revealing the most neatly manicured male groin I'd seen in some time. Jenner went over and above on presentation. He based so much on appearance. Too much. Not that I didn't appreciate the effort.

Wrapping a hand around his straining shaft, I pumped it several times before taking him into my mouth. Holding the base in a firm grip, I dragged my tongue over the sensitive head, flicking and circling before sucking him deep into my mouth again.

From above I could feel Jenner watching. He fisted a handful of my hair, holding it out of the way so it wouldn't obstruct his view. Giving oral pleasure with vampire fangs had come with a bit of a learning curve. If Jenner's husky moan was any sign, it hadn't affected my technique.

When I sensed the rise of his climax I readied for it, but he surprised me by gently touching the side of my face. "Sorry, Alexa, but I'm going to make you work for it." Pulling away, Jenner motioned for me to rise. "Get out of that dress and get on the bed."

I was flushed with arousal as I started to slip out of the black dress. It fell in a puddle of fabric around my feet. The bra that forced my breasts together followed. I slid my hands down my body to hook a finger in my underwear. Naked, I climbed onto the bed he'd indicated and lay in the center.

"Spread your legs," Jenner commanded, coming to stand at the foot of the bed. "Touch yourself. But not how you think I want you to. Touch yourself the way you would if you were alone."

Maybe he wanted me to feel vulnerable, as he'd felt. Or maybe he just liked to watch. Either way, I felt terribly on display when I spread my legs for him. So intently he watched as I slid a hand between my legs, a finger stroking my wet folds.

"I just want you to know," I said softly, a catch in my voice. "I wouldn't do this for just anybody."

Placing both hands on the mattress, Jenner leaned forward and grinned. "Nice to know I'm not just anybody."

Pleasuring myself for his enjoyment was both liberating and embarrassing. Oddly both at the same time. Seeing the lust-drunk haze in his eyes and feeling it on the atmosphere made the uncomfortable aspect fall away. With a fingertip I traced light circles around my clit. Jenner groaned and shook his head, causing tiny water drops to spray my legs.

"Enough with the teasing, your highness. Use those fingers. Two at the very least." He wrapped a hand around my ankle, circling it tight in a needy, demanding grip.

Every order Jenner gave heightened my arousal. A cycle of it flowed between us, growing stronger with each rotation. Pulling us further under.

I dipped two fingers inside myself, a teasing glimpse before sliding them deeper. With one hand Jenner held tight to my ankle, but the other fisted his cock like a vice, pumping it slowly.

The drug-like energy filling the room swelled beyond it, overflowing into neighboring suites. If the occupants were currently inside, they wouldn't know what hit them. Ecstasy had nothing on us.

"Like what you see?" I asked with a sultry smile, eating up the hungry expression he wore.

"Fuck yes. Don't you dare come until I'm inside you." Even Jenner's control wasn't good enough to withstand much more. Not after what had happened back at the club. Too much tension had to eventually be released.

Growing impatient, Jenner barked, "On your knees. Ass in the air."

Unable to hide the anticipation from my face, I did as instructed. The bed moved as he crawled up behind me. His fingertips dug into my ass as he entered me in one furious thrust. I held tight to the blanket beneath me, gasping when he grabbed hold of my hair and tugged my head back.

Jenner rolled his hips as he filled me, hitting several key points inside me on both exit and reentry. The man knew how to fuck. He'd proven that during our first encounter and promised there was more where that came from. It hadn't been a lie.

There was a sensual aggression to the way Jenner fucked me. Like he wanted so badly to bring me endless amounts of pleasure while wanting to punish me at the same time. I couldn't help but want both of those things as well.

The first slap on my ass startled me. The initial sting subsided to a pleasurable burn that tingled. The second slap on my ass coaxed out a growl.

"Submission doesn't come easy to you, does it?" Jenner asked, caressing the spot he'd just smacked. "It brings that wolf snarling out. You might be surprised by how good it can feel to hand control to someone else."

He caught me off guard by pulling out. The touch of his hand followed, gliding over my throbbing clit. I shuddered and moaned, hating that I couldn't just throw him down beneath me and ride him.

"Yeah, I kind of like my control." I tried to sound playful but mostly just managed to sound like a needy sex kitten.

The hot, wet sensation of his tongue delving between my folds seriously tested my will. On my hands and knees as I was, all I could do was try not to collapse from the sheer pleasure.

"Do you trust me?" he murmured against my needy flesh. "Give up that control you still cling to. Let me roll you."

Now that was a dangerous request. I laughed, a small breathy sound that became a moan. "Is this not enough for you, Jenner? You need me completely helpless and at your mercy?"

"Yes, and don't pretend you're not the same damn way, succubus. It's what we are." The cool air bathed my hot skin as he withdrew his touch, leaving me quivering there. "Turn around and look me in the eyes."

I sat down on my butt and turned around to face him. Apprehension warned me against allowing him to pull me under. I could fight it, but if I let it happen, I wouldn't want to.

"Jenner," a warning rang in my tone.

He cut me off with a finger on my lips. "Trust me, Alexa. I think you'll be glad you did."

Such confidence in that claim. So when he pushed my legs apart, I let him. And when he caught my chin and gazed deep into my eyes, I never stopped him.

It took some effort to let down my defenses and let it happen. But when Jenner hit me with the dizzying effect of his thrall, I went under hard and fast. I was all his, nothing but a wanton vixen who desired only to please him.

I ran my hands over his chest before pulling him in for a messy, drunken kiss. With a sexy chuckle, he forced me flat on my back and pulled me down so my ass was at the edge of the bed. Standing before me, Jenner lifted one of my legs and thrust hard and deep.

The position allowed him to look down at me, to feed the power flow that held me captive while watching me beg and plead for release. With each thrust he brought me closer but intentionally left my clit neglected. If I'd been in my right mind, I'd have questioned his motives. As I was completely smitten in that moment, I didn't comprehend that his goal was to make me beg.

At one point I reached down to touch myself, and he slapped my hand away. "That's not how this works, your highness."

With a grasp that was somehow rough but gentle, Jenner rolled me onto my side. He got in the spoon position behind me and reached across with one hand to hold my wrists together. My back was pressed against his chest. Jenner leaned in close as he entered me from behind, pressing his face to my neck.

At some point he'd go for my throat. As his trembling, moaning victim, I couldn't wait for it. But he could. Holding my wrists in front of me, Jenner took claim of my body. Furiously, he fucked me like maybe if he did it hard enough he'd somehow purge his hunger for me. If that was the case, then the joke was on him. The more they got a taste of me, the more they needed me.

"Please," I heard myself beg, needing more of him. More contact. More power. But I was the victim now. I didn't get those things.

"Please what?" Jenner groaned into my ear, his breath hot on the back of my shoulder. The sharp points of his fangs followed as they grazed the surface of my skin.

My thoughts were jumbled. I saw through a cloud of lust. I didn't know what I was asking for, just that I had to have it now. "Jenner." His name was a cry on my lips, and it seemed to be his undoing.

Snarling obscenities into my ear, he released my wrists and slid a hand over my breast and up to grasp my throat. He jerked me into just the right position for a well-placed bite. His mouth was hot and eager on my skin as he sucked gently on my jugular. The passion and yearning in that act alone sent me hurtling toward euphoria.

Jenner molded and manipulated the energy flowing around us. It writhed with the desire for blood, sex, and release. With his mouth fastened to my neck, his hand descended between my legs to rub my clit. Timing the rhythm with each thrust, he easily brought me to a mind-numbing orgasm.

Feeding on the power of my climax, Jenner sank fangs into my neck so he could feed on the power in my blood as well. The room spun, and I closed my eyes against it. Without the visual I felt as if I were falling endlessly. My vampire lover took from me, and I simply gave, taking nothing in return.

With punishing thrusts he fucked me while my blood filled his mouth. A ragged moan preceded his release inside me. Jenner stayed buried within me, unmoving as his tongue worked the perfect wounds. Only when he'd had his fill of my blood did he pull free of my body.

We lay side by side on the bed, each caught up in the power of what we were. The power of what we'd just done. A high-frequency squeal rang in my ears. As I came back to myself, I wondered how the neighbors were faring.

After several long, silent minutes Jenner said in a husky whisper, "From just the right angle, you do look like her. I kind of hate that."

I adjusted myself so I could look at him. Our limbs were entangled, and since he'd made no effort to pull away, neither did I. "Who? Rebecca? Was that her name?"

Jenner glanced absently at the name tattooed in pretty script on his chest. "No, Rebecca is someone else. This wild hippie chick I knew in the sixties."

"Wow, stud, do tell. Inquiring minds want to know." I flashed him a playful smile, certain that I looked as high as I felt.

He graced me with a rueful smile that lit up his eyes so they dazzled in a way I'd never seen before. "What is this? The Life and Times of Jenner Malone?"

Malone? So the vamp had a last name. And two lost loves of his life. Assuming they'd both been lost.

Curiosity piqued, I wanted to pump him for more while the high had him talking. Despite how long I'd known Jenner, he still remained a mystery. I didn't know him well. It felt like time for that to change.

I dragged my finger over the letters on his chest. "Tell me about her. Tell me about both of them."

CHAPTER SEVEN

SHAZ

"How much have you had to drink?" Arys leaned in the corner of the elevator, hands stuffed in his pockets, looking so devil may care.

With an arched brow, I studied our reflection in the mirrored walls and swirled the melting ice in my whiskey glass. "I don't know. A few. What do you care? Planning to take advantage of me?"

Arys's reflection grinned. "Always."

The elevator eased to a stomach-jostling halt and opened. A middle-aged couple stepped back so we could exit. The woman ogled Arys so hard I thought her eyes would pop out of her head Roger Rabbit style. Her husband bumped her with an elbow and cleared his throat. With a blush she hurried into the elevator we'd just vacated.

Then I felt it. Heavy incubus vibes crept over me, seeking to seduce. We turned down our hall only to be greeted by loud, raucous sex from several neighboring rooms.

"They've got the entire floor fucking," Arys mused, grim but impressed nonetheless. A quick slip of his keycard, and he shoved the door to our suite open. He paused near the hall that led to Jenner's room, but one hand on his shoulder and I got him moving again.

Walking through the living room felt like wading through rushing water. It took effort and focus to stay upright against the rolling tide of sexual energy that filled the place to capacity. Even though Lex was down the hall and around a corner, it felt like she was right there with us. Her muffled moans traveled through the wall, and I grew hard at the sound.

"Holy shit," I muttered, slugging back the rest of my drink. As I went to the minibar for a few of the tiny liquor bottles piled in there, I kept an eye on Arys. "It feels pretty fucking intense in here. Maybe we should head back down."

Arys laughed this dark little laugh that felt like a finger tracing the bones of my spine. "I'm pretty sure I can get off by the sound and smell alone. He better be respecting the hell out of our lady."

A shot of whiskey burned its way down my throat. Coupled with the primed sex vibes, I was feeling tipsy and turned on. "It doesn't sound like he's disrespecting her. Pretty sure she wouldn't put up with that."

Arys's gaze continued to stray toward the adjoining hall. "It doesn't bother you?"

"Not as much as it bothers you," I answered honestly. "We're the core of the group, Arys. You, Lex, and me. I like to think of the others as the outer circle. They're tied to her whether we like it or not, but that tie creates a ring of strength around the three of us. It makes us stronger. Safer. You know that. It's only Jenner that bothers you because it's personal with him. Not to be a dick, but it is because of you that he's linked to her."

That penetrating vampire stare bore into me, his face expressionless. He always hated it when I was right.

"You call Falon outer circle, Shaz?" Arys scoffed, a dark brow lifted in wonder. "You're not paying close enough attention."

Refusing to allow his personal issues to become mine, I grabbed the empty ice bucket from the table and headed for the door. "Let me grab some ice. Then we can go talk in the bedroom. Maybe that extra ten feet between us and them will help."

When I returned from fetching ice from the machine down the hall, Arys was already in our room. The sexcapades were still going strong in Jenner's room. I paused near the hall and listened, feeling like a creep. The sound of a slap and a snarl brought my own wolf clawing up to the surface. I forced myself to move.

Arys and Gabriel had found Willow and me playing blackjack in the casino. After filling us in on their brief meeting with Loric, Willow and Gabriel had left together to hunt down a vein to open. Arys and I had come back here to talk to Alexa and Jenner about what our next move would be.

Apparently that discussion would have to wait.

I opened the door to our room to find Arys in the middle of undressing. He tossed his shirt on top of his suitcase and reached for his belt. Closing the door, I said, "It's a bit early for nudity, don't you think?"

Despite my words I couldn't tear my gaze away. I wasn't into men, but the vampire transcended being merely man to being something else entirely. Dark and fascinating, Arys Knight baffled me. I still asked myself why I wanted him the way I did, and I kept coming up with the same answer: I'd fallen for him. It was information I was still trying to process. Arys had been patient, content to allow me to do that in my own time.

Being constantly surrounded by amped up vampires didn't make that any easier.

"You can't put a time frame on nudity, pup. Anything goes, any time." He jerked a thumb toward the door before tossing his belt aside. "Besides, we'd be fools not to ride this wave."

I couldn't argue that. Arys and I didn't get as many opportunities to be alone as Alexa seemed to think. She was usually there with us. Was I ready to be alone with him? Only one way to find out.

"You're right," I agreed. "So let's ride it."

I laughed when he did a double take. He hadn't really expected me to be on board.

"Are you sure you're not drunk?" he asked as his pants hit the floor. In only a pair of black boxers, Arys strode to the bed and peeled the top blanket back.

"Maybe a bit drunk on the two vampires intent on forcing orgasms on the entire floor. Like you said, gotta grab that wave and ride it. They've already done half the work."

Keeping up with this vampire took immense effort. But I wasn't the type to back down from a challenge, and this was personal. Setting my glass on the desk beneath the television, I hooked a finger in the collar of my t-shirt and tugged it over my head.

Arys lounged in the bed, propped on a mound of pillows, hands beneath his head. The way he watched me made me feel like a buffet of pleasure on display for him. Like he didn't know where to start. "They've barely scratched the surface."

The things he wanted to do to me, I saw them all in his dark-blue eyes. My cock twitched as I kicked my jeans off. I left my boxers on and joined him in the bed. Sitting up against the headboard, I left a few inches between us. Enough to allow for personal space. Not so much that it made for any weirdness.

"It's probably good to have some time alone." The words spilled out, encouraged by lowered inhibitions. "For them, I mean. I'm sure it's good for Jenner to be alone with her."

Arys didn't miss a thing, and he was all over that slip like white on rice. "So this is something you want? To be alone together?"

I had to think about how to answer. Arys wasn't always the easiest guy to share feelings with. This was still new. "I think so. I mean, yes. I just… I'm still not sure how far I want to take it." Probably a good idea to just get that said and out of the way.

Arys sat up next to me, and the motion itself felt like a static charge. The fine hairs on my arms stood on end. We sat angled to face one another. He touched my jaw, lightly scraping a fingernail over the faint stubble.

"We take it as far as you want to. There's no pressure here. I want you to enjoy being with me, Shaz. Whatever that includes is up to you."

Relief eased some of the pressure I'd been putting on myself. None of which had come from Arys. As sex hungry as he was, he'd always been patient and respectful of my boundaries, which made me want to push them that much more.

Without waiting for him to make the first move, I kissed him. Arys was content to let me guide the kiss, at first. I took my time with it, teasing him by flicking my tongue over the silver ring in his bottom lip. He responded to me with an all-consuming passion as he let the wave take him.

Too soon he grew impatient with the tease. Grabbing a painfully tight handful of my hair, Arys plundered my mouth. His tongue lashed against mine. He caught hold of it, sucking gently, an unspoken promise of what lay in store if I opened myself to it.

Releasing my lips, Arys made his way down my neck where he lingered for just a moment over my pulse. Then he moved on, nipping the hollow in my collarbone, licking an exploratory path down my chest.

Not only did Arys let the sex wave from next door pull him under, he added his own power to the mix. I didn't stand a chance, not that I wanted to.

He pushed me back against the pile of pillows and continued to explore my body. Together we would find out what we wanted from each other. The vampire infused-lust was like a shot of the best, most fucking pleasurable drug in existence. I succumbed to its siren call, wanting nothing but more when Arys's tongue flicked over my nipple.

Holding himself up over me, the vampire shook from his efforts to take it slow. Sinking my hands into his ebony hair, I growled softly when he trailed a finger over my abs, drifting lower. Arys understood my growl as pleasure rather than a warning, and it encouraged his affections.

I'd imagined this several ways several times. In some scenarios I took the lead and proved how much I wanted him. In others, he did. None of them had prepared me for the reality of it.

He had yet to go any lower. I could feel his hesitation. Was he doubting that I wanted this? Because I sure as hell wasn't.

When I made no move to stop him, Arys continued his trek down my body, pausing to kiss a rib at random or lick my navel. My entire body flushed with heat. A need only he could satisfy gripped me, and I was more than ready for it.

The flick of his tongue along the waistband of my boxers had my cock straining to be free of them. I groaned and tensed, nervous but exhilarated.

Arys paused then, lifting his head to meet my gaze. "Tell me to stop and I will, but I sure as hell don't want to."

"No," I mustered on a sigh. "Don't stop."

My consent was all he needed. Arys grabbed my boxers and tugged. Before either of us could enjoy the line we were crossing, a loud pounding on the hotel suite door busted in to ruin the moment.

"Is this a fucking joke?" Arys muttered. "It's like a constant cock block in this fucking place."

So demanding and incessant was the banging on the door that we both fled the bed in a hurry. Disappointment and irritation crashed through the high. Whoever was on the other side of that door better have a damn good reason for the interruption.

Without wasting time getting dressed, Arys flung open the bedroom door and bolted out. I rounded the corner behind him in time to almost collide with Alexa as she flew out of Jenner's room wrapped in a sheet.

"What's going on?" Hair disheveled, makeup smeared, Alexa had the bewildered look of someone harshly ripped out of the thrall. Yeah, I knew the feeling.

Behind her Jenner emerged, tugging his jeans up. "Who is it?"

Arys peered through the peephole and shrugged. "Vampire. I don't know him. Do you?"

He moved aside to let Jenner take a look. "Yeah, I do."

Jenner dragged the door open while the rest of us hovered close enough to hear and be seen should anyone start trouble. Right away the vampire held up a hand to show he meant no harm. Bullshit. There was no such thing as a vampire that meant no harm.

"Sorry to disturb you. Loric requested that I personally deliver this message to you." The guy held out a white envelope, stretching to pass it over the threshold. Eyes wide and pupils dilated, he'd gotten enough of a taste of the power in this suite to know he didn't want anymore.

Jenner ripped the envelope out of the vampire's hand and slammed the door in his face. We all waited for him to tear it open. He scanned the paper inside from top to bottom before handing it to Arys with a bitter laugh. "It's a warning. If we try to leave town without accepting Loric's invite for tomorrow night, he'll have us intercepted. It's not an invite so much as a command. He must really want us to see his changes."

"He promises it will be worth it." Arys read over the note and chuckled. "I am going to kill that asshole. This was not worth the interruption."

With that statement he drew Alexa's attention to our state of undress. She met my gaze and lifted a brow before flashing me a knowing wink. "So do we actually go back?" she asked. "It could be a trap."

"Of course it's a trap. It's always a trap." Arys scanned the three of us, lingering on me. "We most definitely go. All of us. Like I said, I plan to kill Loric. I'm not in the mood for games. We go in, get this done, and go home."

With a nod, Jenner jumped on board. "I'd rather not drag this out any longer. I just want my life back."

I stifled a laugh. This guy was kidding himself. After the encounter he'd just had with Alexa, there was no way in hell he'd simply go back to his life here and forget all about her. Nope. I wasn't much of a betting man, but when in Rome, right? My money was on Jenner underestimating how much more Alexa would own him every time he had her. He'd never last a week without her now.

"We need a plan." Clutching her sheet, Alexa trudged into the living room, one end dragging like a train behind her.

She plopped down on the couch looking ridiculously perfect in her makeshift dress with her sex-tousled hair. A fresh wound drew my nose to the bite on her neck. Despite the glassiness to her eyes, Alexa jumped right into analytical mode. She tapped her bottom lip thoughtfully. "I need to bounce some questions off Willow about this Seven Deadly Sins stuff. Loric has got to be up to something."

"Probably intending to kill us," Jenner muttered. "He knows you weren't impressed with him tonight, and he knows he can't take us. Whatever demon party he's got going on downstairs, it gives Loric the advantage."

Arys clapped a hand on Jenner's shoulder and gave him a slight shake. "Relax, Jenner. If it's not a party already, it will be when we get there."

CHAPTER EIGHT
FALON

Alexa's nightclub was a god-awful place. Although not as bad as the horror show in Las Vegas, which stank of booze and desperation. I sat at the bar taking shots of the most expensive scotch the bartender could give me, watching the cesspool of humans and vampires that flowed about.

It looked like business as usual to me. Not sure why she worried about this place. Even if someone burnt the building to the ground, they would be doing her a favor. Although it would turn into open season on the streets, so I suppose it served its purpose.

After a few more shots I rose to leave, tossing cash on the bar to cover my drinks. Alexa's money maker was operating just fine without her. I considered going back to Vegas to let her know but decided against it. Watching her roll that vampire had left me with blue balls and a bad taste in my mouth.

Okay, so blue balls is bullshit. But leaving there with a raging erection and the desire to be the one on my knees in front of her pissed me off. Every time I fucked that woman, she embedded deeper into me. And yet, I couldn't quit her.

I wasn't sure I even wanted to anymore. That's where shit got complicated.

A call from the Circle's watchdog chased Alexa from my thoughts. Smudge hated my ass. She only called when she had to.

I stepped outside to answer it. "What's up?" I stood in the parking lot of my hybrid lover's blood den. Of all the damn things. I'd never have believed it if someone had told me this was where thousands of years of battle, service, and experience would lead me. Right between the legs of a vampire queen.

Not one to waste time on small talk, Smudge got right down to business. "One of my people got word of another ritual circle found in a city cemetery. Jez and I are on our way there now. Can you meet us?"

"Yeah, which cemetery?" Another ritual circle? Those fucking witches must think themselves brave, but they were just stupid.

This was the third ritual circle to pop up. Alexa and I had scoped out the first one together. The second one I'd taken care of alone. Alexa didn't know about that one. I'd asked Smudge to keep it from her, hoping this shit would stop. It hadn't and it wouldn't. Not as long as Lilah's followers knew she was free.

Despite my many contacts—and I prided myself on having all the inside information—I had nothing. The demon bitch excelled at keeping a low profile since she'd convinced her twin flame to abandon his light. Once Salem embraced the dark, they formed one of the most powerful demon duos in existence.

When they turned up they would bring hell with them.

If I knew Lilah, and to some extent I did, she'd hide out somewhere she felt safe and plot. The woman was patient, a real planner. Being a psychotic bitch made her unpredictable. Most of all, she was vengeful. It was only a matter of time until she came after those who'd wronged her, Alexa and myself at the top of her list.

Getting close to Lilah hadn't been easy. She'd been closed off, trusting no one. It didn't help that Shya had taken advantage of her lowly status when she'd been cursed to live as a vampire. Their history together made it difficult to get one-on-one time with Lilah, until I started fucking her.

It's amazing what people will share when you bang a few orgasms out of them. Still, she remained a step ahead of me, sharing only what she wanted me to know. All the shit she wanted me to feed back to Shya. Needless to say, there had never been any affection between us. We were each in it for our own gain.

Walking around the corner, I made sure I was out of sight and then made a translocation jump, appearing at the graveyard with little more than a thought. Humans would call it something idiotic like teleporting.

A jump involved the dissolution of the physical form, similar to how it was when I wanted to remain unseen. Incorporeal. Spirit energy with full awareness. A jump took knowing where I wanted to go and willing it to happen to project myself there. That's it. Simple on the surface but complex in execution, a translocation jump required a significant amount of energy. Even immortals have their limits and every power comes with a price.

I didn't take a corporeal form upon landing the jump. I never did. As soon as I arrived, I took a moment to scope out the scene. Only once I was as sure as I could be that no other immortals lay in wait would I reveal myself, if at all.

Too often it was not as it appeared with angels and demons. Some immortals can hide their presence while others can use a glamour to present as something or someone else. I could obfuscate myself but not mask my presence entirely, my abilities limited by my fallen status. Should I choose to embrace the darkness and go full demon, those limitations would cease.

So why didn't I? I had my reasons. Several of them. First remaining as I was enabled me to get close to people who would otherwise never allow me an iota of trust. It wasn't the main reason though.

I simply didn't have a motive to fall any further. I'd need a damn good reason to take that plunge. Because I'd seen what it had done to my brothers. What it had cost them. Maybe I was in denial remaining in between or maybe I just knew better than to let power make my decisions.

I can't say that I wasn't tempted when Bane cursed Winter and me. Embracing my power at its fullest, at its darkest, would have put Bane and me on a level playing field. But Winter had begged me not to sell out that part of myself for someone like him. She made me promise her that I never would, not for anything less than a hero's sacrifice, which she refused to allow me to make for her.

"Promise me, Falon. Let me hear you say the words."

"Get the fuck out of my head, woman." I stepped onto a stone path in the middle of the city's largest cemetery. The memory of the woman I used to love haunted me more these days than she had in a long time.

The ritual circles had all been found here. No surprise. It was private, secluded, and crowded, making it easy for a coven to scatter, getting lost in every direction. The heavily treed graveyard provided numerous places to hide.

An otherworldly frequency drew me to the ritual circle Smudge had mentioned. Nobody remained. Walking the outside of the pentagram, I expected to find signs of a summons attempt. Instead, hovering a fireball over the circle, I found traces of sulfur and chicken blood sprinkled about. Someone had used ritual magic in what felt like a locator spell. Lilah's followers perhaps? They'd tried a summons and it hadn't worked. So why would they think a locator spell would work?

Two women laughed as they approached. Their mirth carried on the night, reaching me before Smudge and Jez rounded the bend in the path. The obvious sound of kissing followed.

Despite my penchant for a little voyeurism, I didn't glance up. A bit of fluff had caught my eye.

"Find anything new?" Smudge asked as they walked up on the other side of the circle. Holding hands, the two of them batted eyelashes at each other. How they got any work done, I'd never know.

"Professional," I remarked, eyeing their joined hands. "Isn't it a rule that we're supposed to separate our personal and professional lives?"

Jez nailed me with a fierce feline stare. "Says the guy who fucks his partner on a regular basis. Hypocrite."

Dismissing her with a shrug, I stepped into the circle, steeling myself against the residual black magic. From the center of the star, I plucked what appeared to be small pieces of a broken feather.

I gathered them in my palm, waving my fireball closer. It was indeed shreds of black demon feather, some of it singed. It stank of sulfur and someone familiar.

"Yeah, I found something new." I held up the scraps of feather. "This belonged to Shya. Someone's trying to find him."

"What?" Jez surged forward, skidding to a stop when her toes touched the edge of the circle. "Who would be looking for that bastard?"

Stepping out of the circle, I motioned for her to back up. Then I redeposited the remains of the feather and waved a hand over the circle. The entire contents burst into flames, which quickly devoured the evidence before dying out.

"Lilah's followers," I began. "They knew about her affair with Shya. They're made up of witches, vampires, and demons all over the world. I can't imagine what they think they have to gain by finding Shya. If they were to release him, he'd make them sorry they'd ever looked. Or maybe at the behest of Lilah herself, though I can't fathom why she'd want to see him."

Smudge shifted her weight from foot to foot and pursed her lips uncertainly. "Nobody can find him, can they?"

"No," I assured her. "They can't. Not as long as he's hidden on consecrated ground."

Even though I knew it to be true, something about all this didn't feel right. I stared at the burnt-out remains of the ritual circle. Spring would bloom in full soon, and green grass would grow to hide the desecration here. But these spells were just the beginning. Something was coming down the wire.

"You have to tell Alexa about this. Have you seen her tonight?" Jez eyed the circle with a nauseated expression. A nephilim new to her necromancy, the half-demon leopard shifter had potential. If she proved able to master her abilities.

"Yeah, I saw her. I saw her force Jenner to beg for her in front of the man who's taken over his nightclub. So her trip is off to a lively start." I rolled my eyes, somehow still able to be annoyed by the woman with fifteen hundred miles between us. Because she was always just a jump away, and staying away from her got harder each night.

"Sounds like someone is jealous," Jez teased in a sing song. "What's wrong, Falon? Are you afraid that Jenner will take your place as her favorite hate fuck? If it makes you feel any better, I happen to know that nobody gets under Alexa's skin the way you do."

Her words were meant to mock and cajole, but they did bring me an unwelcome shred of comfort. Nothing pleased me like driving Alexa crazy. It was only fitting that I return the favor seeing as she'd made a mess of my head.

"Nobody gets inside her like I do either," I quipped, only half able to enjoy the matching scowls each woman wore. My true audience wasn't present. She was back in Vegas, probably doing that fucking vampire.

Smudge stared at her phone, texting one of her many contacts. But Jez stared at me, a knowing glint in her bright eyes. The longer we made eye contact the more that gleam grew.

Gritting my teeth, I finally snarled, "Why the hell are you leering at me like that?"

"You're so obvious" Stuffing her hands into the pockets of her jacket, Jez rocked forward on the balls of her feet with a laugh. "You might hate Alexa, but you love what she does to you. I'd even go so far as to say you've gotten attached."

Smudge snorted without looking up from her phone. "Yeah, you marked her like property. I'd call that attached. I wonder what The Circle's powers-that-be think about that."

But Alexa had marked me first in her own way, and I didn't give a flying fuck what The Circle of the Veil thought. I didn't say that. "I wonder what they'd think if they knew how much time the two of you spent slacking off and screwing around. Don't you have shit to do? A city to watch? That kind of thing."

"Actually, yeah." Shoving her phone in a back pocket, Smudge caught Jez's elbow and pulled her back to the walking path. "We've got a couple of werewolves fighting at a pub downtown. Gotta split them up and send them home before someone gets too beastly."

"Tell Alexa about this, Falon," Jez called back, pointing a finger like that would make me take her order more seriously. "Don't keep shit from her. Not if you want her to trust you. And seeing as nobody else does, you should want that."

"Get bent," I muttered beneath my breath. Jez's unsolicited advice offended me. If she thought I gave a shit who trusted me, she was wrong.

That included Alexa.

No, it fucking didn't. Even as I walked alone through the cemetery I couldn't convince myself that I didn't want her trust. It might be the only thing I did want from her, aside from that sweet pussy.

Attached. What a filthy word. I wanted to protect her from a demon who made a game of tormenting people like us. That didn't make me attached. It made me less of a piece of shit than they all thought me to be.

Denial. Another ugly as fuck word.

I would tell Alexa about the continued activity among Lilah's followers when she was ready to come home. No point worrying her just yet.

Maybe I should go back to Las Vegas tonight. Then again, no, Alexa knew how to reach me if she needed me.

CHAPTER NINE

"Are you kidding me right now, Lex? I'm not leaving without you." Shaz's keen wolf stare followed me about our room as I searched for my phone. His blatant refusal had been expected.

"I knew you'd fight me on this, but it's safer if you go home," I insisted for the third time as I bent down to peer under the couch, feeling about. "I don't want you to become a target, Shaz. It's not worth the risk."

In the quiet that followed, I knew he and Arys were exchanging a look. It was confirmed when Arys jumped into the argument. "Sending him home without us could make him a target. That's the risk we shouldn't be willing to take."

On my hands and knees scouring the floor beneath the furniture, I huffed a strand of hair out of my face. "So you guys are teaming up against me, huh? Guess it had to happen sometime."

I popped my head up from between the couch and coffee table to find them grinning at each other. No, it was more than that. Shaz's cheeks flushed slightly, and his heart rate ticked up a notch. "Maybe teaming up without me too?" I teased.

Shaz's face grew redder, and he avoided my eyes by digging through his suitcase. Arys's devilish blues found me. He raised a dark brow and nibbled the silver ring in his bottom lip. Yeah, they'd taken it further, though not all the way, or else Shaz would've been more obvious about it.

"Well, we had to find some way to pass the time without you," Shaz tossed back. Pulling two pairs of dark pants out, he assessed them both before tossing one aside in favor of the other.

"Can't argue that." Crawling along the length of the couch, I made my way around the seating area of our room.

On my hands and knees with my yoga pant-clad ass in the air, I felt them both watching. So just to tease them a little, I paused and gave my rear a shake.

Arys took the bait. "Now that's an enticing visual." He crept around the back of the couch to perch on the arm of it. "What do you say, Shaz? Wanna take that pretty ass or that sweet mouth? I'm more than happy with either."

"Hey now," I warned, waving Arys off with a finger. "I'm looking for my phone. This is not an invitation."

Playing along with Arys, our wolf snickered. "Flip for it? We'll trade off halfway through anyway."

Spying my phone tucked between one of the sofas and a small end table, I fished it out, raising it in victory. Then I flipped them each the bird. "Who the hell said I have to be the center of this sandwich? Sounds to me like we can switch off on that too."

"Funny, Lex." Shaz gathered his clothes under an arm and headed for the shower across the hall. "It's always going to be hotter with you in the middle."

I waited for the bedroom door to close behind him before saying, "I don't know about that."

Arys delivered a playful slap to my ass as I stood up. The slight sting brought a squeak and a giggle from me. "He's right, my love. It will always be the hottest with you in the middle."

I quickly replied to a few texts from Jez. Nothing much going on back home. No news was good news. Unfortunately, we had a terrifying demon party to get to, and I couldn't feel more unenthused.

"So how much teaming up without me did you guys do?" I asked, curiosity getting the better of me.

"Not nearly as much as you think we did." Arys caught my hand and pulled me close for a kiss. "We were interrupted by Loric's messenger at the door."

"And if you hadn't been?" I prompted, encouraged by his naughty expression.

"Let's just say that if I find myself in that position again, I won't be answering the door." With a caress of my ass, he gave me a gentle push toward said door. "You better go give your vampires blood. We don't want to be late. Or maybe we do. See if Gabriel can get anything from a touch."

We had no idea what we were walking into since receiving Loric's demand to return. Willow suspected there might be some ritual play, which was why I'd wanted to send Shaz home. I'd been outvoted so it was a moot point.

I left Arys to get ready and went in search of Willow and Gabriel. We couldn't walk into a demon playground without everyone being at their strongest.

Jenner stood in front of the large living room window, staring down at the Strip while snarling obscenities into his phone at some unlucky sucker. A lot of his staff had turned on him in his absence. Even if he wrestled control of his club back from Loric, he could never trust them again.

The door to the second bedroom stood open. Poking my head inside, I found Willow and Gabriel seated on the couch, engrossed in discussion.

"… in mind, no two Sins are alike," Willow said as I entered. "Some are bottom feeders with very little impact. Others have more than enough power to cause mass effect. Unfortunately, a city like this tends to draw every kind."

Hands on hips, I said, "Not sure I'm liking the sound of that."

They both glanced up and gaped at me. I felt disheveled, with my hair wild, still wearing what I'd slept in.

"Hey." Willow's face softened into a friendly smile. I saw it more these days than I had during his short but painful stint as a demon. I'd missed it. "Sorry it's not better news, but it never is with demons."

"I know. Keeping my fingers crossed for bottom feeders though." Wishful thinking at its finest. No such luck I knew.

Willow had come back to the suite to find us brainstorming Loric's insistent invitation. He suspected Loric lured the Sins demons by offering them that which they most sought: Sin. He had it in abundance inside that nightclub. What he got in return was power and protection.

According to Willow, the Seven Deadly Sins demons operated by sowing sin wherever they went. That sin grew and spread like a virus among humans and any other creature in its path, like us vampy types. As each individual demon spread its sin, its power grew, enabling it to spread even more sin. A vicious and terrifying cycle. It took only a look at the world in its current state to see the truth of it.

The angels fought against the Sins demons, keeping sin from encompassing the entirety of every being. As a Hound of God and a Light Flame, I would be expected to fight them too if necessary, to the best of my ability. As a vampire with power rooted in lust, I was just a little nervous about how I might do that.

"I have no doubt that you can hold your own." Willow slid over a bit more, creating a larger space in the middle for me to sit between them. "As bad as the Sins sound, they're petty annoyances compared to Lilah and Salem."

I flinched at the sound of their names and the reminder that I had yet to face my greatest battle. Taking a seat between the two vampires, I let my gaze drift out to the view of the Strip. This city never took a break. Even during the day, with the sun high and the drapes shut, the city was in a constant state of unrest.

Night was when it really came alive. Like the monster beneath your bed, invisible when the lights were on but still there.

"Sorry," Willow hurried to add. "I didn't mean to bring you down."

As soon as I sat his aura spiked with apprehension. Making this easy on him was important to me, which was why Gabriel was there. One on one always proved more dangerous when trying to stay in control. Avoiding that should make it easier for Willow, but surely he knew that it only prolonged the inevitable.

He wanted me. They all did. That want grew every time they tasted me.

What would happen if he continued to hold back?

"No worries." I patted Willow's arm, easing him into my touch. This would spiral fast once we got started. Turning to Gabriel, I searched his dark eyes, finding them cool and calm despite his obvious yearning. "Are you guys ready? We don't have a lot of time. Freakshow to get to and all."

It was Willow I needed to hear it from. He sat stiff beside me, several inches between us. I wanted to relax him but didn't want to force it.

"Ready when you are," Gabriel said, content to sit back and let it happen as it happened.

So quiet and vigilant. Not a big talker. Gabriel noticed more than he let on. Observation could be a power all its own. I still questioned Hurst's warning about him. If the reclusive old vampire reached out to me again, I planned to grill him about it.

"Yeah, I'm ready." A nod of his dirty blond head and Willow adjusted on the couch to face me.

I extended a wrist to each of them, letting calm vibes seep forth. "If you need something from me, anything at all, tell me. I don't want you guys to be uncomfortable, and I sure as hell don't want you to suffer. That's not who I want to be with any of you."

Except for maybe Briggs. I couldn't let myself think about what it meant that his hungers for me were growing. Or what it meant for Juliet.

"I know that's not who you are." Taking my offered arm, Willow clasped my hand comfortingly between both of his. "Don't ever worry about that, Alexa."

Gabriel took my other hand and stroked a finger over my palm. It tickled, and I almost tugged my hand away with a laugh. When I met his studious gaze, I found myself struck silent.

"Never believe that you're anything less than a goddess." Gabriel slid his fingers between mine in a slow but sensual caress. "There's a reason you're the queen."

So smooth was the erotic pulse of power he slipped me. It rolled through me to Willow, joining the three of us. Just enough to bring a relaxed ease over the room.

Willow held my wrist gently, like it was a delicate baby bird, while Gabriel gripped tight, forcing the vein to bulge. They both moved closer to me on the couch. It just went without saying that they needed to taste my desire.

Still, Willow held himself back. He pressed his lips to my wrist, feeling my pulse. The promise of blood wasn't enough. Not anymore. I felt it in his hesitation.

On my other side, Gabriel did not hold back. Brazenly he dragged his tongue over my wrist. The memory of his mouth between my legs brought the rush of arousal he sought. Gabriel was eager to please. The succubus in me wanted a taste of that enthusiasm.

Willow couldn't help but succumb to the rising tide. The tension in his shoulders melted away, and he became someone else. Some*thing* else.

With both hands he gripped my forearm. His lips moved on my skin, the faintest flutter like butterfly wings. The more he touched me, the more touch he needed. Light kisses became hungry sweeps of his mouth and tongue over my skin, swirling along the blue veins in my wrist.

Though neither man had touched more than an arm, a needy throb rose between my legs. Because my power was a double-edged sword, as their need for me grew, so did my need for them.

That could get tricky. *Do not think of Briggs.*

I could just kill him. I'd much rather kill him. *Do not think of Briggs!*

Then Gabriel nipped the sensitive inner curve of my elbow, and that other guy was the furthest thing from my mind. Long black hair fell to hide his face, enhancing the mystery that was Gabriel. Both hands held my arm as he teased the veins in the nook of my elbow.

Willow's hand on the back of my neck drew my gaze to him. I turned to find him much closer than I remembered. Had I even felt him move?

I fell into those gold-flecked eyes. Lost in their green depths, I somehow became aware that I'd fallen under his spell despite never feeling the obvious rush of his thrall. How the hell had he done that? I always knew when I was being rolled.

He stared at my lips like he wanted to kiss me. Torn between my light and dark sides, I both wanted and didn't want him to do it.

But mostly I wanted him to do it.

Being between Willow and Gabriel on the couch set loose every dirty desire and hidden fantasy I harbored about them. A few more than I realized. I wasn't used to being between anyone but Arys and Shaz like this, and it felt addictive.

Gabriel's hand slid across my waist and up to my breast. Without warning, he bit into my inner elbow. I flinched and gasped, which was all Willow's hunger needed.

Grabbing my chin in a bruising grip, Willow kissed me. Before I could decide to kiss him back he bit my lip. The sudden sharp sting brought my dark side bubbling up in a wicked way. He sucked my bleeding lip into his mouth and groaned softly.

Before either of us could take it further, he pulled away with a grimace and bit the wrist he still held tight in one hand. Chest heaving as I spiraled, my entire focus was encompassed by how it felt to have their mouths on me as they drew on my blood and power.

The sound of wind rushed through my ears. Overhead the ceiling blurred and grew farther away. I basked in their hungry attention while trying to keep my own reined in even as the dark taunted me: *Put them both on their knees; make them both beg for it.*

Willow broke away first. He tore his mouth from my bleeding flesh like a man waking from a nightmare. Sudden and with a gasp. For a strange moment he held my gaze, looking both uncertain and mesmerized. Then he kissed the back of my hand and rose, leaving me alone with Gabriel.

I waited until I heard Willow's voice in the living room with Jenner. Then I turned to Gabriel who released my arm and licked my blood from his lips.

"Have you seen anything?" I asked. "From touching me just now? Or any other time."

Feeling like a nag, I smiled apologetically. I couldn't help but wonder what he saw every time Gabriel and I touched, if anything. Most of the time, I didn't ask. Because I didn't want to know. Uneasy about what we were walking into tonight, I had to turn every stone I could.

Before he spoke I saw it on his face. My insides tightened in suspense.

"Yeah, I saw something. But, Alexa, you have to understand that it doesn't always make sense. Sometimes it's nothing more than an image or a flash of sound or smell. Other times it's more in depth. Part of a conversation or detailed action." Leaning back against the arm of the couch, Gabriel shook the hair from his face.

Something about the way he watched me set my nerves on edge. It drove me a little nuts that he could see and know things about me, never sharing if he so chose. I had to trust him. He'd earned that. But trust didn't come so easy.

"And?" I prompted, motioning for him to keep talking.

Still he watched me with that strange intensity of his. Part of him was still thinking about fucking me. Taking my blood was mere foreplay these days. Yet even when affected by me, this studious side of Gabriel remained always at work. Quietly analyzing everything.

Always trying to put together the pieces of what he saw perhaps?

"What are you wearing tonight?" he asked with a quirk of a grin.

"Assuming there's a valid reason for this question, I haven't decided yet. Why?"

Despite his best efforts, Gabriel blatantly ogled my breasts through my thin tank top. Without a bra it didn't leave a lot to the imagination. "Give me some time to piece it together. I've learned the hard way that sharing a vision taken out of context can lead to a fuck ton of trouble."

Again with that whole trust thing. Still, I could see how a random visual could easily be misconstrued. Conclusions could be wrongly jumped to.

"Okay, Gabriel, I'm trusting you to tell me what you saw when it makes more sense." Before I stood to go get ready, I leaned in to kiss him, letting him taste the bloody cut on my lip. "Don't let me down."

CHAPTER TEN

Seeing as an evening like this usually called for attire fit for feeding, fighting, and fucking, I'd leaned toward fighting. In a little black dress with a knee length skirt that allowed me to move with ease, I'd gone with a sultry, smoky eye makeup. No lipstick. I wore boots made for kicking some ass. I'd managed to tame my hair so it fell down my back in gentle curls.

The guys were in various states of dress, mostly casual and comfortable. Everyone expected a fight. With four vampires and a werewolf surrounding me, I approached the front door of The Wicked Kiss apprehensive but ready.

Arys's plan was to kill Loric and head home. Arrogant as that vampire could be, even he knew it would never be that easy. Nothing ever was. Not in our world.

"Is that feathered asshole seriously going to let you walk in there without him?" Arys snarled. He walked on my left, protectively close. Almost too close. "So he'll fuck you but he won't fight for you? If that mark draws demon attention, I'll gut that useless angel every night for a month."

When Falon still hadn't shown up as we left the hotel, a small niggle of disquiet worried at me. Was something keeping him, or had he just decided that he was bored of Vegas and I could handle it without him?

There wasn't a man present who was a fan of Falon, so aside from some muttered agreement, nobody had anything to add.

Except for Falon himself.

He stepped into view in time to block our entry to the writhing pit of a nightclub. A hand on the door, he nailed Arys with a vicious silver glare. "Watch yourself. Too quickly you forget everything I've done for her. For you. I bounce back pretty fast from a disemboweling. Do you?"

Arys drew up close to the fallen angel, mere inches away, trapping him against the door. Alarmed, I grabbed Arys's arm but he wouldn't be moved. "Not the time for this shit, guys," I warned.

On my other side Shaz tensed, ready to grab Arys if he snapped. But my dark half just smiled into Falon's face, baring fangs.

From behind us Jenner hissed, "Do you think your ego could possibly wait for a better time, Arys? My livelihood is on the line here, and you fucking owe me."

The vampire and angel staredown was admittedly hot but just as terrifying. Neither of them were the type to bluff. Lucky for them, they weren't stupid either.

Arys backed off so Falon could open the door.

As a group we drifted through the main floor where people crowded slot machines when they weren't trying to find a vampire hook up. Right away a vampire approached Jenner and handed him a keycard for the elevator. From beneath us the energy within the building swelled. Like sudden noise in my head, it was a cacophony of muffled sensations. Like they escaped whatever barrier held them contained below.

Fear. Rage. Greed. Lust. Too many vices, rife with darkness, like a thousand voices talking all at once inside my head.

"What the hell is going on down there?" I asked, aiming the question at Willow and Falon.

"Hell indeed," Falon muttered, keeping his distance from all of us. His silver stare shifted to Willow. "If I were you, Hound, I wouldn't worry about the demons taking an interest in you. The angel you turned hybrid will get all their attention."

Calm but defensive, Willow scoffed. "I don't know. A known traitor in their midst might prove quite the attraction."

"No." Holding up a hand, I cut off Falon's retort and spun to face all of them. "We're not doing this now. While we are in this building, we watch each other's backs and bite down the snide remarks. This might be tough for some of you to accept, but as you're bound to me, you're bound to one another. We have to make this work. All of us."

I turned to keep moving. The grumbles and insults ceased.

As Jenner swiped the card and the elevator door slid open, Gabriel took the opportunity to grab my arm and murmur in my ear. "Whatever I saw, I don't think it's from tonight."

Somehow I felt both nervous and relieved. With an appreciative nod, I gave his arm a friendly squeeze. I trusted him. Despite the many reasons not to, I just did. Although gazing around at the men surrounding me as we crowded into the elevator, the same could be said about most of them.

The elevator door slid open, and we stepped into a whole other world. One of high roller humans, vampires, shifters, and more demons than I cared to see gathered in one place.

We were all momentarily stunned speechless, except for Jenner who uttered, "What the fuck?"

Sin was on display everywhere. The fight cage remained in its place as a central focal point. However, it was no longer the only focal point.

To either side of the fight cage, an altar of sorts had been erected, two raised platforms draped in black carpet. Over them, black stone statues of grotesque creatures loomed, peering with sightless eyes at those upon the altar, offering themselves to evil.

On one a man lay naked and bound while half-a-dozen vampires feasted on his blood. They drained him dry and he was removed, only to be immediately replaced with another human from the waiting lineup.

Behind the table, watching it all, stood a frightfully tall demon with a pig's head. Hooves for feet and an apish body, it was a truly hideous thing. Gluttony.

"Vile," Willow hissed, fearless in the face of so much evil. Wingless but an angel still.

On the other altar a woman and a man were each tied to a Saint Andrews Cross that held their limbs stretched in every direction. Two men, human, tortured them with various tools made to rip, shred and burn. A demon with a goat head watched with glee, three long, skinny tails whipping about behind him.

I glanced to Willow with a raised brow.

"Envy," he said, tone thick with disgust. "Those people have something others want. Money. Success. Anything. The envious derive joy from the pain of those who have what they desire."

"Twisted shit," I muttered, rubbing my arms. Despite shielding as hard as I could, there was no keeping this level of darkness from breaking through. My head began to feel heavy with the pressure of it all.

The perimeter of the room was sprinkled with poker and blackjack tables. A demon with a bushy fox tail peeking from between his wings moved among them, encouraging high rollers to place bigger, riskier bets. Greed.

A bald demon with red snake eyes hovered close to Greed, ambling along behind him. Doing absolutely nothing at all. It took several moments of studying him for me to realize this had to be Sloth. His mere presence seemed to discourage the gamblers from doing anything else.

One demon stood outside the fight cage but close enough to touch the metal bars, watching with disinterest. Wait, disinterest? I peered closer, curiosity stoked.

Deer-like antlers perched atop a head that was both man and cat. Sharp feline features defined a rugged, masculine face. Like a wildcat shifter caught between forms. A long black braid fell down a mostly humanoid body that included a thick ebony tail. Unlike the other altar demons, he wore robes that one might expect on a warrior or even royalty. The air of power danced stronger around him than the others.

Willow took one look at the demon and said something in the language of the immortals. I didn't have to be fluent to know it was a curse word. Falon slid him a sidelong glance that was both inquisitive and amused but said nothing.

That one was Wrath, I realized, and a cold hand of dread touched me.

"So where is Lust?" Shaz asked, accepting a drink that a passing waiter forced into his hand. When the waiter got lost in the crowd of sin worshippers, he ditched the glass on an unoccupied table.

Most of the tables that offered a place to sit were empty. Everyone clamored around the altars or gambled. A static-like noise preceded Loric who burst from the crowd before us.

His suit dripped a deep blood red. Black shirt open to his navel, Loric's blue eyes dazzled as he poured out the charm. He was most certainly high on the intoxicating vibes that flooded the building.

At his side stood a demon with a lion's tail and a mane of blond hair to match. Pride. He reeked of it.

"Arys. Jenner." Loric fired a sly glance my way. "The Queen. So good to have you tonight. I always did have a fondness for Harley's vampires. Please, enjoy the evening as my special guests. Anything you want, it's yours."

Pride's gaze drifted over each of us, lingering on Willow. Fuck me. If turning Willow got him killed, I'd never forgive myself.

"Fascinating changes you made to the place, Loric. Thanks for the invite." Arys swept forward to extend his hand in a friendly gesture that was anything but.

Their hands touched, and I could feel the friction as Arys gave Loric a warning pulse. Subtle but palpable. And Loric smiled right through it.

He couldn't take Arys in a power struggle. He used his words instead. "I must inform you that the building has been spelled. Nobody leaves until sunrise." With a slight bow, Loric beamed with pride, and it suddenly made so much sense why the demon of the same name had latched onto him. "So enjoy yourselves. Later in the evening we'll be having a visitor of sorts. I can hardly wait."

Arys laughed along with him but shook his head both impressed and wary. "You are a crazy motherfucker, aren't you?"

Loric tipped an imaginary top hat to him, but his piercing gaze landed on me. "Wait and see."

The one refreshing aspect of Loric was that he didn't marvel over me, scrutinizing or lusting after the hybrid queen. Of course, he cared so little about my power because he was smitten with the demons. He wanted what they had. Because whatever strengths Harley had received as a vampire, Loric didn't. So naturally he wanted bigger and better.

Continuing on like a carnival ringmaster, or perhaps a used car salesman, Loric waved a hand toward the buffet of sin. "Feel free to indulge in any and every one of your hungers. And I do mean any. Nothing is off limits tonight, though you might find what you like in the theatre."

Lust was in the theatre. So why couldn't I feel it?

The wrathful, envious, and gluttonous vibes battered at my shields, seeking a way to influence my emotions. I kept an eye on

Shaz, the only one of us who couldn't fend off the assaulting forces in any manner other than sheer will. However, he was possibly the only one who might stand a chance of keeping his head together without the darkness that streaked through the rest of us.

Shoulders squared with tension, Shaz stared at the fight cage. Remembering.

I reached out to touch his hand, and he whirled to face me, his eyes wild with wolf. Shit. Holding his hand tighter, I aligned my energy with his, doing all I could to shield him.

A commotion broke out near the fight cage. Wrath overflowed from two vampires fighting it out inside, infecting those who watched. Several more fights broke out among the spectators.

Raising a too perfect, definitely plucked brow, Loric appraised the ripple effect with approval. And yet, the Wrath demon remained unimpressed. Almost bored with it all.

"I have other guests to see to." Loric smoothed the lapels of his jacket and nodded for Pride to follow. "Enjoy yourselves."

Pride's scarlet stare passed over us once more, this time pausing on Arys. So curious were his lion-like eyes. So devious as well.

With his demon in tow Loric strode away, too confident for my liking. As he approached the Wrath demon, his confidence faltered. He feared these demons, and yet he stupidly invited them in to cause mayhem. He had no control here. Pride hadn't said a word, and still it was obvious that he had Loric firmly under his thumb.

"What's his end game?" Directing my question to Falon and Willow, I braced against the growing rage spilling from the fights. "Will those demons reward him for this? Give him power?"

The seven of us stood at the back of the room. We hadn't made it far from the elevator. Trapped until sunrise. And even then vampires can't walk in the sun. Clever trick, asshole.

Falon answered first. Silver wings cloaked him like a shield. Was he concerned? He'd never admit it anyway. "They'll give him something all right, but it will always come with strings attached."

"That doesn't deter everyone though." Sounding detached, Willow stared at the altar where vampires gorged themselves on human blood.

If he wanted to join them, could I stop him? Would I even want to? The longer I let myself follow his gaze, the more appealing it became. I forced myself to look away, seeking reassurance in Arys who had drawn closer to Shaz.

"Why don't you take Shaz and try to get out of here?" Arys suggested, more uncomfortable now than when we'd first arrived. Pupils looming large and black, he was feeling the effects of this place, as we all were. "Take Falon too. Just go."

"Arys, I'm not leaving you," I protested.

Falon threw both hands in the air. "Are you really that fucking stupid? What part of twin flames do you have a problem understanding? Twin as in two. As in don't be caught apart at a wackjob circus like this."

A muscle twitched in Arys's jaw. Irritation flashed across his face. That irritation could burst into an all-out fight to the death pretty fast around here. Shaz seemed to think the same thing because he put a hand on Arys's arm.

Willow nodded. "He's right. Twin flames have to stay together. Don't get split up."

"We won't be getting out of here," Gabriel spoke up. The quiet observer. He waited for us to turn to him before shrugging and stuffing his hands into his jean pockets. "Not until sunrise. So we might as well figure out our next move."

The scuffle that had broken out near the fight cage had been subdued. For now. Two vampires faced off against two werewolves. Supernatural blood hung heavy on the air, mingling with human scents to create an aroma that started plucking my fingers off the ledge, urging me to fall into my bloodlust.

Vertigo hit me. My head spun.

I held tight to Shaz in an attempt to stay on my feet. The closeness of him, the scent of wolf and man, it brought visions to mind of tearing into his flesh. Letting the blood flow.

Just as fast as the dizzy spell hit, it subsided, taking with it the sudden hunger for Shaz. Suddenly awash with fear, I pulled away from him. The influence here was too strong. How long would we be able to keep from succumbing completely?

"We need to get Shaz out of here." I squinted as another wave of blood-hungry urges struck. Did nobody else feel this?

"Lex? Are you okay?"

I couldn't answer Shaz because I didn't know. A suffocating sensation of total darkness shook me. When he tried to touch me, I had to pull further away to stifle the urge to hurt him. Not since before the restoration of the twin flame balance had I hovered so precariously on the edge of control.

"It's the war of light and dark." Falon's arm went around me, ready to keep me from going at my wolf. "The fight arises inside her all the time. Perhaps more keenly now than ever before."

Even Arys, who lived with a spark of light due to our bond, couldn't relate to what I went through. Being his Light Flame while bound by darkness to so many deadly and dark men, it flew in the face of all that was natural.

Though Falon and I never touched in front of others, I found myself clinging to him. A wing curled protectively around me, and I dared to stroke a hand over the feathers. Falon felt safe in my mind. If this place drove me from Jekyll to Hyde, he was the one person I couldn't kill.

"Sounds like madness," Jenner muttered absently. But it echoed in my ears, repeating itself over and over.

"Indeed." Touching the side of my face, Falon drew my gaze to his. "You're the Queen of Light and Dark, Alexa. You rule them both. Remember that. The power must obey you. Don't make me slap it into you again. Although I'd gladly do so."

In the depths of those silver orbs, I found only truth. He believed the claim he made. Somehow, he made me believe it too.

Arys and Shaz wore matching expressions of disbelief and fury. They didn't know the depth of the relationship Falon and I had formed. Hell, we didn't even know.

They might have given over to the wrathful temptations spiraling about in their heads. Another few seconds of watching Falon ground my scattered thoughts, they would have tag teamed him right there. Sadistic envy and domineering wrath, two supercharged powers that sought to claim each one of us.

My two loves never had the chance to act on their sinister urges, however. We had been spotted.

A demon glided through the crowd, his sights set on our group. A party like this must draw several kinds, I imagined, but I hadn't let myself imagine a familiar menace stepping from the crowd of chaos and maniacs.

All kinds of regal in dark-blue robes. A gold and jeweled crown of sorts woven among his horns, two on either side. Black wings flared behind him, making his massive frame loom larger. Red eyes glittery with amusement.

Bane.

CHAPTER ELEVEN

Falon shoved me back and blocked me with his body. I stumbled into Willow who caught me. Alarm sang through me, driving every thought from my head but one: keep Bane's attention on Falon and me. That's all that mattered.

I smashed through the mental door between Arys and me, all but shouting inside his head. 'If this gets bad you take Shaz and go. Upstairs. Anywhere. Just fade into the crowd.'

Arys resisted. But when I fixed him with terror-filled eyes, he nodded. Reluctantly. 'I'm not going far.'

"The Queen of Light and Dark and her faithful subjects," Bane boomed in a jovial, loud voice that made my knees shake. "A pleasure to see you again, Alexa. Falon… You not so much."

"Small world," I managed to say. Stepping away from Willow, I came forward to greet the dark prince. "I can't say the feeling is mutual, Bane."

"It could be. You seem to be missing a demon from your harem." Much to my relief, Bane seemed relatively uninterested in my men. Aside from Falon of course. The two immortals looked each other over, two men with a thousand-year feud they would never let die.

Steeling myself against the many temptations popping holes in my defenses, I gathered my power tight in my core. Using it in a crowd of vampires and demons would draw deadly attention. I was caught here.

"I can't miss something I'm not looking for." I delivered the verbal blow with smooth precision and confidence that I did not feel. Showing weakness wasn't an option.

Bane's laugh thundered, making my skin crawl. The silver feather on my neck began to tingle when his gaze fell upon it. He sobered quickly. "Damn, Falon. I didn't think you were so serious about this one. What's so special about her that you would take a risk like that?"

A risk? Despite being afraid to take my eyes off the demon, I glanced to Falon for his reaction. I didn't understand what Bane was getting at.

"Move on, Bane. She's just a hybrid with power." Falon didn't look at me when he insulted me. He delivered his lines with ease. "A succubus with a nice touch and warm hands. Nothing to concern yourself with."

Bane didn't buy Falon's flippant act. Dark hair moved about his shoulders like a lion's mane as he shook his head. "You expect me to believe that you'd put your mark on some common succubus? That you'd risk what meager scraps you have left at the table for a sullied hybrid queen?"

"Who the hell are you calling sullied?" I bit out, my wolf bursting into my vampire-blue eyes.

Falon's tight-lipped expression shut me up. His face had gone ashen. A nerve had been struck. What was it about this mark that I didn't know?

The angel's response came in the language of the immortals. Whatever he said, it was delivered with venom.

"Hey, none of that." I pointed a finger at both Falon and Bane in turn. "Don't leave me out of the conversation."

"Oh, did you not get that?" Bane asked innocently, smirking like the supreme douchebag he was. "Falon defended your honor. Quite colorfully too, I might add. But it's just a ploy to get around the real subject at hand, that pretty mark on your neck there, sweet snowflake."

The term had no effect on me other than to creep me the heck out. Falon though, it sent him from leashed guard dog to rabid wild beast in seconds.

Snowflake. Winter. Oh, dear God. It was a trigger.

He lunged at Bane, and I threw myself in his path.

"Falon, don't!" My shout was lost amid a raucous cry from the fight crowd. With each fight their hunger for more bloodshed and rage grew. "Don't do this. It's what he wants. You know that."

In my peripheral view Arys held Shaz in place, trying to keep him calm. Willow and Gabriel stood ready to jump in if needed. But Jenner, he'd disappeared. I couldn't be bothered with that right now.

Hands raised, I used a push of energy to keep Falon from getting past me, hoping it wasn't enough to draw attention. Bane delighted in our display as it fed everything he thought he knew about us. When I touched Falon's face, he tried to jerk out of my grasp.

"I never thought you'd do it." Bane sounded both impressed and surprised. "I mean, you didn't do it for Winter."

All I had to hear was her name. I threw an energy wall up to separate Bane from us. Then I turned to grab Falon's face and forced him to meet my eyes. "Look at me, Falon. Do it!"

He complied but only just.

"You cannot give him what he wants. Don't give in to the wrath. Not here. Not now."

In his eyes I saw a torrent of pain and hatred. All because of Bane.

I whirled back to face the demon. "What are you hoping to achieve here?"

"You're a cute little thing." Bane swiped a drink from a passing waitress's tray and downed it in one swallow. "Powerful too. Feels like something I'd like to get better acquainted with. But you clearly don't know shit. That mark on your neck is Falon's promise to protect you at any cost. A pretty bold declaration for someone who claims that you're nothing to him, don't you think?"

Without care, he tossed the empty glass. It shattered on the floor several feet away.

"I am nothing to him." Those words felt hollow. I struggled to wrap my mind around what Bane meant.

Enjoying Falon's discomfort, Bane casually stretched his wings. "If that were true, why would he be willing to complete his fall for you after a millennium of walking the line? Seems to me, snowflake, you must be worth it. Which leads me to wonder what's so damn exceptional about you."

Complete his fall for me? Falon's face revealed nothing. This couldn't be right. He would never.

Brushing me aside, he stormed right through my barrier and up to Bane. "Call her snowflake one more fucking time."

The burly demon smirked. There would be no stopping them now. Wrath had taken hold.

"You push her away and talk like she's underworld scum," Bane taunted, extending a hand toward the fight cage. "It's a lie. If she means enough for you to go dark, Falon, maybe you'd be willing to prove it. Defend your mark."

Challenge issued, Bane folded thick arms over his chest. He took such joy in sticking it to Falon. It shone in his eyes. I hated him. If worry hadn't struck harder than rage, I'd have gone at him myself. He saw it too. With a chuckle he regarded me thoughtfully.

"Fine." Falon shrugged out of his trendy jacket and tossed it over the back of a nearby chair, ignoring the vampire who sat there. "Let's get in the cage."

"What? No, this isn't happening." Neither of them paid me any mind, despite my frantic protest.

"Don't worry, snowflake," Bane assured me with a sinister wink. "I'll go easy on him, just for you. And I'm sure you'll find a way to show your appreciation."

Falon's fist smashed into his gloating face. The blow snapped the demon's head to the side. "I told you not to call her that."

Wiping blood from his nose, Bane's humor vanished. "And last time we spoke, I told you what I plan to do to that tight little body of hers. She's not going to care what I call her when I rail her into submission."

Now my temper flared. As the flow of sins taunted my dark side, I contemplated nailing Bane with a psi ball between the eyes. Behind us Shaz growled and snapped fangs, and I turned to find Arys pushing him away from the rising commotion. I motioned for Gabriel to go with them.

My eyes locked with Arys's angry blues. He gave one nod. I had to stay with Falon, and he had to get Shaz away from the fight cage before he wolfed out and joined in the melee. Bloodlust burned hot in my dark flame's eyes, and I wondered if the two of them would be safe with one another.

So quickly our group had become separated. Too many temptations in a place designed to lure out one's darkest desires. Of course we would turn on each other, infected by the madness. Trapped inside until dawn, even then we couldn't all leave. Somehow we had to survive this shitshow until sunrise.

"Go with them, wolf," Falon snarled at me. "You don't need to see this."

Like hell I didn't. As he strode toward the fight cage, I rushed to keep up. "You don't need to do this, Falon."

"Actually, I do. Beat it and let me handle this." His silver wing, which had shielded me a moment before, now knocked me aside. Raising a hand, he caught the attention of the wrath demon. Jerking a thumb at Bane who ambled up cracking his knuckles, Falon shouted over the din. "We fight next."

Now Wrath seemed interested. For the first time since we arrived, his face registered something more than boredom. Two immortals would surely be a far more entertaining fight than vampires or werewolves.

"I'm not going anywhere." Refusing to be pushed around, I caught Falon's jaw with clawed fingertips.

He stilled in my grasp, his expression hard and unyielding.

"We have to fight the temptations here. Don't give in to Wrath."

Falon gently pried my fingers from his jaw. His eyes were wild with fury, but he was still himself. "You heard Arys and Bane. I have to defend my mark. If you weren't such a perpetual dumbass, you'd get the hell out of here while you can. Find a way out."

"Why though?" I persisted, unwilling to stand back and do nothing. "Why give me a mark that you have to defend? What's this about you going dark side? I need answers, Falon."

The current fight ended. The crowd roared as a pair of twisted creatures dragged a body from the ring.

Falon crushed his lips to mine in a head-spinning kiss. "I told you, Alexa. You are mine. My mark proves that, and I will defend what's mine against anyone who dares challenge me." He left me standing there, staring after him as he entered the fight cage, where Bane already waited.

I had not received an answer to my question.

Eager for a battle between immortals, onlookers flooded to the cage. Immediately I was crushed by the mob. Tossing bodies out of my way, I fought through the crowd.

I emerged to find Willow waiting with teeth clenched, his face crumpled in the effort it took to fight the dark vices that sought to get inside us all. The vampire feasting frenzy that continued to appease Gluttony had Willow's attention. He wanted to be part of that bloodbath, and I didn't blame him. My guardian had never been the type to indulge in either sex or blood, and surely never the kill, but the hunger from those wicked urges was eating him alive. If I hadn't reappeared when I did, he would've joined those on the excessively insatiable altar.

Lightly I touched his arm, and he jumped. "Willow, are you okay? Maybe you should find the others."

Standing on my tiptoes, I tried and failed to see over the heads of the crowd. Arys had headed toward the theatre. I could feel him but I couldn't see him. I chose not to tap into his mind, afraid that anything he was feeling would roll over into me and vice versa.

Between the thickening aroma of fresh blood, the screams of the tormented, and the cheers of Falon and Bane's audience, I was using a lot of power to block it all out. At some point my strength would wane, and the only way to replenish would be to partake. A catch twenty-two for sure.

"I'm not leaving you." Rubbing his face, Willow shook his head, trying to clear the brain fog. "And I know you won't leave while Falon is in there."

"I can't." A heavy, sick sensation hung in my stomach as I waited for the fight to start.

The Wrath demon raised a hand to the crowd, inciting their growing excitement.

Willow studied me, bloodlust dragging his gaze to my neck more than once. Clearing his throat, he forced himself to meet my eyes. "Are you in love with him?"

"What? No. We can barely stand each other. Why would you ask me that?" My face burned at the suggestion. Had Willow lost his mind?

As he searched me for the truth, I got the strange feeling that he was trying to choose his words carefully. "Alexa, the silver feather is a symbol that tells all other immortals what he's willing to give up for you. This feather says he's willing to embrace full darkness, full power, to protect you. Whatever is going on between you two, it's no longer a begrudging fling."

I swallowed hard, dragging my gaze to the fight cage. So badly I wanted to look away but I couldn't. Things had changed between Falon and me. I knew that, although I hadn't let myself think much about it. It felt safer not to.

Falon was willing to go full dark? For me? From fallen angel to full-on demon? How could that be? My mind refused to accept this new and ridiculous concept. It was just too farfetched.

"Did you know that when he first marked me?" I asked, certain of the answer already. When the Wrath demon incited another cry from the crowd, my blood ran cold.

A bell rang and my skin prickled as the fight began. I didn't want to watch but I couldn't look away. Not even when Willow said, "Yes. But it wasn't my place to tell you."

Bane didn't play around. He didn't taunt the crowd's hunger by dragging out the first blow. He attacked. A fist loaded with power connected with Falon's jaw, and he stumbled back a step. His recovery was quick as he blocked the next hit and delivered a solid punch accompanied by a force that thrust Bane against the cage.

"He's not in love with me," I insisted, raising my voice to be heard. "Whatever this is with him, love is not a word I'd use to describe it."

"What about possession? Obsession? Need?" Willow too watched the fight, though I wondered who he really wanted to see win. "Maybe it's something darker than love. More dangerous."

More tragic and broken.

I couldn't say those words to Willow. Falon and I had formed a strange relationship, no doubt about that. We'd gone to places with each other that nobody else could take us. And I didn't feel the need to give it a name.

I bumped my arm against Willow's and became much too aware of the power flowing in his blood. Goddamn this place.

Watching the fight brought me an unwelcome mix of emotions. Both Bane and Falon used physical and magical attacks, though there was no doubt that Bane's power was stronger. Darker.

He nailed Falon with a sharp psi ball that slashed open a cut on his cheek. It dripped a few drops of blood and healed. A fight between immortals could take some time. Eventually they would wear one another down, and the wounds would take longer to heal.

Just how far would they let this go before a winner was decided? Could an immortal be sent back to the other side if we were all supposedly trapped here until sunrise? The thought of Falon wounded beyond repair, trapped inside this shithole, it sickened me. I wouldn't let it happen.

A realization hit and the heavy weight in my stomach spread. I'd have Falon's back, whatever I had to do. My fingers traced the outline of the feather on my neck, and I let out the breath I'd been holding.

I'd claimed Falon as mine when Salem came for him. In this very moment he claimed me as his before any underworld creature that dared to question it. Yet our entanglement wasn't love. It was not the heart-rending devotion of a loyal partner or the soul-deep affection of a soulmate. It was wanting, needing, yearning. A twisted thing, more vines and thorns than roses. It was basking in the blood of wounds that would never heal. Falling apart over and over again and putting each other back together. Being unable to walk away from the web we'd weaved.

Was this darker and more dangerous than love? Yeah, I'd say so.

CHAPTER TWELVE
FALON

Why did she have to watch? I could feel her out there, refusing to leave, even to save her own sanity. And I hated her for it. Well, I hated her for many reasons. Currently, this was it.

What gave Alexa the right to put her ass on the line for me? To stand in the face of a storm of sin battering her shields to nothing, despite my order for her to go. Like she owed it to me.

We owed each other nothing. So what the fuck was I doing in this goddamn fight cage?

I could no longer convince myself that she hadn't infected every part of me. Like a sickness with no cure. I'd allowed it. I'd sought her out. Now I couldn't get her out of my system.

She was my drug. My therapy. My solace. My worst fucking nightmare.

But fuck anyone who tried to take her from me.

Bane and I had fought numerous times throughout the centuries, most of which occurred during the time he'd cursed Winter and me. We hadn't crossed paths for a long time since.

But I hadn't lost track of him.

The underworld loved to talk. Everyone was a disloyal fuck. Not sure why I had such a shitty rep for it.

Bane had continued in his torment until Winter caved to his will. Of course it didn't take him long to forget her and move on to other unsuspecting victims. Unfortunately, no one mentioned that he'd heard about Alexa. But of course he had, because the goddamn underworld loved to talk.

She was a collectible to him. A rare gem to parade about and take advantage of until it either bored him or she ended up dead. That was the thought that fed the fireball I thrust into Bane's face when the cocky cunt got too close.

He jerked out of reach, laughing as he slapped the flames from his mangy hair. "You know you can't win this, right? I'm going to fuck you up, and she's going to watch me do it."

Bane's efforts to intimidate were lost on someone like me. I'd worked alongside a sick fuck like Shya. I blocked the sudden and expected retaliatory attack. The next ball of blue crackling light smashed into the fight cage behind me.

"She'll probably enjoy it too," I said, lip curled in a sneer. "I'm not sure what kind of reaction you're hoping to get from her, but you'll be disappointed."

I fell for his feint then and received a mouthful of meaty knuckles for it. Pain ricocheted through my head. I blocked the next few, choosing to wait for my moment rather than burn myself out early. As every demon I'd ever known liked to remind me, they had more power than I did.

For now.

Not for a minute since my fall had I believed I wouldn't go all the way with it. I just hadn't been in a hurry. Having less power than people like Shya and Lilah had allowed me to get close to them. It had served me well over the centuries. I'd suspected that I'd complete my fall when my back was pressed against the proverbial wall. No other way out.

That moment had drawn closer since my fall, hunting me at a slow, certain pace. A flinty voice in my ear, it whispered promises of great power and eternal darkness. It was inevitable really.

Bane left his right side open, and I nailed him with a shard of ice. Having a few elemental powers at my disposal made me a well-rounded opponent, although I didn't like to show them off until I had to.

Gripping the ice shard like a knife, I plunged it deep into his side, sliding it between his ribs. I let go and jerked back out of reach, setting off a small smoke bomb in his face. A noxious substance that got him gagging and choking.

It was enough to rile him. Usually when we fought several immortals broke us up before we could destroy the place or a bystander. Nobody would stop us here.

With a guttural snarl Bane launched himself at me. Unable to brace for the impact, I went down beneath him, the air crushed from my lungs. Those giant hands wrapped around my throat and squeezed.

"So you're telling me the little hybrid out there isn't going to so much as flinch if I squeeze until your eyes burst from their sockets?" Putrid breath in my face, Bane banged my head against the floor. "I don't buy it. Guess I'm going to have to call your bluff."

Tighter he squeezed until the bones in my neck began to crack. When he thought he had me, I brought both hands up and grabbed each side of his head. A scorching hot, brain-searing attack had him reeling back. I brought a foot up and kicked him just below the ribs before he escaped my reach.

With a flap of my wings, I was back on my feet.

Shouts and jeers from the crowd made it clear they thought me the underdog. Fair enough.

I could feel Alexa watching. Still fucking watching. Why didn't she go find her twin flame?

A shot of dark magic came my way, a spell to paralyze. My rapidly erected barrier deflected it back to Bane. The entire exchanged happened in less than a blink. Paralyzed by his own magic, Bane stood there dumbstruck. Unmoving. I spared not a second in smashing my fists into his face, each hit loaded with enough power to rend flesh from bone. It took a vast amount of strength, but I saw no alternative.

"Call my fucking bluff," I spat into Bane's slack face as I pummeled it bloody. "Call my bluff on the mark. Test me, Bane. See how far I'm willing to go."

It didn't take him long to break free from the magic holding him. But it was long enough for me to leave some lasting damage. The blood stopped flowing quickly but the marks remained.

Bane smiled through the blood staining his face. "Your biggest mistake will be showing me how much you give a damn."

His next shot wasn't for me. He whirled away to fling his next attack out of the cage. Straight at Alexa.

I jumped, my focus on her. When I resumed physical form, Bane's shot hit me instead. It bowled me over, throwing me into Alexa, who hit Willow in a domino effect that knocked all three of us down in a heap.

With wings spread to block the other two, I was on my feet in time for Bane to appear right in front of me. When he hit me, I let him. I let him pound my face until I tasted blood.

Suddenly Bane's fists were gone. Ripped away from me mid-blow by a tiny blonde shitstorm of power. Alexa slapped Bane with enough force to take his legs out. She didn't stop there. Before he could rise, the feisty spitfire leapt atop his fallen form and slashed at his throat with deadly claws.

With an infuriated shout the demon flung her away with a smack of his thick arm. He grabbed his bleeding throat, though it had already healed. That dumbass wolf was going to get herself killed. Or knowing Bane, something much worse.

I grabbed Alexa's arm and hauled her away from the raving demon. Her blue wolf eyes flashed wild. Nobody was immune to the effects of the sin magic here.

"Find your other half and beat it," I snarled, having no patience for her attitude. "Don't make me hurt you."

Intrigue gleamed in the wicked expression that crossed her lovely face. "I'd love to see you try."

"No you wouldn't, and this is not the time or place for th—"

Bane barreled into me. He thrust me aside and grabbed for Alexa.

She hit him with a point-blank blue and gold psi ball that exploded in his face. The light flame power in her touch scorched Bane's skin, leaving ugly oozing blisters that did not heal. Dumbfounded, he stared at her. Really stared at her. Like so many of them did, he'd underestimated her.

Wiping skin, blood, and ooze from his face, Bane leered at Alexa like he'd just found his new favorite toy. "I am going to enjoy listening to your screams."

Willow snapped. He could put up with a lot of crap talking from me, but that one uttered remark from Bane and the guardian lost his shit. His fingers barely moved. Still the power darted forward at his command. A black rope-like tendril wrapped tight around Bane's body, pinning his arms to his sides. Willow stepped closer, fangs bared.

For a moment the air seemed to quiver behind him, right where his wings would have been. Did anyone else see it? They didn't seem to.

"I don't care what your issue is with Falon, leave Alexa out of it," Willow seethed, hands raised for another attack. "She belongs to many people, but you're not one of them. Pick your battles wisely. You won't win this one."

Even with a face full of blisters and cuts, Bane proved unable to take anyone or anything seriously, other than himself. He spat blood on the floor at Willow's feet. "You must be her angel. Yeah, I know about you. I like to know everything about the women who catch my interest. Pretty sure you're out of a job now. Due to obvious circumstances."

Willow's glower assaulted Bane with such righteous angelic disdain that I had to chuckle. He'd never been like the others who'd fallen. Most of them embraced the fall, relishing the illusion of freedom. Giving up the good fight. Willow never had. Not even in a building filled with demons who would tear him limb from limb should they discover his identity. For the tiniest spec of a moment, I respected the hell out of him.

"I suggest you find other interests, you pissant, piece of shit, demon scum," Willow snarled and snapped massive wolf fangs inches from Bane's face. His eyes were all beast. In each hand he held a livewire of power.

From where I stood I could feel it. Hybrid. A vibe on the same frequency as Alexa's but with a hum all its own. Beneath that hum though, I sensed something more. Alexa too watched Willow with a sudden curious arch of her brow, soft pink lips parted in wonder.

Before Willow could drive his point home, several demons descended on us. They surrounded both Bane and me, grabbing us by any limb they could reach before dragging us back to the fight cage to finish what we'd started.

There were bets placed on us after all. Couldn't disappoint the greedy crowd.

I went willingly, a grin on my face. Yeah, let's finish this.

CHAPTER THIRTEEN

I cursed as they dragged Falon back to the fight cage. He didn't resist though, letting the demons pull him along. Glancing back over his shoulder, he winked a silver eye and blew me a sarcastic kiss.

Falon was on his own. Clearly he wanted to do this. All lit up with piss, vinegar, and wrath, he leaped back into the ring with both arms raised. But I couldn't watch because several of the demons in our vicinity had taken notice of Willow.

"Come on." I grabbed his arm and dragged him along with me as I walked backward, slowly, keeping an eye on those who paused to take a harder look. "Let's find Arys."

Part of me felt bad about walking away, but Falon could handle himself. No matter what happened to him, he couldn't die.

Not like Willow. He had enemies among demons. Any who did not yet know him didn't need to.

Slipping through the crowd, we made our way toward the theatre. I cast a risky glance back as we neared the door to find just one demon who still watched. *Fuck.* Could they tell that he'd started out like them? An angel gone dark? Did they know?

Panic kickstarted my heart and I reached out to Arys in my mind. 'Status update. Headed for the theatre. It's demon central out here and too many eyes are on Willow. Where are you guys?'

The two demons standing off to either side of the theatre doors stood back to allow us through. One of them bowed to me and with a respectful nod said, "Succubus Queen."

They thought I was here as a willing participant, come to have some sinner party fun. How very wrong they were. Lips pressed into a tight line, I grabbed Willow's hand before either of them could study him too closely and all but burst into the theatre.

In the same moment came Arys's warning. Too late. 'Don't come to the theatre. Not with Willow.'

We were already in. The demons manning the doors immediately closed them behind us. Shutting us in with a literal orgy of lust.

I couldn't be sure what hit me first, the visual or the metaphysical.

The theatre had become an all-out sex fest. The seats had been replaced with a plethora of sofas, chairs, beds, and furry carpets. There had to be well over a hundred people fornicating all over the damn place. Two hundred maybe. Hell, I wasn't about to stand there and count. They rutted in groups of two and more. Many more in some cases.

The steady flow of sex in my own small nightclub back home was more than enough to test one's control. This? This was like nothing I'd ever experienced. Nothing I was prepared for. The swell of lust hit me hard, digging its way inside me, finding the place where my succubus power lived.

There had to be a ward on the theatre for the insurmountable level of sex magic to stay contained. Otherwise it would flow throughout the entire building, perhaps the whole city block. Or further.

Willow tore his hand from mine and spun back to the closed doors. He rushed them then, slamming the doors with a psi ball that did nothing. Panic gripped him and he beat the door.

We weren't getting out that way.

I knew better than to touch him so I hovered close enough to speak over the cacophony of moans and cries. "Willow, stop. You have to save your strength if you're going to stay in control. There's another way out. A fire exit on the other side of the theatre. Come on." Gritting my teeth, I struggled to shield against the onslaught.

Standing on my toes, I searched the writhing bodies for Arys or any sign of Shaz's platinum hair. I shuddered as I fought the sudden, strong urge to impale myself upon the shaft of one of my lovers.

Or Willow.

My gaze darted to him. His green eyes were solid wolf. He shrank back against the doors, staring at me with teeth clenched. "I can't fight this, Alexa. Judging from the way you're looking at me, neither can you. We have to get out of here."

Why did we have to fight it? If we just unclenched a little and let it happen, the high would last for days. And the things we could do with all the power we'd draw from this group? Limitless. So why did we want to leave?

Fuck. Arys and Shaz were in here. Were Jenner and Gabriel too? The thought snapped me out of my dark and lusty mind frame. I reached out to Arys again. When I felt him there, slip sliding into desire's arms, I prodded him for some kind of response. Nothing.

"Do you see Shaz or Arys anywhere?" I searched the dimly lit theatre. Once I focused on my tie to Arys, I took a step toward him.

Except my gaze landed on the stage, and I fell captivated. Enthralled. Enamored. All of the above.

The Lust demon sat on a tall, red velvet throne at the center of the stage. A woman knelt before him, her head in his lap, bobbing up and down. A man lay on the floor, pleasuring the woman. Hair the color of crimson fell about the demon's shoulders. Black horns curved up on either side of his head from somewhere within those red locks. Scarlet eyes appraised the sexual frenzy. In contrast to the many red shades, his robes were of the deepest black.

He was gorgeous. Sinfully so. Because of course he was. Every angle of his face had been perfectly cut. Every line and curve flawless. An illusion. It had to be.

I couldn't tear my gaze away.

He felt it. Before I could avert my eyes, his locked onto mine, and I knew Willow and I were screwed.

"I think I see them over there." Willow pointed, but I wasn't paying attention. "Looks like they're having some difficulty getting out."

The way he said it made me want to look to where he pointed, but I couldn't. The Lust demon's red gaze bore into me. I couldn't even blink. As he took me in, appraising me from head to toe, I felt it like he'd touched me himself. Skin on skin.

I shuddered and the demon smiled. With a finger he beckoned me and my feet started moving. Like I had to go to him.

Willow caught my arm, jerking me back. "Alexa, no. What are you doing?" His hand trembled where he touched me, like it took everything in him to hold back. Still, he didn't let go.

"I have to go," I whispered, too aware of Willow's proximity. His wolfy scent. The dark spicy hint of cinnamon in the cologne he wore. The way his energy throbbed with need. "He's calling me."

"I can't hold back much longer." Willow's voice was husky with both wolf and the lust for blood and sex.

The Lust demon sat up straighter in his grand chair, assessing us both now. Too intently. He raised a hand and snapped his fingers. Immediately two demons popped into form on either side of us. We weren't given a choice as they physically forced us along to the stage.

I realized that those surrounding the throne on the stage were almost all otherworldly creatures. Shifters. Vampires. Demons. Power types.

Including Jenner and Gabriel. The two of them had a human woman stretched out on a chaise between them while they feasted on her in a variety of ways. The heat between my legs felt like a betrayal. I couldn't help but respond to them. To all of this.

As the demons ushered us up the stage steps, I caught a glimpse of Shaz's white hair across the theatre. He had Arys pressed against the fire exit door, the very door they should be using to get the hell out of here. Instead of fleeing, they were engaged in a heavy makeout session. I couldn't see their hands.

Not that I had much of a chance to look. Standing in front of the Lust demon, I felt no fear. Much to my horror, my panties were drenched. Somewhere in the back of my mind, I knew I needed to get away. Convincing the rest of me to make it happen was another matter entirely.

Somehow I still had enough sense left to break into Arys's lust-hazed thoughts. 'In a bit of a predicament here. Willow and I have drawn attention. You guys have to go. Upstairs. Anywhere. Away from this goddamn theatre.'

We all had to go, but Shaz had come so far in finding his comfort zone with Arys. If he stayed here much longer, it wouldn't be his choice anymore. He'd do whatever the heady rush told him to. Like everyone else.

Obeying Lust's command.

Helping the sin to spread and its power to grow. Through all of us. But perhaps most especially through those of us linked to lust. Empowered by it ourselves. We were so fucked.

I felt Arys take notice. My eyes were glued to the strangely perfect demon sitting before me. With a careless hand he pushed the woman's head from his lap, dismissing her.

From beneath his robe a tail twitched. A serpentine tail. Leaning forward, he beckoned us to come closer. When we didn't budge, the demons who'd escorted us gave us a shove. I tripped but didn't fall. Willow snarled and bared fangs, receiving a smack that knocked him to his knees. Well, this was off to a great start.

"The hybrid queen. Interesting. Not quite how I pictured you." Hands steepled before him, the Lust demon assessed me with a scrutinizing once over that included a prodding of my aura. His eyes widened slightly and he nodded in approval. "Better than I pictured you. Nobody who was ever human has power like that."

Crap.

"The angel whose mark you bear. Where is he?" A slender finger tapped a full bottom lip as he eyed Falon's mark.

"He's around." It was all he'd get out of me without forcing it.

The demon turned his curious scarlet stare on Willow who rose, braced for a fight. I tensed while he received the same analytical poke and prod. My entire being was alive with the many wants of the flesh, but in that moment I still knew fear for Willow.

Whatever the demon found in my guardian, it interested him enough to bring him to his feet. Tying the multiple layers of ankle-length robes with a gold sash, the demon glided forward. He stopped right in front of Willow and searched his face.

Disappointment struck me. He knew.

Without asking, our Lust representative from Hell placed a hand on Willow's forehead.

Willow jerked back. "Don't fucking touch me, heathen."

My jaw dropped. Had he lost his mind? Calling out the Sins demon was not going to help him keep a low profile.

"Brother," the Lust demon purred, flashing a grin that boasted eight fangs, two where most animals had just one. "I wouldn't believe it if I wasn't seeing it for myself. Tell me how you came to be a hybrid like the queen here. I imagine it's a hell of a tale."

"I'm not your brother," Willow snarled, low and menacing.

His aura hummed with arousal. Unable to release the tightly wound tension, it would burst out as rage. The problem was that he abstained too much. Willow's morals clashed with his needs as an incubus vampire.

"Oh, but you are. Still new to all this, are you?" The demon gave a sinister chuckle and nodded. "I understand. In time you'll happily accept your role as an instrument of my power."

Willow wouldn't back down. I got the feeling that his beautiful wings would have been flared right now, if he still had them. "The only role I accept is that of serving my queen. Our power might be rooted in the sin you spread, but you are just one of many Sins demons. A dime a dozen. We owe you nothing."

Inside I was dying. What was he trying to do to me here? Willow had always been a little feisty and temperamental, usually when drinking tequila. He hadn't been reckless or stupid. This felt a bit like both.

"I beg to differ. What you owe me is a gift." Gesturing to the fornicating masses, Lust's gaze darted between us. "Much like the rest of these good people, you are here for my pleasure. So by all means, serve your queen. I'm eager to taste her desire."

Hold up a minute. Did I hear that right?

"I don't follow your orders," Willow growled. Yet his resolve wavered, his fierce facade cracked. The brain-melting, panty-dropping force inside the theatre beat at his defenses as surely as it beat at mine.

Lust blinked a few times and tilted his head to studiously reconsider Willow. "You're so fucking new I can smell it on you. Like a newborn baby fresh from the womb. Practically virginal." When Willow failed to react, the demon snickered. The horrid sound meant bad things. "Let's see what we can do about that." His face shone with psychotic delight. He planned to torment the former angel, and he planned to enjoy it.

For a fraction of a second, I glanced over my shoulder to Arys and Shaz. Gone. Hopefully that meant they made it out. When I turned back to the demon, he promptly threw both hands in the air, black reptilian wings stretched out behind him. Power rippled out from him to nail Willow and me at point-blank range before sweeping to encompass the unbridled orgy.

Lust's magic reached inside to the dark succubus side of me and tore down every last shred of inhibition and self-control. It freed the most raw, carnal parts of me. The badass hybrid queen was rolled by a Lust demon in a mere blink without so much as a struggle. Then the demon returned to his elaborate seat to observe.

It wasn't me that I would have been concerned for if I'd been able to think clearly. Willow and I were friends, and though being bound to me possibly made a sexual encounter inevitable, having his desire encouraged by a demon was not the way this should happen between us.

But I couldn't stop it. I was a victim here too.

Some inner part of me wanted to tell Willow not to give in, that we could fight this. Instead we locked eyes and froze for a matter of one second. Then his mouth was on mine.

CHAPTER FOURTEEN

Willow was my friend before he was anything else. He also happened to be mine. My vampire. My creation. Mine to take from and to give to, as the power that ruled us demanded.

But I was his too. His friend, sire, and queen. And I'd only become those things by first being his charge. No doubt in recent weeks Willow had come to the same realization I had. Not one of the men bound to me would cease to want me. My blood alone would never be enough.

Which brought me to the potentially awkward conclusion that they all had to find their place with me, in and out of my bed.

Willow's lips moved on mine, sensual and soft. With a hand on each cheek he held my face gently. He devoured my mouth like it harbored the key to the lock that held him. I kissed him back, high on the rush and hungry to satisfy the deep-rooted need to have him between my legs.

Neither of us were in the right headspace to fight the pull or bring this to a stop. We were completely enveloped in Lust's dark magic. And yet somewhere in the recesses of my mind, I had this awareness that we were only doing what we truly wanted to do. The Lust demon didn't force a fake desire. It uncaged the true wants we possessed, the ones we stuffed deep down out of shame or obligation.

I did want Willow. I had wanted him since his turn. Since his personal energy had become tainted with the potent sensuality of our bloodline. Our friendship as we knew it had been forever changed that night.

Tonight it would change again.

It shouldn't happen this way. But that didn't matter. And in the moment, we didn't care.

Not when we stumbled to an empty chaise and not when Willow eased me down upon it. We were nothing but a power trip to the Lust demon, acting on our primal urges like animals. Willow's tongue dipped into my mouth, and when he filled his hands with my breasts I had no doubt how far under he'd fallen.

Inhibitions ceased to exist, our personal comfort zones stripped away. No hesitation or holding back, dirty-blond hair slid between my fingers. My head fell against the arched back of the chaise as Willow kissed his way down my neck. Like every vampire, he lingered over my jugular. Smelling the blood beneath the surface of my skin.

He gave a hungry growl that was both beastly and erotic as he pressed his face to my cleavage. My hands sank into his hair.

I trembled with want, almost shaking with it. That first-time anticipation hit hard. I ached to taste all of him.

As my arousal swelled and flowed, Jenner and Gabriel took notice. They drew on my energy, never needing to cross the short distance between us. In turn I drew on them, taking my excitement higher. Drunk on their favorite sin, they quickly drew others to their not-so-private party. The two of them quickly had more women than they could handle, whether their egos would accept that or not.

"I've wanted this… since the first time I laid eyes on you after I rose," Willow murmured, his breath hot on my skin. "I try to ignore it, but it's gotten so much harder."

I nodded, tripping over my tongue when he tugged the thin straps of my dress and bra down together to bare my breasts. "It's okay. We knew the risk we were taking."

Words tumbled out of my mouth, but I paid no attention to what they were. Lust would make you say anything. Do anything. Whatever it took to get what you most wanted.

A red-hot passion drove us. Wild and untamed. Dredged up from a place beyond this world. We were possessors of it. We used it in both love and war. Yet we were but conduits. Keepers of the power though not creators. Not its masters.

The lust was the master. It reminded us of that with every kiss and caress.

Willow spread my legs so he could sit on the chaise between them. My skirt rode up my thighs to flash the watching Lust demon a glimpse of my red underwear. His constant ogling didn't bother me as it normally would have. It barely registered at all. The heat of

Willow's mouth upon me as he swirled his tongue around my nipple kept me firmly entrenched in the pit of desire.

A soft moan fell from my lips when he slid a hand beneath my skirt. Though he might have been guided by a hurricane of lust, Willow deftly sought out the wetness between my thighs like a man who knew what he wanted. Hiking my skirt as high as it would go, he abruptly stripped off my panties.

Biting my bottom lip, I gave a little squeak of anticipation when he dropped them and stroked a finger over the sensitive place where my leg met my groin. At his teasing touch I grabbed at his shirt, yanking it up, over his head, and off. Clothing was an unfortunate and unnecessary barrier. I sat up straighter to feel him, needing to run my fingers over the ridges of his chest, down to a place I hadn't dared let myself think about.

Catching my hand, Willow pushed me back against the chaise. Then he slung one of my legs over his shoulder and without hesitation, dragged his tongue over me from one end to the other.

An explosion of light before my eyes momentarily blinded me. I threw my head back, holding my breath. Every sensation burned with a fire hot intensity. Scorching.

This couldn't be happening.

Willow's mouth moved on my needy flesh with the same hungry yearning as when he'd kissed me. Deep and passionate, he plundered me with his tongue before flicking my throbbing clit.

No, this was definitely happening.

With one hand he grasped my breast, kneading firmly. The other joined his tongue in making me writhe on the chaise. I felt eyes upon us as Willow licked me. Several sets of them, including Gabriel and Jenner.

Strongest of them all was the lecherous stare of Lust. If I made it out of this in one piece, I'd make him sorry. Somehow. When I could muster the give-a-damn to do it.

Willow slipped a finger inside me, and I came suddenly, a spontaneous climax that didn't recede for long before it started again to build. It was both pleasure and pain. Too much intensity. Almost torment.

His name was faint on my lips. I could barely form words.

Sitting up, he quickly finished disrobing. Of course he was as beautiful as I'd expected. A work of art, as the immortals tended to be. Needing to taste his pleasure, to feel it on my lips, I groped hungrily for his gorgeous erection. Willow might be a vampire, but I knew he'd fuck like an immortal.

Again Willow caught my hands, kissing me as he eased me back against the arch of the chaise. "I serve you," he whispered against my lips, a slight quiver to his voice. "That's all he gets."

Realization struck, and I settled back on the chaise, regarding Willow with lusty intrigue. He didn't want me to perform a sex act on him in front of the watching demon. Because it involved submission, the most personal kind of intimacy, and he refused to allow me to give the demon that. I gawked at Willow in a state of desire-soaked confusion. He wanted me to appear the worshipped queen. And somehow he still had enough control to make that decision for both of us.

Even now in the belly of the beast, Willow made choices that put me first.

I didn't deserve him. As a guardian or a friend. Or a lover for that matter. I'd given him what he wanted when I turned him, and still it would never be enough.

"Willow." With sudden desperation I grabbed onto him, holding him close. I kissed him several times before saying, "It's okay to enjoy this. It's okay to enjoy me."

Unlike the others, Willow didn't believe that. I saw it in his gold-flecked eyes. So I kissed him again, a deep melding of our mouths. I draped him in my own thrall, reminding him who he belonged to. It sure as shit wasn't that Lust demon.

When he pulled back something in his demeanor had changed. Relaxed. He held my gaze evenly. Part wolf, part vampire, and a little dash of angel. But all Willow. And then some.

Straddling the chaise, he lifted my hips to place me in his lap. The curve at the back of the chaise propped me upright while a smaller curve at the foot of it pushed Willow forward, forcing an intimately close proximity. To hold onto him comfortably, I had to wrap my legs around his hips. The strange chair had to have been designed for nothing but sex; it presented options for at least a half-dozen positions.

I held my breath, unable to release the pressure in my lungs.

Lust shifted in his seat. He snorted out a sharp breath as he waited for Willow to bridge the gap left between us.

For a moment I thought maybe Willow would hold eye contact, but he didn't. Instead, he buried his face in my hair, pressed his lips to my neck, and tenderly thrust inside me. After the shortest pause, his soft sigh caressed my ear.

Was it relief or regret? I couldn't tell.

One arm slid around to hold me close. Our bodies were already so tightly aligned, but Willow pressed closer, leaving just enough space between us for him to move inside me.

Squeezing my eyes shut, I let sight and sound fall away. Other than the soft moans in my ear, I heard nothing. All I smelled was man, wolf, and sex. All I felt was the otherworldly embrace of a friend, now a lover. Someone I trusted undoubtedly. Someone I loved and wanted to see happy.

Together we crossed the line that would take us beyond friendship to something else. Willow hooked a hand under my knee so he could pull my legs wider apart, angling deeper. His mouth moved hot on my neck. Spilling my blood in this place would be a mistake, and Willow seemed to know that. His fangs never came into play. Although it wasn't blood that he wanted from me now.

This was far more erotic than blood alone. An exchange of pleasure. Of trust and respect. I hoped Willow remembered it this way, regardless of the demon's involvement. Guilt and regret wouldn't serve us.

The way he pressed me between his body and the chaise, he still needed to protect me. Protect my honor in a den of demons that had none. Like he didn't want them to see me exposed and vulnerable in the throes of mindless pleasure. If he'd still had his beautiful wings they'd have been curled protectively around me.

A swell of regret at his loss brought the sting of tears. Like a drunk girl crying in a bar bathroom. More emotions rose, irrational feelings and yet still real. I didn't cry though. It was just one of many overwhelming sensations that struck as we found our rhythm and rode it to friggin' oblivion.

Overcome with it all, I moaned and gasped his name. Harder Willow thrust, but not once was he anything but sensual. Some of my lovers got dirty and aggressive, rough and predatory. Some enjoyed playful, feisty fun. Yet they all stood apart, having their own sexual personality and flare. This was nothing like any of them.

Willow was a force of mad, erotic passion. As if deep down he harbored the soul of a lost romantic who loved a woman with every single piece of himself when he was with her. He gave everything he had to the intimate encounter.

No wonder he'd been so damn lost since the death of the woman he'd loved. Willow had so much of it to give. I felt it in his touch, his kiss, his energy. He may have fallen, but he was still exactly who he was always meant to be.

I couldn't help the feelings that overtook me. Placing a hand on his cheek, I drew Willow's face to mine. With every stroke the flurry of sensations, both emotional and physical, grew into something I didn't recognize anymore. I moved with him, gasping as I opened my eyes.

Perspiration dotted Willow's brow. Our eyes locked, and before I could run the risk of letting myself see anything I didn't want to see within his pretty greens, I kissed him.

He held me tighter, thrusting faster and moaning softly against my lips. So close we were. And then we were there. Sliding into the abyss with an orgasm I felt to the bottom of my soul.

My cry echoed in the cavernous space above the stage. After the initial shock of my climax faded, only then did Willow release inside me with a ragged groan that hurt me to hear.

So much pleasure and pain in that one sound.

Power exploded from us to cascade over the surrounding orgy of insanity.

Crap. This twisted party didn't need any more juice. But it wasn't really for them. It was for him. Lust. Who watched us with venomous satisfaction.

Through me the lust flowed out to target each of my vampires. Like the many strings of a web, the demon-fed power hit every one of them. Gabriel and Jenner were lost amid a pile of naked ladies who moaned and shrieked as they begged and bled for the two of them. Somewhere Arys took the hit as well. Somewhere with Shaz.

I threw my arms around Willow's neck and just held him. Chests heaving, hair disheveled, we hung in the strange afterglow that wasn't really an afterglow at all. The need for more waxed higher between us. As long as we stayed here, it might never be sated. Were all these people going to fuck themselves to death for this asshole's enjoyment?

"Don't stop now." Lust's slick voice broke in, reminding us that we were far from alone. "I haven't even begun to dirty you up yet, Willow. We're just getting started."

"I'd say you're fucking finished." Falon's voice cut through the blanket of desire suffocating my brain.

Bleeding, battered and bruised, he stepped into sight. Somehow he was unaffected by the lust magic or the orgy of bodies engaged in carnal acts. He stepped forward, drawing a sword that seemed to appear from nowhere.

Lust studied Falon, interested in the newest specimen to join his party. Unfazed by the sword he said, "So it's your mark the succubus bears. This just keeps getting better. By all means, join them." A twirl of his finger and the demon sent a shot of sex magic spiraling toward Falon who deflected it with the blade of his sword.

Mouth open in wonder, I knew without a doubt that blade was of angelic origin.

"Pull yourself together, Alexa," Falon ordered, never taking his eyes off the demon.

The sharp edge to his tone cut through the fog, enabling me a moment of clarity. Willow and I scrambled to pull our clothes into place. Heat filled my face. Falon's arrival had roused me from the demon's spell, but it was still there demanding that I stay and fulfill my obligation to feed it. The worst part was how desperately I wanted to.

So did Willow. That desire lurked in his hurried movements and the furtive glances he shot me.

No sooner had we dressed than the urge to undress took me. "Falon." His name fell from my lips as a plea, both sensual and scared. I couldn't fight my way out of here if I couldn't keep my clothes on.

Silver wings flared, Falon pointed the tip of his sword at the Lust demon's face. "They're leaving with me."

Lust pursed his lips and furrowed his brow, like he couldn't decide how seriously he should take Falon. "Nobody leaves the building until sunrise."

"We're leaving the fucking theatre then. Now back the fuck off before I slice and dice your pathetic carcass and bring a gruesome end to your freak show of filth." Brazen and unafraid, Falon didn't back down. He stepped closer, bringing the tip of his sword within inches of the demon's left eye.

"Do you have any idea how much power I can glean from a succubus like her?" Unimpressed by Falon's display, the demon relaxed in his lavish seat like he didn't have a care in the world. "Why should I give her to you?"

"You can't give what was never yours in the first place. See the mark?" Falon spat blood on the floor in front of the throne. "I just finished defending it against someone who got a little too close. Looked a little too long in her direction. Your cute little stunt beats the shit out of that. What do you think I'm going to do to you?"

The seething mask of vengeance Falon wore turned my lust in his direction. Later I'd be clear headed and offended at being discussed by immortals like I was nothing but property. With my head slipping back into the clouds of desire, I just wanted to climb my fallen angel and ride him to paradise.

We really had to get out of here.

To my surprise, Lust relented. "She's not worth the fight. Take her."

Falon lingered, and I was certain he'd ram that sword into the demon's eye. Easing away, he held the blade ready. "Get moving, wolf. Hit the exit."

Snapping into motion, I pulled Willow with me, before Falon could sweep us along with his massive wings. We had no choice but to leave Gabriel and Jenner behind. They were besotted with women, a tangle of limbs. Hardly in any real immediate danger. I hoped.

Falon marched us to the fire exit on the exterior wall. Not once did he take his narrowed gaze off Lust. Not until we'd shoved through the heavy doors into the stairwell beyond. The back exit was unmanned, probably because nobody made it this far when they didn't want to leave.

No sooner had the doors swung closed and latched with a heavy thud than the fog in my head cleared like the sun bursting through the clouds on a summer day. I glanced at Willow, afraid I would see shame on his face. It would gut me.

He offered me a smile to appease my concern. It didn't reach his eyes. Before I could search them, he turned away, rubbing both hands over his face and into his hair. Shoulders hunched, he let out a breath that sounded strained, like it came from between clenched teeth.

The stairwell, which led all the way to the top floor, had an emergency exit at ground level. But seeing as we were trapped until sunrise, we wouldn't be going out that way. We needed to find Arys and Shaz.

Falon paused at the bottom of the stairs, sword still in hand. His face was unreadable as he looked the two of us over. "Are either of you hurt?"

"No." I shook my head, rubbing my arms as a shiver crept over me. Everything felt wrong.

Shrugging out of his jacket, Falon draped it over my shoulders. "Then let's get moving. You two will have to unpack this suitcase of shit later."

Colorful. Also correct. What Willow and I had just undergone would have to wait despite the fact that I could still smell him on my skin and feel him between my legs. But the way he'd turned away before I could study him further made me wonder just how bad the repercussions would be.

CHAPTER FIFTEEN

The stairwell was disturbingly quiet. I reached out to Arys, feeling him there but receiving no response. Were the two of them caught up in the lust that had overflowed from me to Arys?

We reached the main floor, and because we had to try it, Falon gave the exit to the street a shove. It opened. But when he went to step through, an unseen barrier stopped him like a brick wall.

"That ward will hold until dawn," Willow observed, reaching to hover a hand over the barrier. "There's no point fighting it. I'll check the main floor if you two want to check the top."

Surely he knew that I could track Arys with a little focus.

His gaze darted to me in furtive glances. Willow was dying to get away from me.

Not wanting to force him to stay when he clearly wanted to be alone, I nodded. "Stay safe, okay? We'll meet back on the main floor. Nobody goes back to the basement alone."

Willow turned to Falon, his face an emotionless mask. "Do not leave her side." Without waiting for a reply, he opened the door to the main floor, releasing the muffled sound of slot machines and music.

As the door swung closed behind him, the sound once again faded. I stared at the closed door, trying to hold together the splintering fragments of my heart as it broke for Willow. What if he could never look me in the face again? What if this proved more than he could handle?

"And I thought I was a mess after the first time I fucked you," Falon muttered, fussing with a wing that wouldn't tuck nicely behind his back like the other. A slash of red revealed an ugly gash on the inside. "Somehow I suspect the beating Willow handed out to me wasn't half as bad as the one he's going to hand out to himself."

I let out a long, slow sigh and massaged my temples. "That's helpful, Falon. Thank you."

"That's me. Always here to help." His hand was warm on my back as he ushered me along to the top floor where the private suites were located.

"Hey, wait." I paused a few stairs above him and looked down, head cocked as I eyed him with suspicion. "How did you go unaffected in the theatre?"

Falon's brows drew together, and he gave me that look, the one that conveyed how stupid he found my question. "Um, hello, I'm an immortal. I might be fallen, but I'm not a powerless hack. There's a lot you still don't know about me."

All other immortals present had been demons happily consorting for their master's enjoyment. Still, the pull had been so strong.

I refused to budge. "If you can't resist my thrall, then there's no way in hell you could have resisted the boatload of sexed up power down there."

"Oh, for crying out loud." Sword blade dragging against the concrete stairs, Falon stepped up another, bringing us face to face. "We all have our weaknesses. Our personal sins. Lust isn't one of mine. It's only you, you dense wolf. I've met my share of Lust demons and succubi. Nobody affects me like you do, and we both know it was never just about lust for us. Now can we go?"

It was never just about lust with any of the men tied to me, was it? My connection to all of them had become so much more than that. Lust formed the base of my power as a vampire, but it only drew them. It wasn't what bound them to me on the deepest level.

Sucking in a long, shaky breath, I turned to sprint up the rest of the stairs on legs that threatened to fail me. I couldn't help but be struck with a sense of déjà vu. The last time I'd come up this stairway to the top floor, I'd been searching for Jez. It was impossible to shake the sense that I'd find Shaz and Arys in a similar position. Jez had been running a little fast and loose during that Vegas trip.

Falon stopped me at the top of the stairs. Sword still clenched tightly in one hand, he dragged open the door at the top and peered down the hallway beyond. Finding no obvious danger he entered, waving me along behind him.

Right away I felt Arys. His cool vibe within me swelled, and I knew he was close. I was almost afraid to find them. Afraid of what I might walk in on. And yet also afraid to leave them alone if an interruption would save them from feeling like Willow did right now.

"Maybe they don't want to be found, Alexa. They sought out a private room. Your efforts might be better spent finding and killing Loric." Falon slid the sword into a sheath hanging from one hip. While I walked down the hall, letting my senses guide me, Falon stopped to fuss with his bleeding wing.

Arys's tantalizing vibe grew stronger. My gaze landed on a door halfway down the corridor. They were in there.

My hand touched the doorknob and trepidation filled me. Would I be ruining a private moment better left just to two? Should I walk away?

A visual of the orgy downstairs made my decision for me. If they were caught up in the swell of Lust's influence, an interruption might be welcome. Slow and silent, I turned the knob and cracked the door open.

What I saw almost nailed me to the wall.

The room was lit only by two small lamps in wall sconces. The bed was empty. Shaz stood, leaning against the wall beside the bed, as if they'd never made it that far. Head thrown back, his hands were lost in raven-black hair.

Arys was bathed in shadow. Although the lamp light didn't reach him, there was no mistaking what I saw: Arys on his knees for our white wolf, pleasing him as he growled.

Lust only called forth one's true inner desire. Just like it had for Willow and me. Regardless of how it happened, they wanted this.

I took a step back to leave except Shaz's head turned my way. Brilliant jade wolf eyes found me, and I froze. Even if I hadn't so recently been mindfucked by a Lust demon, I'd still have found the scene before me unbearably sexy. My breath caught, and I held tight to the door frame like I might hit the floor without it.

Shaz's gaze smoldered, unflinching and without regret. He watched me while Arys pleasured him, and it was about the hottest damn thing I'd ever seen.

From behind me, Falon guided me back into the hall, then gently closed the door and pressed me against his hard chest. "Let them have their moment. Then we start rounding up all of your damn vampires. If Loric made a deal to host these demons, then only he can break it. Unless you kill him. Then his deal passes to you."

Demon business sucked. There were so many rules and loopholes, not unlike the human world, although far deadlier.

I heard Falon and understood his message: our predicament was grave. It didn't stop me from trying to lay a lusty kiss on him.

He pinned me to the closed door, his forearm across my chest to hold me in place. "I'm not fucking you here, and most definitely not after what I witnessed downstairs." Teeth clenched, Falon ruffled his wings and winced with pain. Even with his injury and adversity to picking up where Willow left off, my fallen angel oozed arousal. "Stop looking at me like that."

I couldn't help it. With one look at my dark vampire on his knees for Shaz, I was right back in the headspace of downstairs. Straining against Falon's arm, I taunted him with a grin. "You might have to slap me. Seriously."

"You don't have to tell me twice." Falon's hand cracked across my face. It was a nice smack but he was holding back.

"How much did you see?" I rubbed the stinging spot on my cheek, trying to focus on the burn of it rather than the tingle between my legs.

Taking my hand, Falon led me down the hall. "Enough to be grateful that I didn't see more. Let's go downstairs. Seems like the main floor might be the safest place to clear your head."

A shriek rang out from behind one door. Blood hunger clawed its way up to demand my attention. One thing after another. It hadn't been that long since I'd fed. Still the scream twisted in my head. I quickened my pace.

Falon jerked to a halt, forcing me to stop dead in my tracks since he still held onto my hand. Wincing, he stretched out the injured wing with a curse. A wave of pain tainted his ethereal aura, leaving a bitter taste in my mouth.

"Let me help." I held out a hand, waiting for his nod before touching the silver feathered wing.

Healing had never been my strongest skill. The effort required precise concentration. However Falon wasn't healing, so his injuries exceeded what he could mend without his return to the other side to recover. I had to try something.

Falon's expression remained guarded as I touched his wing. Parting the feathers carefully, I examined the wound. The gash was deep and long, at least six inches. Caused by a blade of some kind I presumed. It had cut deep enough to sever some vital bits needed for the wing's proper function.

For the first time since he'd interrupted in the theatre, I really took in Falon's appearance. Blood dried in crusted patches here and there on his face. Both eyes were bruised, one worse than the other. The bridge of his nose had swelled, and cuts slashed through both eyebrows.

"What the friggin hell did you two idiots do to each other?" Placing one hand on top of the other, I held them both over the wound in his wing. I reached for his energy, needing to feel it.

Falon sucked in a sharp breath and flinched. "What does it look like? We beat each other bloody. It went a little worse for Bane when I hacked his fucking head off his shoulders."

I laughed softly in disbelief. "Did you really? I can't imagine he'll be too thrilled about that next time we see him. There will be a next time, won't there?"

"Count on it."

Tuning into the immortal spark of his energy, I focused on the injured wing, pushing my energy into Falon, guiding it with specific intent.

Healing energy started off warm and grew in intensity. It was pure Light Flame power. But I was dark too, so when that lovely trickle of sensuality flavored the flow Falon muttered, "Figures."

Beneath my hands the thick gash slowly knit back together. It wasn't perfect, but the pain should've been gone. Turning my attention to his face, I kept the healing force flowing and ran my hands gently over his cuts and bruises.

"Show me the rest," I commanded.

Without question or snark he did so. Another nasty blade wound in his side gaped to reveal muscle and tissue. Important stuff that should not be seen. I hovered my hands over that as well. For me healing took more effort than other forms of energy manipulation. The high-strung encounter downstairs kept me from being completely depleted, but I momentarily felt faint when I'd finished.

Falon scrutinized his wing, flexing it a few times. "Nice work, Hound. You're kind of handy to have around. Who knew you'd be good for more than one thing?"

A blow that low from just about anyone else would've brought my wolf out snarling. With Falon the insult rolled right off my back. "That's right. I'm more than the best lay you've ever had. Surprised?"

"You have no idea." Falon caught me off guard with his lips against mine. Not a kiss driven by physical urges but one fueled by real affection. It clung to him, a light but pleasant hum of warmth.

Before I could marvel over where the hell that came from, we were accosted by demons. Several of them filled the hallway on each end, trapping us. They made no move to attack so we made no move to defend. Still, I braced for it.

"Loric requests all guests join him downstairs," barked a demon with a pig-like snout of a nose.

My gaze darted frantically to Falon whose face revealed nothing. If he was concerned he hid it well. Although he'd had oodles of time to learn how to do that. My nerves began to jitter.

We were being rounded up. For what I could only imagine. But I wouldn't have very long to wonder.

CHAPTER SIXTEEN
ARYS

I felt Alexa before she opened the door. My back was turned to her, but I knew the moment she made eye contact with Shaz. The scent of his arousal grew stronger, and he gripped my hair tighter.

I couldn't be sure how long we'd been in the theatre. From the time we'd walked into the orgy party until the time we left, our hands were on each other. Arrogantly, I'd believed the Lust demon's effects to be nothing I couldn't handle. It took only moments to show me how wrong I was about that.

We had fled the theatre when the demon took interest in Willow. Leaving Alexa behind never felt right, but I knew she'd face whatever was thrown at them and guide Willow through it. Though the distraction had given us the opportunity to slip out, we hadn't made it far before Alexa's lust roared through our link, erupting in me like lava. Her molten fire moved fast, intending to devour anything in its path.

Shaz and I stumbled into the first empty room we'd come across. Kissing him hard, I'd promptly slammed him against the wall, pinning him with my body. His sexy growl rocked me to the soles of my feet. My want for this wolf had gone unsated for too long. I needed to feel him, to taste him.

Shoving my hands beneath his t-shirt, I grazed the line of hair above his boxer shorts. He sucked in a breath and groaned, submitting fully to the moment. We'd both waited long enough.

All I wanted was to taste his pleasure. To roll it around in my mouth and savor him. I went to my knees before him, pressing my face to his abdomen, nipping at his navel until he trembled.

I was done with interruptions. Done with waiting for the right moment. This was it.

My patience had been stripped away. Fueled by a lust as old as time, I unzipped his jeans without any slow, careful movements. The passion that drove me would not be made to wait.

I had him in my hand, then my mouth.

Shaz's husky moan had my already hard cock straining inside my pants. His hands tightened in my hair, and I thought I might come just from the sounds he made. I didn't care if the wolf never laid a hand on me. If I could simply enjoy the way he felt in my mouth, I'd be happy.

When the door opened my lovely she-wolf found us in a lover's embrace of sorts. The heat of her response echoed inside me. Oh, she damn well loved the visual. I understood completely. I too enjoyed watching my two loves together. A moment later the door closed, followed by Alexa and Falon's muffled voices in the hall.

Against my better judgment, I risked a glance up at Shaz.

Eyes alive with his wolf, he growled down at me with a mouthful of beastly fangs. "Don't stop."

No better invitation could have been issued. All too happy to oblige, I feasted on his ravenous flesh, sucking him deeper into my mouth. When his breathing grew labored and his pulse pounded, I braced for his release, ready for it after so many damn months of buildup.

The potency of his orgasm rocked me. I savored the heady swell, chuckling softly as he drew me back to my feet. My head swam with everything Shaz when he crushed his mouth to mine.

We were prisoners in the eye of the storm, but I don't think we'd ever felt as free with each other as we did right then. His hands went to my belt.

Other voices joined Alexa and Falon in the hall. We froze.

I was ready with a psi ball in my palm when the door to our room burst open. A hulking demon filled the space, grunting something about Loric insisting we return to the basement. I let the psi ball dissipate but remained ready as we were ushered from the room.

As we emerged into the hall, Shaz leaned in and whispered, "I guess I owe you more than one."

"I will gladly take you up on that. Maybe one of these days, we'll get five minutes alone without a fucking interruption." Yeah, I was bitter. My hard-on faded as my disappointment grew.

"We're definitely going to need more than five minutes." Shaz's smile was feisty and playful, unafraid of whatever lie ahead. The wild spark in his wolf eyes set me ablaze. Would he ever really know how much I admired him?

Loric's demon muscle already had Falon and Alexa marching down the stairs ahead of us to the main floor. Patrons continued to drink and gamble, oblivious to the darkness that dwelled below. They were just cogs in the machine, feeding the beasts. As long as they got drunk, laid, or lulled by the hope that the machines might pay out, what did they care?

A demon waited near the elevator with Willow who waved both hands in a 'come at me' gesture. The five of us were crammed into the metal box with more demons than I felt the car could safely hold. Seeking out Alexa's gaze, I found her sneaking peeks at Willow. The two of them smelled like sex and each other. The tension between them was palpable.

Brow furrowed, Alexa nibbled her lip. That woman worried too damn much. She'd make herself crazy fussing about Willow's struggles with the incubus life. I understood. She loved him. And she loved so fucking hard. But he'd made his choice. He had to have known it would come to this.

Feeling my gaze upon her, Alexa's head whirled toward me. Right away her expression changed, morphing into something less uptight. She slipped me a small half smile and a wink.

The elevator reached the lower floor, and like a night that would never end, we once again stepped into Jenner's worst nightmare, his ridiculous nightclub in squalor under someone else's thumb.

Where was Jenner anyway?

Demons weren't new to Vegas. The city itself was likely a portal to hell. Harley had kept them out of his nightclub, never giving them the opportunity to use him like a pathetic lapdog. No doubt he'd never been a good man, but he'd had his own standards and he'd upheld them.

As soon as we were all free of the elevator, I put myself next to Alexa, shoving a demon who lingered too close. "I guess now we find out why Loric really wants us here."

"Something tells me we're about to be blindsided." She slipped her hand into mine and squeezed. The touch of her power slithered up my arm. Every time I felt it was like waking up from the dark and finding my light.

Shaz stuck close to her other side while Falon followed behind, watching our backs. Willow kept his distance as we were ushered to the den. Or what had been the den when Harley was in charge. Jenner had turned it into a private party room for bloodletting orgies, and he must've loved what they did to his theatre.

The den had now undergone yet another renovation. No longer was it filled with eager and willing bodies ready to serve anyone with fangs in Jenner's VIP playroom. The large bed and lush carpet had been replaced with hard stone tile and a sacrificial circle.

Alexa's sharp gasp was quickly muffled by her hand. An inverted pentagram had been painted inside the circle in blood. Human blood.

Three demons stood at various points around the circle. Loric stood at the head of it, awaiting us with Pride at his side. The demon's tufted tail whipped lazily about, like a cat who knew he was worshipped. It didn't surprise me that he clung to Loric. Or vice versa.

Most alarming of all, and what had Alexa so horrified, was the occupant of the circle.

Hurst.

Bound to a stake much like those used during the witch trials, a farce if I ever saw one, Harley's sire had been positioned in the dead center of the star. A sacrifice. Well, now we knew why Loric had wanted us here.

Clothed in a black cloak, Hurst bore a few superficial wounds, likely from the struggle it had taken to get him here. Hurst was a loner who'd gone underground decades ago. Nobody saw him unless he initiated contact. During our last visit he'd reached out to Alexa, something I wished he'd never done. All it had done was leave her with questions and unwarranted suspicions.

Loric strode forward to greet us with hands spread. "I hope you've all been enjoying yourselves. You have no idea how happy I am that you're here for this." Jenner and Gabriel were ushered in behind us, disheveled and stained with lipstick and blood. Loric grinned broadly. "Good. Now we can begin."

Most of the demon muscle left the room to guard the door from the outside, granting us a little breathing room. I glanced at Jenner to gauge his reaction. Neither of us had an especially strong connection to Hurst. He was Harley's maker, not ours.

"I trust you both know my sire," Loric addressed Jenner and me in turn. "I've invited you here to witness his final moments. Since I'm laying my claim to the city, it seems only fitting to give the former ruler a final send off."

Jenner bristled and pressed his lips together like he reined in a scoffing protest. Hurst hadn't ruled this city in many years. We all knew Loric wouldn't even be here if Harley weren't dead.

Did he expect us to buy this puffed up ego display? Yeah, the demons standing by to protect him proved that he did. It was all for show. They didn't give a damn about him. It was business, and Loric would end up on the losing end of the deal.

"Is this really necessary?" Alexa bit out, oozing empathy for the vampire in the sacrificial circle.

As much as I adored my other half, I didn't share her concern for Hurst. He and I had never forged a real relationship. Everything I knew about him had been whatever Harley had to say. Though I certainly didn't wish death on him, my people came first. I wouldn't risk them to save him.

Loric met Alexa's concern with skepticism, like he couldn't believe anyone would feel for his sire. "Obviously, my dear, you don't know him. Don't fall for the wisdom-spewing ancient act. I promise you he's never said or done a damn thing in his entire existence that didn't come with an ulterior motive."

Alexa's face tightened, and she shot a fearful look Hurst's way. "Tell me that's not true."

Hurst stared silently at her for so long I thought he'd gone mute. After lengthy consideration he gave a slow shake of his head. In a low, gravelly tone he said, "Never trust that any vampire has your best interests at heart, Alexa."

"I need to know just one thing," she went on without addressing his cryptic remark, having held this question close to her heart for far too long. "Why did you warn me against turning Gabriel?" Her voice quavered at the end there. She'd been dying to ask that question.

I was pretty damn curious to hear the answer myself. Not that his warning had done anything to deter me. I'd turned Gabriel anyway.

Everyone present stared at Hurst, but only two people really cared about his answer. Alexa and Gabriel, the latter having been understandably insulted upon learning such a warning had been issued.

Loric watched their exchange with keen interest. He wanted us to join him in the sacrifice of his sire. Sensing Alexa's unrest and suspicion, he stood back and allowed her to ask her question.

Long black hair matted with blood, Hurst wore defeat well. Proudly even. He knew that his prodigal son had returned, and it wasn't to seek forgiveness. "Because the fates knew that he sees things. You already walked so close to self-destruction, I could practically taste your death on the air. I couldn't take the chance that he would see how to save you." Head held high, Hurst looked Alexa right in the eyes and said, "I hoped you and Arys would destroy yourselves before you could ever reforge your flame."

CHAPTER SEVENTEEN

"But why?" I asked, trying to put it together. "Why the hell would you do that?"

Finding Hurst tied to a stake about to be sacrificed in some kind of demon ritual was not what I'd expected, despite the screwed-up shit we'd experienced already tonight. My initial shock at seeing him had turned to a sickly uncertain twinge.

Hurst still had the friendly appearance of a grandfather figure, only now I questioned why I'd ever trusted it. From the first time we met, he'd set me at ease. But he wouldn't be the first person to deceive me.

He took so long to answer, or perhaps the seconds just felt like eons. Calm hazel eyes looked out of a warm, welcoming face now ugly with the truth. Had he fed me nothing but crap along with oatmeal cookies? Shit, I was such a fool.

"You killed the last person in this world that I loved." Each word came slowly, like he rolled it over in his mouth first, tasting its impact. "I could have simply destroyed you myself, but I wanted you to suffer until you destroyed yourself."

I squeezed Arys's hand in mine hard enough to feel the bones grind. Because he was such a trooper, he allowed it without so much as a grunt. "You lied. You played me like a naïve idiot, and I bought it. And all those nice things you said? Telling me about Lena's stone? Why any of it?"

Hurst frowned, the many lines in his forehead wrinkling in deep furrows. Abhorrence washed over his face. "It cost me nothing to mix truths with lies. It earned me your trust, did it not?"

My ears rang with the crash of adrenaline. I'd gone numb to everything but the pain in my own hand as I crushed Arys's fingers in a desperate attempt to ground myself. All along Hurst had wanted vengeance on me for killing his precious, sadistic offspring. Not once had I suspected him of harboring such sinister intentions.

Trying to absorb this horrific revelation, my gaze darted first to Arys. Whereas I felt stunned and betrayed by my misplaced trust, he had this stony, unfazed expression. He'd learned long ago to trust nobody.

All this time Hurst had played me for a fool. He'd proven to have the ability to see things as well, and I'd stupidly believed that meant I could trust him. I'd been so reluctant to let Gabriel in, to allow him to prove himself despite his pleas and insistence that he would be loyal to me.

Gabriel had been the one to see how our flame could be reforged. Without him, Arys and I would be dust and ash by now. I caught and held Gabriel's gaze. His stoic expression revealed nothing, but I knew his feelings had been hurt.

I owed him so much more than a mere apology.

Hurst's seeds of doubt could have cost us everything. It almost did. I'd only taken a chance on the information that saved our flame because Falon had delivered it.

"Harley was a vile, selfish piece of crap." Shock gave way to rage. I wasn't sorry. I'd never be sorry. "He didn't deserve to live another night, and if I could kill him again, I would."

Through our connected hands I felt the jump in Arys's energy. Inwardly I cringed. I couldn't forget that Harley had meant something to him despite their rocky relationship.

Loric, however, enjoyed my outburst. Grinning from ear to ear, he stood back and let me have my moment. It was the opening act for whatever grand finale he had planned.

Hurst's face crumpled. His eyes widened before narrowing suddenly. From kind old man to fang baring, seething monster in a blink, he hissed, "The fate of one who possesses both light and dark is the fate of one surely doomed to madness. I hope you suffer long after I'm gone, Mad Queen."

They were the angry words of a man who felt robbed of vengeance. There was nothing certain or prophetic about them, and yet they struck a chord. Something inside me recognized truth there.

"You have no idea who this woman is or what she's capable of," Arys snarled, releasing my hand to approach the edge of the circle. Two demons moved to ensure he didn't try to cross it. "You're a bitter, pathetic old recluse who spent the last few hundred years in hiding because you couldn't handle Harley's attachment to me or anyone else. He always knew you killed Anya, and he never forgave you for that."

Anya. Harley's twin flame. And more than likely the reason he'd been so drawn to Arys.

Stunned fury rippled over Hurst's face. Jenner and I wore matching expressions of confusion. Apparently, Arys had just revealed a secret.

"He knew nothing," Hurst protested in a near shout. "I never laid a hand on that wretched woman."

"You lie." Arys clenched both fists, the muscles in his forearms flexing as he held back from taking a shot at the bound vampire. "He watched through her eyes as you killed her. You could never understand their connection. It threatened you so you destroyed it. Harley went half mad and you went underground. Did I miss anything?" Arys held himself tight, like he might explode with the weight of the secret he'd carried for so many years. A secret that hadn't been his but had burdened him just the same.

"If that were true," Hurst countered. "Why would you have sent Alexa to see me alone? You'd never have trusted me to return her alive."

"I was always destined to be the one to kill Alexa. It was never going to be you." Jaw clenched, Arys pulled away from the demons blocking his path and turned to Loric. "He's all yours."

"Wait." I rushed forward, shoving through massive demon bodies until I stood at the edge of the circle. "What about the angel with black wings? And saving my wolf? That was all part of your scheme to get inside my head?"

Hurst's evil grin stripped away the last of the lies I'd believed about him. "Did it work?"

Yeah, it had worked. Saving my wolf had only been half the battle. It hadn't helped me save my light. Only Willow's sacrifice had done that, causing him to become the angel with black wings. Even now on this very night, Willow and I suffered the repercussions of that time.

Because Hurst didn't deserve an answer, I turned away from his deceitful, lying face. I met Loric's arched brow and lazy grin. He loved this, exposing Hurst for the manipulative asshole he was, not so different from Harley in the end. I hoped this wickedness died with the two of them.

"Now that we're all on the same page here," Loric said with a clap of his hands, "shall we get started?"

When nobody protested, Loric strode into the middle of the room like some ringmaster from hell, ready to send his maker off with a flourish. His twisted grin broadened when we made no effort to stop him. He mistook our silence for alliance.

I hung back against the wall near the door, as far from the ritual circle as possible. Willow and Shaz joined me, with Falon lingering somewhere in the middle of the room. Arys and Jenner though, they wanted a front row view and lingered as close to the circle as possible.

They had loved Harley, both of them, in what certainly had been a toxic and abusive relationship. He had made them what they were today, and then he had tormented them ruthlessly until his eventual demise at my hand. But the evidence showed that Harley too had been a victim.

I didn't want to feel anything akin to sympathy for that man. Knowing now that he'd been a lost twin obsessed with filling the void left behind, it made me both ill and angry. Harley had tried to blood bond with me, the closest move he could make to binding himself to another man's twin flame.

It was fucked up. And just the darkest kind of sad.

Standing in front of the circle, Loric studied the vampire inside. His maker. In a strangely wistful tone he said, "If that's the kind of shit he did to his favorite, can you imagine what he did to me?"

I didn't really care to, but I had a feeling we were going to hear about it. Playing along with Loric had gotten old right about the time Falon entered the fight ring. And when Willow was forced to face his desires in front of an audience, I had reached my limit.

Somehow I'd keep up the act until we could escape this shindig from hell. It was one thing to fuck with Jenner, Arys, or me. Doing anything to hurt Willow crossed every line I had. Loric would die before I left this city.

"I saved you, you ungrateful waste of skin." A harsh cough racked Hurst. He spat blood and what might have been a tooth. "You'd have been dead within a day if I hadn't turned you. I should've left you to the plague."

"Saved me? You spent the next several hundred years tormenting me every chance you got." Loric snapped his fingers and two demons came forward. "I've waited so long for this. My only regret is how fast it will happen."

One held a chalice; the other, a dagger. Pretty standard for rituals in my limited experience.

Both items were placed into Loric's waiting hands. He glanced around at those of us gathered. "Anyone have any final words for Hurst?"

I had many things I could have said, but he didn't deserve the satisfaction. Nobody had anything to add other than Jenner who simply said, "Harley was a fucking mess, and because of you, he made our lives a fucking mess too. So, you know, burn in hell."

Being present for anyone's execution felt wrong. Despite how much I wanted to hurt the bastard myself, this entire scenario unsettled me. If I knew I could walk out the door, I would have. Sensing my discomfort, Shaz ran a hand over my arm. That subtle, simple touch proved more than enough for me to feel his calming wolfy vibes.

With a demon at his side, Loric crossed into the circle.

Hurst watched his approach with his chin held high, having no regrets. Even now. "Do you know why Harlan was my favorite? Why I could barely stand to look at you?" He chose to go down with fighting words. "Because you're weak. Not half the vampire he was. You could never measure up to him. You never will."

The dagger in Loric's hand shook slightly as his fingers trembled. "My strengths lie elsewhere. If you'd taken your head out of Harley's ass for even five minutes, you might have noticed. You may have been powerful once, but now you're nothing. No one."

Moving fast, Loric slashed with the knife. It cut across Hurst's jugular, spilling blood down his front. Loric pressed the chalice to the crimson stream, catching the flow. The atmosphere hummed with the power released in the old vampire's blood. It felt aged and worn, dusty in my mouth. Like he hadn't used it for a very long time. Being a recluse had made his power dormant.

"You've always been nothing, Loric. Killing me doesn't change that. You can't even do this on your own. Still a pathetic disappointment after all these years." For a man facing his final moments, Hurst had a surprising amount of moxie. He was going out his way, and on some level I could respect that.

Before he could utter another insult, Loric slashed the blade over the other side of his neck, opening up a gruesome gash that severed arteries, veins, tendons and anything else unlucky enough to be in the way.

Letting the dagger fall to the floor, Loric reached out to dig a finger into the gushing wound. Eyes bulging, Hurst stared hatefully, mouth agape. We all watched with mixed reactions as Loric rubbed the blood beneath his eyes, over his forehead and chin, a line down his nose.

As soon as he finished, the demon who waited next to him began to chant. I didn't recognize the words, though a few of my companions certainly did. Willow and Falon visibly stiffened, but Gabriel sidled closer to the circle for a better view.

After the demon finished his unusual monologue, Loric lifted the chalice to his lips and drank from it before pouring the remainder on the floor in the center of the star. Sulfuric smoke rose up as the blood splattered the tile.

"All I wanted was for you to see all that I am, Hurst. All that I'm capable of." Loric ducked his head, turning the dagger over in his hand. "Now you have to find out the hard way."

Light glinted off the blade as Loric whirled and plunged it into the sternum of his maker. Blood dripped from Hurst's mouth. He didn't try to utter another sound. But his hazel eyes remained fixed on Loric.

Withdrawing the dagger, Loric hesitated for one excruciating second before slamming it into Hurst's heart. There was that horrible final moment before his body dissolved into dust and ash. It shook me, tearing the scab off the still raw wound within. This reminded me too much of plunging my own dagger into someone I loved. For Loric surely loved Hurst still. Otherwise none of this would have meant so much to him.

Hurst's body collapsed into a pile that dispersed throughout the ritual circle. Loric stared at the remains. Something about his macabre stance struck me as wrong. When he turned back to face us, his eyes were solid black.

The frequency in the room had taken on a pitch so shrill I wanted to cover my ears. But it was more than audible. That energy clawed its way beneath my skin. It was palpable, digging its way inside my skull. This sacrificial death carried a heavy, murky vibe. Like dirty oil.

I itched to be away from it all.

From outside the circle Pride watched with exactly that. Pride. He beamed like a proud father at Loric, satisfied that he'd gotten so deeply inside the pathetic vampire's head. Hurst had been right about that. Anyone who needed to align with demons to bolster their power was pathetic.

"As you've all witnessed, the head of our bloodline is dead." Loric's voice boomed through the room, lower and more guttural than before. "I will make this city what it once was, a lawless haven of darkness where anything goes. Unless any of you have something to say about that." He paused, surveying us each in turn, lingering longest on Jenner.

In my head I pleaded for Jenner to keep his mouth shut. We needed a plan. Fighting it out here and now wouldn't result in a win for us. We needed a chance to consider our best options.

When several moments passed and nobody spoke up, Loric continued. "It's been lovely having you all. Enjoy the rest of the night. Shortly before sunrise you will be able to leave with more than enough time to reach your hotel. Come the following sunset you will leave my city until you're invited to return. There is no room for negotiation."

CHAPTER EIGHTEEN

"I say you go home on the first flight out of here and deal with your own shit. It's not your problem, Alexa." Without asking, Falon opened the minibar and helped himself to a bottle of vodka. He grabbed a disposable cup emblazoned with the hotel's logo from the stack on the counter and poured a generous amount.

As Loric had said, we'd been able to leave his nightclub an hour before sunrise. With thirty minutes to spare, Falon was using the last of his time on this side of the physical realm to sass and spew opinions. However, he'd also put a ward on our suite as soon as we'd arrived. Something to keep Loric's demons out. Just in case.

I'd promptly collapsed on the couch, grateful to be off my feet. The evening had been a drain on me in just about every way.

Jenner threw the fallen angel a scathing glare. "Why the hell are you even still here?"

Without acknowledging him, Falon sipped his drink, silver gaze upon me. I shook my head and looked to Arys. He'd been awfully quiet since we returned to the hotel. I could see that he was wrestling with this. Of course he wanted to be there for Jenner, but just how much of a personal risk could we take? Too much trouble brewed back home. We needed to be there.

Arys shoved away from the doorway where he'd lingered. Crossing to the window, he stared down at the Strip below. "The place is loaded with demons every night, Jenner. How much is it really worth to you? Your life? Ours?" Whereas earlier Jenner had gazed out that window eager to see the view he called home, Arys seemed to be getting his last good look. He didn't plan to come back here.

Jenner leaned against the back of the couch, arms crossed. Stains of lipstick and blood remained from his time in the theatre. "Go home then. I get it. It means nothing to you. This isn't your city anymore, Arys. But it's all I have. I'd rather die here than flee like a coward."

Arys let out an annoyed breath but didn't turn from the window. I knew that he was torn between obligation to his old life and his new one. If he had wanted to stay and fight, I would have supported that, but all I wanted right then was to get the fuck out of Dodge.

"If we go home now and do nothing, then we are just as guilty as every demon inside that nightclub." Willow sat in one of the chairs at the dining table, eyeing the drink Falon held with envy. "I'm afraid I can't do that."

Something about the stubborn and dedicated way he said that picked at Falon who scowled into his paper cup. "It's not your fight anymore, Willow."

"Then why the hell are you known as a traitor among the underworld?" Willow countered. After the events of the evening, he seemed to have reached the end of his patience. "Because you still pull strings for the light even though you tread in darkness. Working from the inside, so to speak. Tell me I'm wrong."

Falon could tell him no such thing. It was true. Although I did not know the extent of the details, Falon himself had admitted as much to me the night we were trapped together in the FPA building.

He stared at Willow over the rim of his cup. "Watch yourself, asshole."

While all I wanted to do was run home to my own damn demon problems, I knew that Willow was right. Leaving and going on about our business would be tacit approval, no less evil than the demons inside Loric's sin party. Fuck.

"Stop." I held up a hand to silence them. "You guys saw what was going on in there. Experienced it firsthand. We can't just leave—trust me, I want to—but that's not who I am. I have to fight this, but anyone who wants to go home can go."

"Don't be an idiot, wolf," Falon scoffed. "Get your ass on a plane and leave. Whatever is going on in your own city is far more important."

My eyes narrowed in suspicion. "What do you mean? Do you know something I don't?"

"What I know is that this city is not worth dying for. Do you honestly expect to walk back into that place and kick everyone's ass? It's never going to happen."

Dismissing Falon with an eye roll, I turned to Willow, though he'd barely looked at me since we left the theatre. "If we stay how much can we possibly do against that small legion?"

Briefly his eyes met mine before flicking away, to Falon. The two of them held a long, uncomfortable stare. Finally Willow said, "The only way to defeat a Sins demon is to challenge the sin."

From his place on one of the easy chairs, Shaz shook his platinum head. "I don't like the sound of that."

"It's exactly what it sounds like. A stupid fucking idea." Crumpling the empty cup, Falon tossed it toward the garbage, missing completely.

My brows knit together as I puzzled this out. "Yeah, it's not sounding great to me either. How the hell do you challenge a Sins demon and win?"

"By facing the test of the sin and somehow overcoming it." Willow knew that wasn't as easy as it sounded. He wrinkled his nose and shrugged.

"Keyword being somehow," Falon bit out, irate with this whole conversation. "In case you didn't notice, every single one of us had our asses handed to us tonight. How the hell do you propose to pull that off?"

The room fell quiet. It seemed we were all caught between a rock and a hard place. Exhausted and in need of a shower, I threw up both hands in defeat. Willow and I hadn't stood a chance in the face of Lust. I couldn't imagine how we could return with the sole intent to challenge every sin.

"I think we could do it." Gabriel surprised me by breaking the silence. He sat on the couch at my side, hunched forward as if unable to relax. "There are seven sins. There's also seven of us. Through Alexa we're all bonded, making us stronger than we are alone. We challenge them, winners take all. If we beat them at their own game, they relinquish their hold on Jenner's night club and destroy the contract with Loric. A demon has to honor their own deal."

Falon scoffed. It was no easy feat to convince the stubborn angel that he didn't always know best. Still he must have been intrigued enough to question the idea further. "What makes you so sure we could face whatever challenge they throw at us?"

Gabriel's dark gaze flicked to me, and I nodded, remembering the vision he'd had earlier. "Nothing makes me sure at all. I only know what I saw. Before we went out tonight, I saw Alexa. With all of us together. In the theatre." He paused to let the unspoken parts sink in.

My lips parted in surprise. The guys had various reactions from scoffing to awkward laughter. Except Willow.

"Group sex." Shaz issued a bewildered little laugh. "Is that what you're saying? All of us with her together? That doesn't sound like we win."

"Doesn't it?" The wickedness in Arys's tone sent a teasing tingle down my spine.

Raking his fingers through his hair in tired exasperation, Falon muttered, "How utterly revolting. Definitely not a win."

Used to the snarky angel after their time with Shya, Gabriel made brushing off Falon look easy. "I don't get the whole story in a vision, but I'm pretty sure it wasn't a failure. Rather an attempt to overthrow Lust."

Could we really do such a thing? Build enough power under Lust's influence to seize control and overthrow the demon completely?

"What about the others?" I wondered aloud, refusing to let myself imagine the scenario Gabriel had seen. Just the thought of it made my cheeks red hot. "Even if we somehow managed to outlust Lust, there are six other sins."

"I don't know. I wish I did." Frustrated, Gabriel rubbed the stress line that pinched tight between his brows. "Maybe if we start with Lust, we could use the power we called to sweep the rest."

Willow spoke up then, his features etched in doubt. "They would never make it easy for us. There would be twists, loopholes. Although, Gabriel might be onto something. Alexa is the one thing that binds us all together. If she could draw on the power of us all, overthrowing Lust might be possible."

Hearing him back Gabriel's vision, if that indeed was what he'd seen, made me look a little closer and harder at him. There was no way that Willow would want to take part in making that a reality. He had yet to even look at me for longer than a flicker of a glance, if that.

"Just one thing." Shaz raised a hand. "Where does that leave me? I'm not magically bound to her the way the rest of you are."

Falon made a noise of disgust, offended at being grouped in with the vampires. Striding past his cup on the floor, he headed toward the door to the suite.

Willow laced his knuckles together, cracking them thoughtfully. "I think you underestimate the connection you have with two incredibly powerful vampires, Shaz."

"Excuse me, wolf," Falon said to me from the doorway, "a word in the hall if you will? I don't have much time."

Sunrise didn't just chase vampires indoors. It forced demons and fallen angels back to the other side. The strong ones could remain here incorporeal for a time, but eventually their energy drained, sending them back to their realm. Same idea if they tried to globe jump to outrun the sun. Eventually, the drain would force them back.

Leaving the others to continue the discussion without us, I followed Falon. Not content to linger close to the door, he led me down the vast hall to the fire exit on the opposite end.

"Tell me you're not going to listen to Gabriel on this one." He caught me by both arms and spun me around, pasting me against the fire exit door. Pressing close, Falon caught my chin and forced my gaze to his.

Enjoying the way he felt against me, I tried to figure him out. "I don't know. Honestly, I think we all need to sleep on it. Regroup at sunset. Be here, okay?"

"Why must you be so damn stubborn? Don't go back into that shithole. Go home, dammit." To emphasize his command Falon kissed me forcefully, thrusting his tongue into my mouth.

I slid my arms around his neck and kissed him back before nipping his bottom lip. "Don't be such a chicken shit. It's just a little group sex, Falon. Why are you so scared of a little sword crossing? And don't tell me what to do. You know that's never going to work."

"What? No." Falon protested, kissing me again. Quick feverish kisses. "No sword crossing. Don't even joke about that."

Laughing against his lips, I said, "I'm dead serious, baby. Don't be such a prude."

His hand was on my throat then, squeezing just hard enough to choke off my laughter. "Do you really think you have it in you to take on six of us at one time? You can barely contain yourself when it's only my cock inside you."

"I'm always up for a challenge." Raising a brow flirtatiously, I pried his fingers off my throat. Truth be told the very thought of what Gabriel had seen intimidated the crap out of me.

"Liar. Willow can't even look at you, and you expect him to get on board with that?" The ever observant Falon might have thought he had me there, but he'd just slipped up.

Did he expect me to believe that he gave a shit about Willow? "Damn, Falon. If I didn't know better, I'd say you're jealous."

In response he slid his thigh between my legs, rubbing against my core. "Better shut that filthy mouth, Hound. None of them will ever fuck you the way I do."

He had that right. Not one of my lovers could replace another, and I loved that. Arys was mad love and possessive power. Shaz could play the dominant or the submissive, and he always loved me with a fierce wildness that was part wolf and all him. Jenner had a dirty streak a mile wide, and I loved the way he brought it out in me as well. The depths of Willow's passion had rocked me. He loved so hard.

And Falon, well nobody set me free the way he did. Nobody saw the broken pieces of me and released me from the pain of carrying them for a little while.

"You're right," I agreed, jerking him closer so I could drag my tongue over his lip. "So what are you so afraid of? If there's a chance we can take on the sins and win, then we have to. Because I'm with Willow. We can't just leave."

Falon kissed me hard, a punishing crush of his mouth on mine. Then he pulled away with obvious reluctance. The sun was rising. "I'll be back when the sun goes down. Try to stay out of trouble until then." He poofed, leaving me to scoff at the empty hallway.

Pretty sure I could make it a whole day without trouble finding me. And since when did we kiss goodbye? Was that what that was?

Baffled but too tired to think on it, I padded back down the hall to the suite. The guys had dispersed. Arys closed the blinds in the living room as I entered.

"Falon thinks it's a bad idea," I stuck the 'Do Not Disturb' sign on the door handle, closed it gently, and flipped the deadbolt. "I told him we'll sleep on it and decide at sunset."

"Yeah, that's pretty much what we decided too. We need to get some rest if we're going back in there." Arys swept me into his arms, wrinkling his nose at the lavender scent of Falon clinging to me.

"You want to go back in?" I'd been so sure he'd want to leave Vegas to the demons.

Guiding me along toward our room, he gave me an affectionate pat on the rear. "Willow has a way of making me feel like a piece of shit for thinking about leaving without even saying a word. How does he do that anyway?"

We entered our bedroom to find Shaz stripping off his shirt. He flashed me an impish grin, but dark circles were forming beneath his eyes. My white wolf was exhausted.

"Willow's just that good. None of us measure up to his ideals." I laughed but my heart squeezed. "I'd hoped to get a chance to talk with him."

I didn't feel right about leaving things as they were with Willow. I needed to know we were okay. That he didn't hate me for what happened, that he didn't hate himself.

"You'll get your chance, my love. Give him some time to process. We all need to decompress." Arys's hungry gaze roamed over Shaz's naked torso. Insatiable.

"Oh yeah?" I quirked a brow and pinched his arm playfully. I couldn't help but tease, "How about you guys? Do you need time to process?" Keeping an eye on Shaz for his reaction, I sidled over to my bag and sifted through for some clean clothes.

The two of them exchanged a look, as expected.

Shaz caught my eye and winked before sliding his pants off. "No, I'm good. I've spent the last few months processing. No regrets here."

Inwardly, I breathed a sigh of relief. Since Shaz had stepped onto an unfamiliar path, I was glad to see he didn't feel lost. "Good. It's about time you two finally touched each other without me. You both needed that."

"For the record…" Arys made a show of fake clearing his throat. "We didn't touch each other. I touched Shaz."

He'd done more than touch, but that was neither here nor there. Shaz and I both saw where Arys was going with this. I smirked while Shaz shot a brazen stare at our dark vampire.

"Like I said, I owe you a couple." Sauntering to the bed in his boxers, Shaz slipped between the sheets and stretched out. "Don't worry, Arys. I always pay my debts." His eyes closed with finality, a sure sign he had no plans to clear their account tonight.

I hit the shower, fatigue settling in. While I massaged conditioner into my long locks, I replayed the most vivid parts of the night in my head: Falon forced to defend his mark, a mark that meant more than I'd realized. Willow shielding me with his body while he claimed mine. Hurst's bulging eyes seconds before Loric plunged the dagger into his heart.

With the many images dancing in my head, I expected sleep to elude me. But when I crawled into bed and settled in between Shaz and Arys, slumber took me fast. I felt safe there with them, though all I wanted was to be back at home in our own bed.

We'd come to see what Loric had done to Jenner's nightclub. Now we knew. Since Arys had laid claim to this city, we had a responsibility to uphold.

And I wanted to. Leaving just wasn't an option. Every fiber of my being wanted to go back in there and kick some ass.

But I was scared too. This was evil on a level I'd never faced. Even so it would still pale in comparison to whatever Lilah and Salem had in store for me.

CHAPTER NINETEEN

FALON

Back in my own realm, I sat in a dumpy demon bar where some jackass played the piano in the corner as if it were a saloon in a bad western flick. It was nothing of the sort. Nothing but a rundown dwelling where demons gathered to get loaded on otherworld swill.

Much like the human world, our side of the spiritual line boasted of the low, middle, and high class. Though I could've sipped expensive liquor in a high-class joint, I'd come here to be left alone. These decrepit, back-alley places offered the anonymity that I craved right then. The places I preferred to frequent had much higher quality booze, but they also drew assholes like Bane.

With a glass of potent whiskey strong enough to blind a human, I tried to wash the taste of Alexa from my mouth. That woman was crazy. She had every intention of going back into that hole, which meant I'd be going back in. After what had occurred earlier, I couldn't take my eyes off her inside that building. Or outside it for that matter. Alexa's ability to draw the wrong attention never ceased to impress me. Although it did grow tiresome.

"Where the hell have you been?"

Nova's irritatingly familiar voice from right behind me incited an inward groan. So much for being left alone. Without waiting for an invitation, because he knew he wouldn't get one, he pulled out the chair across from me at the small round table and sat down.

"When exactly?" I asked, downing enough of my drink to get a nice buzz going.

"You missed the last meeting." Nova waved a hand to the bartender who flipped him off in return. "You and Alexa both missed it. What's keeping the two of you so preoccupied lately? Other than the obvious."

The Circle of the Veil made it their business to know just about everything about its members. Even our personal lives. However, those were usually left personal, until we gave the *quesos grandes* adequate reason to look a little further.

"We get our jobs done. What does it matter?" Refusing to be interrogated by a guy on the same rung as me, I took another drink, savoring the burn.

Nova stared hard, his red eyes boring into mine. "You know why it matters."

"Don't fucking talk to me about the mark. I'm sick of hearing about it. I wish I'd never put the damn thing on her, but it's too late now." My buzz continued to grow steadily as I neared the bottom of the glass. I was not discussing Alexa with this shithead.

"Cut the shit, Falon. You knew marking her would get attention. Why else would you do it?" He paused, but when I didn't respond, he prodded, seeking a reaction. "But the real question is, what were you thinking? Falling in love with that woman is a dangerous game, my friend. One that I don't think you can win."

My fist clenched on the table top, drawing Nova's gaze. "Listen, asshole. I am not in love with Alexa. She'd be the first to tell you that. She's just a pretty face who makes my cock very, very happy every now and then. Not that it's any business of yours."

Nova sat back in his chair, shoving long hair out of his face. He appraised me with a weird little smile that pissed me off. "I hope for your sake that she's worth it."

I slid the demon a vicious grin. "It just kills you that I'm fucking her and you're not."

After having himself a good long laugh, Nova sobered enough to say, "I have no interest in Alexa. Not after seeing what she's done to you. And that, Falon, should scare the hell out of you."

It did. It scared me on a level so profound that I couldn't let myself think about it for too long at a time.

Fuck Nova if he thought I'd admit as much to him. We weren't friends. We were occasional and indifferent partners in various Circle related tasks, and I made sure we rarely worked together if I could help it.

"The only thing that concerns me is your keen interest in who I'm fucking." Letting all form of expression seep from my face, I regarded him with a cold glare. Despite Alexa's surprisingly adept healing skills, I was tired and sore. But I'd still kick Nova's ass if he continued grilling me.

Nova held up a hand and laughed. "Trust me, aside from it fucking up your ability to do your job, I'm not interested. Watch your back, Falon. The Circle of the Veil won't be happy if your fling with Alexa blows back on them somehow."

Ah, the not-so-thinly veiled threat. Nova got up to leave, and I didn't bother with a parting remark. I owed him nothing. To myself I muttered, "You and The Circle can kiss my ass."

A fight broke out in the corner, drawing everyone's attention. Two demons going at it over a female. This happened frequently. Women were rare among immortal kind and highly sought after. Their desirability alone gave them incredible power, which many of them were quick to abuse. And who could blame them? While those two idiots beat each other senseless, the demoness flounced out on Nova's arm.

Unsurprisingly, many demons opted to fornicate with humans and vampires.

Done with everyone and their shit, I ambled outside. The stone streets were empty in this part of the city. Closer to the main street marketplace, there would be more activity. Rather than walk through it to get to my place on the other side, I opted to fly. It took more effort than a stroll through town, but I needed the solitude.

Unfurling my wings, I stretched them slowly. Other than some stiffness where Bane had slashed me, they felt pretty good. I took to the sky with a few strong wing beats and headed for the tall luxury building against the pale purple skyline in the distance.

The Circle of the Veil provided well. They'd set me up in a penthouse suite and allowed me almost any extravagance I wished. Not that I wished for many. I assumed Nova's place, wherever it happened to be, was stacked with extras that I'd never think to request. Like an around the clock maid that doubled as a personal sex toy. If I were to take a wild guess.

As I neared my building, I started to rethink this whole flying thing. I landed on the balcony off my bedroom and paused to check my wards. Still in place.

Once inside, I stripped off my clothing and dropped everything in the corner before collapsing on the bed. Pressing fists to my gritty eyes, I spread out on silk sheets and muttered a few choice words. To Nova. To Alexa. To myself.

I'd quit asking myself how she and I had gotten to this strange hate-fueled attachment. We thrived on it, both of us. Every new and clever insult, every dirty kiss and rough fuck. We'd both come to rely on it. To want and need it more with every look and touch.

It was sick, twisted, depraved. But it wasn't love.

It also wasn't ending any time soon. Not as long as she wore my mark, which I had no intention of removing. Alexa picked at my nerves like nobody I'd ever known. Not a night went by when I didn't want to slap her. And yet, the thought of Bane putting his hands on her filled me with an unholy rage.

"Fuck that demon," I swore at my ceiling, clutching a handful of the sheet beneath me. The fabric was among the finest to be had in this realm, but I'd have traded it in a heartbeat for the scratchy cotton sheets from the hotel room Alexa and I frequented.

Slamming a fist on the unadorned headboard, I forced my mind from that hotel room and back to the current moment. Me, blissfully alone. It wouldn't last long, so I had to make the most of it.

I drew the sheet over me. Though I could go several days without sleeping, after the beating I'd both taken and given in that shithole, I needed it. Especially if I was going to accompany that stupid wolf back in there.

Despite my fatigue it took hours to fall asleep. Try as I might, I couldn't help but miss the feeling of that perfect ass pressed against me.

Love and me, we didn't go together. Not anymore. That didn't mean I never missed having a woman in my bed. Loneliness made a real and ruthless devil. One-night stands scratched only the physical itch. Not that I'd touched another woman since the night I had first touched her.

Alexa scratched deeper.

Somehow she managed to slip past my guard and get a peek at my soul. The part of me I'd buried with Winter. Or so I thought. It pissed me off to no end.

What right did she have to be the only one to see the shattered remains of what Bane had destroyed? Who the hell was she to be my only source of any release from this eternal grind? And why the fuck couldn't I stop this thing with her?

I tossed and turned, naked and wrapped in a blanket that felt like a dream, thinking about her in that Vegas suite with five men who didn't have to leave her side at dawn.

I was so fucked.

CHAPTER TWENTY

"I knew you wouldn't come to your senses."

Falon's voice scared the ever-loving crap out of me. Because I was in the bathroom. Alone.

With a shriek, I whirled to find him standing behind me, near the closed door. Clutching my towel tight around me, my fear quickly turned into anger. "What the hell is wrong with you? Who does that? Not fucking cool, Falon."

The bastard burst into laughter, and I grabbed the first thing I could reach off the counter to throw at him. The wrapped bar of soap bounced harmlessly off his chest and hit the floor.

"Looks like I showed up at just the right time." Waggling his brows at me, Falon kicked the soap aside and came at me, reaching for the towel. "How exactly were you planning to kick my ass with an energizing bath bar?"

I held tight to the towel, refusing to be played by that teasing grin. It wasn't easy. "I have my ways."

"Seeing as you're not packing for the airport, I'm guessing you've chosen to go back in there. Typical. You never listen to me." He rubbed the hem of the towel, scowling at the material, like it had failed to meet his standards. The tips of his fingers grazed my thigh, and I twitched at his touch.

When he backed me slowly up against the counter, I let him. Falon's penetrating stare dug into me like a knife. Butterflies tickled my insides at the intent in his eyes. Something was up with him tonight.

Dark dress pants and a navy-blue long-sleeved t-shirt was about as casual as I saw on Falon. He always wore expensive name brands, the kind of shit from fashion magazines. Tailored jackets and shiny loafers. This slightly dressed-down version was good too. No matter what Falon wore, I couldn't wait to get it off him.

Too satisfied not to gloat, I smirked up at him. "Seeing as you're dressed like you're planning a casino heist, I guess you've chosen to come with me?"

"Please tell me you're not going to challenge a full house of Sins demons. Even you can't be that stupid." The lack of effort in his insult made me stare harder at him. He shirked from my inspection. "What? Stop looking at me like that."

"You're stressing about facing Lust." I knew he'd tell me off for daring to call him out on that. "Whatever you're picturing, I'm sure it won't go down like that."

Falon nodded. "You're right. It will be worse than anything I can imagine. And if we do it, the repercussions could be horrific. Have you considered that?"

No matter what happened when we saw Lust again, I most definitely wanted Falon to be part of it. Having him pressed so close while I stood there in nothing but a towel took my mind to naughty places.

"What kind of repercussions?" Eyes narrowed, I searched for any sign of him bullshitting me.

He hesitated a moment before pushing away from me. "Nova sought me out this morning after I left here. Back on the other side. He made it sound like The Circle is keeping tabs on us, Alexa. You know, just in case our relationship botches any Circle business. But I think it's more than that. I'm just not sure exactly what yet."

I didn't like what he was getting at. "Can we not trust them?"

"Of course not. You can't trust anybody in this world. Not when you have any shred of power. The more power you have, the less trust you can afford." His words felt foreboding. Ominous.

Not for a second did I have implicit trust in The Circle of the Veil. No secret society founded by angels, demons, and who knew what else was going to give a crap about those they stuck on the frontlines. Like me.

They'd taken an interest in me right from the start, before I even knew they existed. Just like Briggs and the FPA, The Circle saw my abilities as an asset. For now. I wasn't naïve enough to think that couldn't change in a heartbeat.

"Sounds like you're trying to distract me from the real reason you don't want to face Lust," I teased. Able to pile only so much on my plate tonight, there was no room for The Circle of the Veil. "Are you worried that you won't measure up to the others? I promise, it's really not so bad. Average even."

If looks could kill.

Falon pointed an angry finger at me, and I burst into laughter. "Not fucking funny," he snarled. "I'm well above average and you love every inch. If you insist on making me fuck you in front of your vampires and your wolf, that's fine with me. If you're worried about anyone, it should probably be Willow."

"Ugh, don't talk to me about Willow." Grimacing, I let the towel drop and reached for the underwear, t-shirt, and jeans folded on the counter top. "He's barely spoken to me since last night."

I felt Falon's silver gaze upon me as I slipped into black panties. So I moved a little slower than I would have had I been alone, tugging the panties up my legs inch by inch, making it a show all for him.

"He'll be fine once he has some time to absorb the sudden and horrifying reality of fucking you." With each word Falon's voice grew lower. Huskier. "Just try to go easy on him tonight."

I glanced up to find him watching me with that same expression he got right before he threw me on the bed in our hotel room and forced me to my knees. "What about you, Falon? Should I go easy on you tonight?" Flashing him a flirtatious grin, I winked.

The tiny bathroom swelled with the sudden rise of heat. "Whatever you give, you get, wolf. Try me."

My cheeks warmed, and my grin became a seductive laugh. Falon would rise to any challenge I threw at him, if for no other reason than because he couldn't allow himself to back down. Still I knew he wasn't entirely on board with what we had planned. He liked to have me to himself. I understood that not everyone was as carefree in bed as Arys.

Well, that was a poor example. Nobody was quite like Arys.

"I'm going to need you to be pretty, um, hands on. I might have to take your blood to maximize the power I can raise." I grabbed my t-shirt and bra from the counter and blurted, "You're the only one I trust to help me maintain control in there. I need you, Falon."

Why did I say that? It just slipped out. Then it hung there between us, awkward as hell.

"Is that what you're planning to wear?" he asked, criticizing my clothes as if the previous weird moment hadn't happened.

"Yeah." I raised a brow and shot him a warning look. "Why? What's wrong with it?"

He snatched both the bra and the t-shirt from my hands before I could put either on. Holding the shirt up, he shook his head at the band logo on the front. "It's hardly the attire of a queen. Especially a succubus about to wage war."

I barely managed to refrain from an eyeroll. If I rolled my eyes every time Falon incited the urge, they'd probably roll right out of my head. "Well if anyone would know the proper attire, I suppose it would be you, oh most-fashionably-dressed one. Enlighten me."

A snap of his fingers and a long black dress enveloped my body. The corset bodice fit like it had been made for my curves alone. The skirt flowed in silken waves to my ankles. It felt otherworldly.

Falon stepped forward to release the clip that held my hair atop my head. It cascaded down over my shoulders. "That's better."

I gaped at my reflection in the mirror over the counter. "I'm pretty sure this is an abuse of power."

"I'm fallen, remember? Who gives a shit?" Falon stood behind me, looking at the two of us in the mirror. Our eyes met through the glass as he kissed the back of my shoulder. "You're a goddess." Then he dropped my t-shirt, turned, and walked out the door to the living room where the others had gathered.

* * * *

"This is a joke, right?" Nothing about Loric's face indicated that he found our disobedience funny.

Flanked by demon goons with Pride at his side like a turd stuck on a shoe, Loric had met us on the main floor of The Wicked Kiss Las Vegas, refusing us entry to the floor below. Fine by me. I wasn't ready to go down there yet anyway.

We'd arrived, stated our terms, and now we waited to learn if he would accept or fight. If I had to fight in this dress, I was going to be really ticked with Falon. I still questioned why I'd worn it. I didn't have to, but once it was on me and I'd had a few minutes alone to take it in, I wanted to.

"We're not on a plane out of here," Arys said with a carefree shrug, hands stuffed in his pockets. Unaffected by Loric's muscle, he challenged the other vampire, no hint of fear. "So I'd say we're serious."

"You want to challenge the Sins demons in order to nullify my contract with them and foist me out, and you think I should be ok with that? I can't think of a single reason not to kill every last one of you. Maybe it's best to just bring an end to Harley's bloodline." As he raged around the VIP poker room, Loric flipped a table at random.

"Well, that escalated quickly," Shaz muttered, causing Arys to snicker.

One of the demons standing ready to intervene if we jumped Loric laughed as well, while Pride smiled slyly. He was a calculating asshole. I didn't like the sharp, devious glint in his red lion eyes. Not one of them was loyal to Loric or felt they owed him a damn thing. They were all in it for themselves and would choose whatever best served them.

"It's not such a bad proposition, Loric," Pride said, eyeing us each in turn. "The odds are certainly not in their favor. Their failure would mean our gain. The destruction of such powerful creatures shouldn't be taken lightly. We must glean what we can from it. Don't you think?"

What the heck was happening? I shot a raised brow to Falon who gave me this 'are you surprised?' look. Pride wanted Loric to agree to our proposition. He thought we'd never be able to face it and win. That didn't instill a lot of confidence in me, but Pride was Pride. I mean, did he ever lack confidence? He was the absolute last person to allow inside my head.

The Sins demon surveyed us like a curious cat, sizing us up. He seemed to like what he saw. When his gaze lingered especially long on Arys, it made my gut clench.

Loric didn't like the demon's opinion. He frowned and turned to Pride, both furious and confused. "You want to agree to this? Why not just kill them outright?"

"I just told you why. I didn't gain my power by missing out on opportunities, especially those that literally fall into my lap." Pride nailed Loric with his icy red stare. "Don't be a fool."

The stare down that ensued between them revealed exactly how their arrangement worked. Loric was nothing but a means to an end. One of many I presumed. He had something they wanted. A cushy, steady flow of traffic to feed their sinful delights. Maybe they'd needed an invitation to come in here and take over like this, but now that Loric had extended it, what did they really need him for?

He seemed to come to the same conclusion. "Fine," he seethed through clenched teeth. "You must challenge and beat all Seven Deadly Sins. Then we'll talk contracts and ownership."

"Four out of seven," Arys countered, but his gaze was on Pride, not Loric.

"Out of the question," Loric snapped. Veins in his neck bulged as his ego took a hit.

But Pride overruled him again. "Deal. Four out of seven."

Grinning far too broadly for me to feel good about it, Pride stepped forward and extended a hand. Not to Arys as expected but to me. "The Queen makes the final call. My lady?"

Instinct screamed at me not to take his hand. Except there was no other way. Once we shook on it, the games would begin. Would we fail as Pride believed?

Too bad Gabriel hadn't seen that part. Although he'd taken one look at me in this dress and nodded to himself, so hopefully that could be taken as a good sign.

Showing hesitation would be seen as weakness. So I ignored that voice shouting in my head and put my hand in Pride's. Nausea swept me as an acrid taste filled my mouth. The taste grew stronger when Pride pulled my hand in for a kiss. His lips brushed over my knuckles, and I fought back a shudder.

The queen had made the final call. I hoped like hell we wouldn't regret it.

CHAPTER TWENTY-ONE

We started right there in the VIP poker lounge with Greed. The demon of money and excess worked the room, encouraging the high rollers to gamble with desperate intent. Fluffy fox tail whipping about behind him, Greed looked on with satisfaction as one man lost his Maserati to another.

As Pride and Loric waited, Greed moved among us, sniffing us out each in turn, deciding who he wanted to challenge. It came as no surprise to me when he stopped in front of Jenner. "You want this place more than any of them do. Let's see how well you play poker."

If this wasn't some kind of bittersweet twist of fate, then I didn't know what was. Jenner had forced Arys to play him during our last visit here. Arys's loss had resulted in Shaz's cage fight and ultimately Jenner's binding to me.

A strange smile played about Jenner's lips. "That's it? A poker game?"

Greed's thin lips pursed, and he brazenly stroked a finger over the spade tattoo on Jenner's arm. "You underestimate the power of the cards, my friend. It will be your undoing."

Jenner jerked out of reach. "We're playing cards. Keep your fucking hands to yourself."

While the two of them took their seats at an empty poker table, the rest of us watched with varying expressions of suspicion and disbelief. Shaz and Arys stuck close on either side of me while Falon stood behind, lingering close enough for me to catch whiffs of his comfortingly familiar scent.

Gabriel lurked near the exit where he could watch everyone in the room, and Willow sat right down at the poker table with the others to keep a close eye on Greed. If anyone knew how to cheat or scam the game, it would be Greed.

The dealer was a staff vampire who did her best to hide the fear that trickled from her. I imagined that working here since the Sins demons arrived hadn't been the best experience. Not for those who preferred answering to Jenner as boss.

Loric and Pride stood near the table to oversee the entire thing. Everything about this smacked of bullshit. I got the feeling these games could be designed so that nobody could win. As I watched Jenner and Greed play hand after hand, that feeling grew to certainty.

Jenner's wins came too easily. The chips in front of him grew, as did his confidence. Exactly what Greed wanted.

"He's doomed," Falon remarked utterly without care. "We all are. Deals with demons never turn out how you expect."

Arys's jaw twitched, the only visible sign he was on edge. "Unless you have a better plan, shut the fuck up."

"Well, I did actually." There was no silencing the snarky angel. "My plan was to go home and stay there. I'd think you idiots would have learned to listen to me by now. Instead you have to drag me into this shit along with you."

I felt the rise of Arys's temper in my blood before he rounded on Falon with a clenched fist. "The only thing that dragged your ass into this is the mark you put on my wolf. Would you like to discuss that now?"

"No," I butted in before Falon could open his mouth. Shoving between them, I pushed them both a few steps back in opposite directions. "We're in this together so I suggest you both drop the testosterone-driven crap right now and remember that. Until we get home, you're best fucking friends. And I don't want to hear or see otherwise. Got it?"

They exchanged a glare loaded with vehemence but kept their mouths shut. Arys didn't trust Falon or how close he'd gotten to me. Falon had a grudging acceptance of Arys. He understood our twin flame bond, in some ways better than we did. But that didn't mean he liked my dark half by any means. My theory was that they were too much alike. Headstrong and arrogant.

On the poker table Jenner's winnings had climbed to a few hundred thousand dollars. Maybe half a million. I didn't trust any of this. But as we watched, he gambled everything on the next hand.

"Why would he do that?" I wondered aloud.

"That's what Greed does. It makes you take stupid risks in the name of more." Falon's touch on my lower back made me want to grab onto him in fear that he was right, that we'd made a huge mistake coming back here.

I didn't. I touched none of my men. My personal security didn't lie in them. It lay in me. Not for a second would I send the message that I needed them to protect me like a fragile flower in a hailstorm.

Jenner lost. As Greed swept his entire pile of chips away, the vampire resorted to desperate bargaining. "Give me one chance to win that entire stack back."

"You have nothing else to bet." Greed flashed a sharp, toothy grin.

"This nightclub. It's rightfully mine." Jenner's blue eyes widened as he glanced about for anything to raise the stakes.

"And you're willing to gamble the whole damn thing?" Greed tested Jenner, leaning closer to really peer into him.

Beside me Arys made a frustrated noise. We'd come here for this nightclub. For this city. For Jenner. And he was going to just gamble it away without a second thought?

No, that wasn't right. His will was being influenced.

I darted forward, knowing only that I had to get to him. I'd taken only a few steps when Pride shouted, "Stop her before I do."

Half expecting to be swarmed by demon muscle, I was confused when Falon grabbed both my arms to hold me back. Falon?

Oh, right. Because the immortals saw me only as Falon's property, as his feather on my neck marked me. The hybrid queen who'd faced death twice and lived was a joke to Pride. Because the jackass couldn't possibly see anyone else for what they were, not if it contested his ego in any way. And even knowing that, it pissed me off to no end.

A few demons moved to block Shaz and Arys as they made to intervene. Next to my ear, Falon snarled, "Don't make yourself an easy target."

I struggled to pull away from him, but he held tight until he was sure I'd stay put. "Jenner, don't," I shouted. "It's not worth it."

But Jenner wasn't paying any mind to the commotion around me. He stared right into Greed's beady eyes and said, "Yes. All of it. On the next hand, if I lose. If I win, you give me back that stack of chips."

All we could do was watch in horror as Jenner blindly bet everything he had left in this world without so much as a second thought.

With nothing to raise, the cards fell.

And Jenner fucking lost.

Because of course he did. The whole damn thing had happened so fast. Jenner, who'd outplayed Arys, couldn't outplay Greed.

We all stared at the cards laid out on the table, a flush and a straight, but nobody stared as hard as Jenner. Eyes glued to the losing straight he'd laid down, his hands trembled as emotion shook him.

"I admire your ability to take a risk," Greed purred, leaning back in his seat with hands folded. "Seeing as you just lost any right you have to this business, I don't see any point in continuing this challenge."

My brain raced as I searched for a loophole, anything to keep us in this game. In a sense he was right. Jenner had lost the club we'd come here to bargain for.

Except… "Jenner might have forfeited his claim to this place, but we didn't." I inclined my head toward Arys. "Jenner was here as Arys's acting second. It's not really his city at all. Never was."

Inwardly I grimaced, knowing that shot in the dark would wound Jenner whether it hit its mark or not.

Greed slid a glance at Pride who merely nodded and gave a lazy half shrug. Pocketing his chips, Greed rose from the table without so much as a parting remark.

Pride caught my eye and winked. "Shall we move on then?"

* * * *

Gluttony came next. Chosen by Pride who had appointed himself the ringleader of this whole operation. Back downstairs in the dark heart of the Sin party, we stood grouped by Gluttony's nasty altar while the pig-faced demon decided which of us would face him.

He chose Gabriel.

The choice made me do a double take. Did Gluttony choose Gabriel simply because he was a relatively new vampire who'd been a relatively young thus easily manipulated human? Or did the demons have some kind of insight into our personal sins?

"Your challenge, should you accept it, is to feed from just one human enough to sustain yourself without causing serious harm or death," Gluttony explained, all too happy to participate in our challenge. I got the feeling he didn't lose a lot of these. "You must be able to stop and walk away from my altar of your own strength and will."

"No problem." Gabriel didn't even pause to consider it.

He started to climb the steps to the platform where vampires bled victim after victim, and I stopped him with a hand on his wrist. "You can turn it down if you want to. One of us can do this one."

He gave me this silly little smile, like he thought I was adorably ridiculous, and tugged free of my grasp. "No worries, Alexa. I've got this."

Gluttony went ahead to clear the platform. Waving a hand, he had Gabriel take a seat at the table. Next he gestured for a woman to come forward. This was so messed up.

From where I stood I could see her chest heaving with fearful breaths. Of course she was scared shitless. Who wouldn't be? She'd just watched every sacrifice before her meet a grisly end at the hand of several vampires, most of which did not have an incubus touch.

Gabriel did though, and he knew how to use it. The table was smeared with blood, but when the woman went to sit upon it, Gabriel caught her hand and shook his head. He whispered something to her, but from where we stood at the foot of the platform, I couldn't hear it over the din.

Watching him made me tense, despite Arys's hand on the back of my neck, massaging gently. He could probably feel the steady rise of my anxiety. I just didn't see how we were going to beat these demons. We were already off to a bad start.

When Gabriel used the woman's hand to pull her onto his lap, I couldn't help but feel proud of him. He was keeping it classy, where those who'd gone before him had acted like rabid animals. I hoped so hard that wouldn't happen to him.

Gluttony lingered close, watching every move Gabriel made. Waiting for his moment. Gabriel touched the woman's face, looked into her eyes. Under his spell she blinked glassy eyes at him and slid an arm around his neck like he was a familiar lover.

"If any of you can handle this one, it will probably be the kid." Arms folded, wings tucked against his back, Falon nudged me with an elbow. "Poker face, Alexa. Put it on. You look like you're crapping yourself right now."

I blinked a few times and thought about my face. Yeah, I probably looked completely aghast to anyone watching. This entire ordeal was just so damn surreal. "What makes you so sure he can do it?"

Gabriel had proven himself to be as susceptible to losing control as any of us. He turned Lizzy, the psycho witch who'd almost set Shya free. Still, as far as I knew, aside from the night he turned and Shya had set him loose on a buffet of victims, his track record was better than most, certainly better than mine.

"Gabriel actually learns his lesson when he fucks up. Unlike the rest of you." Arms crossed, Falon watched the young vampire woo the woman in his arms. He didn't speak well of Gabriel often, so I took heart in the truth of his words.

"Why don't you like him?" I asked.

"I don't like anyone, wolf. You least of all." It was exactly the Falon response I'd expected, and somehow it brought me comfort.

The woman hung limp in Gabriel's arms, surrendering fully to him. It was harder to stop when the victim struggled. Her calm manner might help. Or so I thought until Gluttony blew that to shit.

He waited for Gabriel to sweep her hair aside and press his fangs to her slender throat. And he was all too patient when Gabriel sank fangs, spilling her blood. It was then that he leaned forward and spoke close to the vampire's ear.

Gabriel's head snapped up. Dark eyes wide, he bared bloodstained fangs and bit her again. Vicious this time.

My hope sank like a stone.

"Get in his head," I told Arys, frantic with the certainty we were about to lose our second challenge. "Try to stop him."

Arys shook his head and swore. "I can't."

"Gluttony is isolating his mind," Willow explained, the first thing he'd said in quite some time. "Gabriel has to break free of it on his own."

A sudden swell of anxiety gripped me, and I pulled away from the rest of them to pace in front of the altar. Loric and Pride watched from the other side. I knew that if I tried to get on that platform, a dozen demons would tackle me. So I just muttered obscenities to myself, unable to stand still.

My poker face sucked. I couldn't help that I was worried about my vampire and it showed.

The second bite sank deeper but still not a mortal wound. As I watched Gabriel lick and suck at the punctures, I vibrated with the power I couldn't quell. It raced through me, driven by the many surrounding threats. Holding it inside made me feel like I might burst. How the hell would I be able to get through five more rounds of this?

Gabriel jerked back with a hiss, his gaze fixated on the blood that spilled from the punctures. I said his name, but if he heard he didn't acknowledge me. Watching him sit there clutching his victim like a broken doll, waging a war against the desire to drain her dry, it picked away at every fiber of patience I had. Which wasn't a lot.

If I intervened we'd forfeit everything, the entire challenge. I wanted to turn away to collect myself, but I couldn't show that kind of weakness in front of so many demons. Forced to watch, I willed Gabriel to prove himself to be stronger than Gluttony believed him to be.

He wanted to bite her again, to tear her carotid open and indulge in every crimson drop. Tipping her head back further, he eyed her bleeding neck. The muscles in his forearms rippled and bulged as he physically fought the murderous urges.

The hunger for more.

Feeling my heavy stare, Gabriel turned to meet my gaze. Hunger made his eyes a drowning black. All pupil, like a wild animal seconds before the killing blow.

I shook my head. *Don't do it.*

The tightly coiled snake of savage hunger within him turned its attention on me. The one whose blood he wanted most. Knowing I had maybe seconds before he turned back to the woman moaning in his arms, I tugged my hair aside and ran a finger sensually over my jugular, taking a deep breath to make my cleavage swell as I did so.

Was it breaking the rules? I didn't think so. There didn't seem to be a lot of rules so far.

He watched me, slightly entranced, but I sensed that I had yet to hook him. Lengthening one fingernail into a claw, I dragged the sharp tip slowly over my vein and down my neck toward my chest. Slowly. Not once did I break skin.

Gabriel's gaze drowned in an abyss of black.

I had him, although I wasn't entirely ready when he came off the chair so fast it knocked the woman on his lap to the floor. But he didn't notice. Off the platform in a leap, Gabriel was on me in a blur. His full weight he hit me, taking me down beneath him. My head hit the floor as he went for my neck.

Arys moved to grab him, but Willow stopped him with a hand on his shoulder. Gabriel bit into my neck, and I plunged hands into his long hair. Taking hold of his erratic energy, I willed him to calm.

Despite being pinned awkwardly beneath Gabriel, I still felt him harden against me. Typical incubus vampire. Gluttony might have whispered in his ear, but he was still my vampire. I didn't fight his bite. It would only feed the hunger. Instead I lay there, just holding him and pushing a calm vibe into him.

The rough touch of his mouth on my neck softened. His aggressive sucking at the wounds became a gentle lick. A shudder rippled through me.

Gabriel raised his head to look at me, still licking my blood from his lips. I saw him come back to himself as he shoved off me, pushing to his feet. Holding a hand out to help me up, black hair fell forward to hide his face.

"Fuck, Alexa, I'm sorry." He shoved his hair back before checking my neck.

"I'm not." Shaking my head, I turned to fire a scowl at Gluttony. "You didn't kill her. You stopped. That's all that matters."

Gluttony didn't argue. He couldn't. Narrowing his eyes, he sneered. "Well played, succubus."

No contest. Gabriel handed me a bandana from his pocket, and I pressed it against my bleeding neck.

Pride beamed with a Cheshire Cat smile. We were one for one, and we had to win three more times. Maybe it was intuition or maybe it was just Pride's creepy grin, but I had a feeling we'd barely scratched the surface of where the Sins demons would take us.

CHAPTER TWENTY-TWO

No matter who Pride chose to throw at us next, I'd never be ready. There was no readying for this, only reacting. So when he sauntered over to Envy's altar with an especially self-satisfied swagger, I tried to brace for anything. Still, I wasn't ready for this one. Not by a long shot.

"Every one of you knows Envy. You've all tasted that bitter poison in your hearts." With a sweeping gesture suitable for a game show host, Pride waved a hand at the goat-headed demon with its eerie, vacant stare. "A poison that breeds the most sinister of urges to bring pain and suffering to those who possess what you most desire."

I fired a glance around my group, wondering who Pride could possibly have in mind to face Envy's torment. That seemed to be the specialty at his altar. Envious people acting out against those they were most envious of. How did we fit into this?

My mind raced as I tried to guess who Pride was gunning for here. Gabriel was the one who'd admitted to wanting what we had, the sense of family and companionship. By the way he stiffened, he seemed to think the same thing.

But Pride's scarlet gaze landed on Falon. "Our fallen brother. Why don't you join Envy on the altar? You know this one is all for you."

My heart skipped in surprise. Falon?

His wings flared slightly as he braced in defense. "Are you going to have me tortured? That's weak. Nothing I haven't endured before."

Again I was reminded of how much I didn't know about Falon. How many lifetimes he'd lived before I'd ever existed. I couldn't fathom the possibilities of all he'd seen and learned.

Pride laughed, a throaty sound that seemed to come from his toes. "No, my friend, you misunderstand. You won't be undergoing the torment. You will be inflicting it. Upon the one whom you envy most."

I almost choked on the lump that formed in my throat. The tiny hairs on the back of my neck stood on end. We'd come too far to turn back now, and all I could do was wish that we'd just gone home. Like Falon had told us to.

Refusing to be coerced into the reaction the demon wanted, Falon raised his chin, looking down his nose in arrogance at Pride. "And *whom* might that be?"

For a moment Pride didn't answer. He just stared at Falon, trying to worm a way into his mind. When Falon refused to react, a mask of cold, hard cruelty stole over his face, chasing his stupid smile away.

"Why, your queen of course." Pride paused, letting the impact of that little bomb roll over us all. "You were a fool to mark her. I'm sure your intent was to protect her; however, the action itself is incredibly telling."

With a small whoosh of air, Shaz released a breath. Arys muttered a curse directed at Falon. Without tearing my gaze from my angel, I silenced him with a raised hand. As much as I loved my dark half, I wouldn't hesitate to tear a strip out of him if he fucked this up by breaking our show of unity.

Falon almost caught me off guard when he grinned and said, "You want me to torture Alexa? You really have no idea how our relationship works, do you? I'll be more than happy to."

It might have been the wrong time to laugh, but I couldn't help it. A small bark of amusement escaped me, causing a ripple of confusion among my men.

Falon glanced my way and winked.

"Why Alexa?" Willow broke free from the pack, coming forward to face Pride. Unafraid, my guardian got right in the demon's face and snarled, "I'm starting to think you're just making shit up."

"Am I?" Pride stood there unflinching, welcoming Willow's antagonistic demeanor. "Did you think perhaps Falon was most envious of you, Willow? For being her guardian? Her friend. Or maybe he should be envious of the Dark Flame due to his bond with her. Surely those would make much more sense."

Willow's enchanting eyes bled to full wolf. "You're pulling strings and you know it."

"Hardly." With haughty derision, Pride tugged his suit sleeve, as if it had somehow been out of place. "Falon envies Alexa because she is all that he once was, all he longs to be and will never be again. She walks between both worlds like no other can, and he deeply envies her that as well." Raising a brow, Pride added, "Isn't that right, Falon?"

Clever bastard. I knew as the words left Pride's lips that they were true. The expression on Falon's face confirmed it. Stone cold, his mouth and eyes grew tight, like he struggled to keep the truth from reaching his face. But it sparked through his eyes before he could avert his gaze.

Except it was more than a simple truth. He envied me? Was that why he hated me so damn much?

Falon turned away, and with a single bound leaped up onto Envy's platform. "Let's get this over with. Name the stakes."

I didn't wait for Pride to tell me to get on the altar. Steeling myself by avoiding the imploring gazes of my men, I lifted the front of my skirt and ascended the steps. Willow hissed my name but I didn't look back. I stared straight ahead, to where Falon waited, needing him to look at me.

"One more thing." Pride's tone rose with a playful lilt that told me more bad news was coming. "Why stop at two of you when we can have fun with three?"

"Say what?" I muttered, pausing at the top of the steps to glance down at the demon.

He beamed and nodded to Sloth who stepped into view. Where had he been lurking? Sloth's snake eyes glided over my men, and the urge to rush back down the stairs struck me. But Envy's heavy, sweaty hand on my bare shoulder stopped me.

"Get your fucking hand off her if you want to keep it attached," Falon snapped.

Demons knew how to hurt people. They have nothing but time to learn. Envy's hand tightened on my arm, and he threw me up against his cross of torture hard enough to bang my teeth together. Then he turned on Falon, black wings and goat nostrils both flaring.

"Slow down there, boys," Pride laughed from below. "Let's take things to the next level, shall we? How about a little tag team?"

Sloth didn't smile. He didn't do much of anything. I guessed showing any form of expression required too much effort. He did, however, point one long, bony finger straight at my white wolf.

"Ahh, interesting choice, friend," Pride commended. "Why him?"

"Strong," Sloth replied after a moment of consideration. "Unused potential." Directly to Shaz the demon said, "Capable of much but resistant to discovering just how much. Just how far."

Arys stiffened defensively but Shaz waved him off. As each of us were called to face a Sins demon, we knew there was no backing down or having our battles fought for us.

Head held high, Shaz met the demon's gaze evenly. "Bring it."

Enjoying the mixed reactions from Willow's blatant disgust to Arys's rising temper, Pride strutted about with that lion's tail flicking happily behind him. "I like your moxie, wolf. Hold onto that. You're going to need it."

"State the terms," Willow demanded as the air around him crackled and sparked with power. "Your showboating has grown tiresome, and the only one who enjoys listening to your voice is you. Quit wasting our time. We'd like to move on."

Anger flashed over Pride's face. He swallowed it down so fast I almost second guessed seeing it. Next to him, Loric hissed something about calling off this entire thing and killing us on the spot. Pride dug an elbow into his ribs to silence him. The demon had completely taken over the show tonight. It left Loric silently seething.

"Falon faces Envy. The werewolf faces Sloth. What more do you need to know?" The abhorrence in Pride's eyes as he stared down Willow came from a place of deep resentment. It made me admire Willow that much more.

"Not good enough." With a shake of his dirty blond head, Willow held himself back but just barely. "What exactly are you trying to achieve here? I see right through you, Pride."

Pride seemed like the kind of guy who could let a lot of shit roll off his back in the name of keeping up the front he wanted us all to see. Still, he wasn't able to rise above the smug expression on

Willow's face. Despite his current status as a hybrid like me, Willow would always be an angel, and Pride knew it too.

His temper got the best of him, and he lashed out with a black magic attack that sent Willow tumbling across the hard floor. Pride went to stand over him, hands trembling with sudden rage. "You might have friends in high places, but I will still make an example of you."

I wanted so badly to shout at Pride, but Willow's green gaze peered past him to me. He'd already suffered enough because of me. So I clamped my mouth shut.

Willow smiled up at Pride. "I fucking dare you."

Damn. My guardian had some stones. A warrior still and always, he exuded badass confidence. He shot a daring grin at Pride, which caused a faint twinge between my legs. Aw, shit.

Despite the commotion that filled the rest of the place, nothing else existed but that second when Pride had to swallow his and walk away. Turning his back on Willow, the pissed-off demon climbed the stairs to Envy's altar two at a time.

Grabbing me by the throat, Pride shoved me against the beams crossed behind me. My head slammed against one wooden arm. He motioned for Envy to shackle my wrists and ankles to the cross.

"The terms are as follows. Envy will challenge Falon. The werewolf will face Sloth by watching his mate endure the torture of Falon's challenge. Should he wish to bring it to an end, he can do so. By completing one task set before him by Sloth, if he's willing."

Pride gave my throat a squeeze for good measure, and I glared into his arrogant face. He thought he had us beat by turning us on each other. Maybe he was right, but I would not feed his ego.

"Can't I just complete it now and spare her the torment?" Shaz asked, too hopeful in the face of demons who'd mastered the art of soul crushing.

Pride rewarded him with a bitter laugh. "Of course not. Where's the challenge in that?"

While Falon watched with an emotionless mask, Envy roughly secured me in place. The cross smelled of blood and death. The atmosphere reeked with the emotional distress of both the envious and the envied. Fear swelled in my chest, a hard lead weight that wouldn't budge.

My eyes bugged as I took in the tray of blood-crusted tools of torment displayed on a tall black table next to me. Everything from knives and pliers to whips and chains. When my gaze settled on the massive saw, teeth as long as my finger, I lost it.

So much for being a badass.

In the face of that kind of hell, I couldn't keep it together. Unable to bring myself to look at the rest, I strained against the bindings that held me. Pride never said that I had to lay back and take whatever Envy made Falon do to me. Screw that.

Channeling the power that fear pumped through me, I targeted the hard metal encircling my wrists. Absolutely nothing happened.

"Immortal bonds require immortal power," Envy sneered, enjoying my panic.

Falon shoved by him. Coming to touch my face, he whispered hurriedly against my lips, "Trust me, wolf."

Then he pushed away because Envy was already on him. A hand on Falon's arm, Envy spun him around and blew a pale-gold dust in his face. Falon blinked in confusion as the demon's magic took him under.

It all happened so fast, there was no time to prepare my mind or my body. Silly me for not sparing a thought for my heart.

Down below on the floor, demons surrounded the guys, cutting them off from Shaz who stood alone with Sloth. Arys's gentle touch on my mind should have brought comfort, but it only encouraged my panic. He didn't need to experience this through me. So I shut him out.

"Tell me about your queen, Falon." Envy prodded the fallen angel, steering him. "Tell me what you most envy about her."

A silver stare drank me in. Despite his words, I didn't think I could trust Falon right now. Not with Envy breathing down his neck. I could still see Falon in there behind his eyes, but I saw something else too. Something sinister.

"I don't envy a damn thing about her," he snarled, jamming an elbow into Envy's ribs when he got too close. "Stop trying to plant false truths in my head, you ugly son of a bitch."

Not knowing how little time I had before Falon lost this battle of wills, I kept fighting and tugging against my bonds. No dice. It wasn't going to happen. Whatever happened next, I had no choice but to endure it.

Envy folded beefy arms over his chest and snorted. "You know how this works. Stop trying to fool the lady. I only draw out true feelings. I don't create them. Now let's try this one more time. What do you envy most about this woman?"

Lips clamped tight, Falon shook his head, fighting against the truth summoned by the demon. Envy didn't ask again. He didn't have to. Simply waiting on the answer seemed to affect Falon, feeding his urge to spit it out. Until he just couldn't contain it any longer.

"I envy that she walks in both light and dark." It burst out in a rush, tearing from Falon against his will.

With a low chuckle, Envy shifted his weight from one foot to another. "No, don't tell me. Tell her. Tell her why."

Teeth and fists clenched, Falon flung his next words at me like an accusation. "You're a killer. A temptress. You have power unlike anyone else, and you don't deserve it."

I flinched. I couldn't help it. His words were loaded with truth, and for some reason, it hurt.

"How does that make you feel?" Envy prodded gently.

A battle raged in Falon's eyes. He didn't want to say any of this, but it all spilled out regardless. Pain flashed across his face. This was hurting him too.

Funny thing, he'd hurled such insults before, and I'd laughed it off as I always did. This felt different. It was more than our snarky banter. It was the true face of his hatred for me.

"Sick," Falon spat. Envy guided his line of thought, but Falon continued to address me. "With myself. For still wanting you so much, even though you represent everything I lost."

"Everything?" That one word was a breathy murmur on my lips.

I might have been the one strapped to a torture device, but I quickly caught onto Envy's tactic. He'd found the source of Falon's initial envy of me, but that was just the surface layer. The tip of the iceberg, so to speak. The demon was going to dig deeper into Falon's psyche, and I feared what might be exposed.

"Status. Purpose. Love. You are everything I'll never have again, and I hate myself for being unable to break free of you." His voice hardened with each word as he slipped further into his resentment.

Envy eased back another step, giving Falon a wider birth. "Why don't you show Alexa how it makes you feel? Give her a taste of your pain."

Falon took a step toward me, caught himself, and jerked to a stop. Anguish washed over his face as he fought the demon's pull. Despite his efforts, he couldn't help giving the black table of implements a once over.

My blood went cold.

"She has everything you want." A sly lilt danced in Envy's tone. "Everything that you worked your ass off for. Taken from you and given to a vile, unworthy creature who has made you her slave. Show her how that makes you feel."

A tremor racked the atmosphere as Envy picked his way deeper inside Falon's head.

I barely had time to scream before Falon was suddenly there. Right in front of me. The cold sting of a blade against my throat had me wishing I could shrink away. Trapped against the boards at my back, I held perfectly still, wary of doing anything to set him off.

"Falon," I whispered softly, searching his wild eyes for something to hold onto. "Please, don't give in. You have to fight this."

His other hand slammed into the wood right beside my head. "You turned me into your goddamn slave. But you're nothing. Just a mongrel of monsters. A false queen on a throne of ash."

I winced as the blade bit deeper, right next to the mark Falon himself had placed on my neck. Talking didn't seem to help, so I held my tongue. I couldn't fight this battle for him.

Down below there were shouts and angry murmurs from the guys. I couldn't spare them a glance. Taking my eyes off Falon was not an option. If he fell completely over the edge into Envy's abyss, I wanted to see it coming.

The blade against my skin quivered as his hand trembled. Because he was fighting the urge to slash me wide open. Holding his gaze, I silently willed him to keep fighting. To prove that he was stronger than Envy.

Doubt flickered over Falon's face. Confusion followed it before envious rage seeped in once again. He was all over the place inside his head.

With my hands bound I didn't have as much precision and control over my power. But some of my best tactics didn't require that kind of focus and direction. Peering into Falon, I willed him to see me. Really see me.

Then I slipped him the slightest bit of what I hoped was a seductive, serene energy. Anything to try to break through the demon's hold without somehow setting Falon off like I'd cut the wrong wire on a bomb.

His eyes narrowed. The battle raged. I could see him in there, torn between what was true and what was right. The way he felt about me was dark and bizarre. He knew that though.

So did I. It was mutual, wasn't it?

Not quite. My hatred for Falon stemmed from his arrogance and bad attitude. Not envy. From the moment we'd first met, he'd been a supreme asshole. It had cemented my opinion of him immediately.

A lot had changed since then.

"You're nothing," he repeated, voice wavering.

Then in one swift motion, he slashed the blade across my throat.

CHAPTER TWENTY-THREE
FALON

Somehow some part of me was able to jerk back as the dagger blade bit through her flesh. A small gash opened up beneath my feather, the mark of protection I'd placed on her. Before I could follow through with the urge to slash her again, I let the weapon fall to the floor.

"Alexa, fuck, I'm sorry." I jerked away from her.

Envy wouldn't let me go far. He shoved me back toward her, and I turned to throw a fireball in his face.

The motherfucker was ready for it, and he countered with a blast that hit not me but Alexa. She yelped, a sound of pure angry wolf. The scent of scorched skin made me ill. A nasty burn marred Alexa's outstretched arm. Something about the sound and sight of her in pain both disgusted and delighted me. Shame crushed my spirit, and I stupidly risked a glance at Willow down below, who glared at me with promises of much worse things.

Her guardian was going to have my ass for this. And who could blame him? I wanted him to make me sorry.

"Don't tell me that you don't enjoy watching her suffer." Envy ambled to the tray laden with macabre devices meant only for harm. His hand drifted over several of them before stopping on a small surgical scalpel. "Why not remove that mark? Have a little fun with it."

Envy tossed the scalpel at me so I was forced to catch it. Everything he said was wrong, but the visual he planted in my head felt right. Despite knowing it was nothing but black magic bullshit, I succumbed like a complete pussy.

Turning back to Alexa, I found soul-drenching fear flooding her pretty brown eyes. She owed me that much, didn't she? The woman had made me her slave. Little more than an immortal side piece. I'd been such a fool to let her get so close.

"Give me one reason why I shouldn't carve that thing out of you," I growled, my own voice foreign and rough.

With fear gleaming in her eyes, Alexa held her head high, refusing to act upon it by begging or pleading. "You said that I was yours. Remember? That no other immortal would lay claim to me because I belonged to you, Falon. Would you so easily give that up? Do your promise and your word mean nothing?"

I flashed back to the hotel room where we enjoyed much of our time together. Her naked body beneath me while I claimed her for all the underworld to see. No doubt that mark had been a stupid move on my part, but I didn't want to take it back. Alexa was mine, and I did not want to change that.

Horror slowly filled me. Flowing in like a torrential mudslide of shit that obliterated everything in its path. So clearly I saw the way to beat Envy at his game. And I didn't like it.

"You are mine," I agreed "That's why I will do as I damn well please."

I held the scalpel tight, staring at the wound that seeped blood down her chest and cleavage, disappearing inside her dress. The dress that I myself had decorated her beautiful body with. Underworld threads fit for royalty and worn only by those with true power and prestige.

Both of which she embodied.

The need to punish her for everything I detested about her was akin to the need for air. So desperately I wanted to make her scream and beg for mercy. Envy had forced an unfortunate truth from me. I did envy Alexa her ability to touch both light and dark. And yet…

She was still my Queen.

Not a queen forced upon me by some power-hungry bitch like Lilah or any of the status-seeking shitcakes like Bane who believed themselves worthy of worship and respect. Alexa was different. Because I had chosen her to be my Queen.

A sick feeling bloomed through me along with a shockingly nauseating revelation. I didn't just desire Alexa. Somewhere in the tangled vines of my hatred, I harbored a deep affection and respect for her.

"I can never love you," I shouted, inches from her face. It was sudden and unexpected. There was no stopping it.

As if only to anger me further, Alexa gave a wan smile and shook her head sadly. "I never asked you to. I never wanted to be whatever it is I am to you. Just like I never wanted you to be what you are to me."

"And just what might that be?" Because I didn't trust myself, I tossed the scalpel aside. Once my hands were empty, I longed to wrap them around her bleeding, gorgeous throat.

The wolf shone in her eyes. I'd come to learn that the wolf was where Alexa's heart lived, all the parts of her that were pure and good. Unlike the succubus vampire. I always marveled that both creatures dwelled within one woman.

Those brown orbs seeped wolf until there was nothing remotely human left. Her husky voice reached inside me when she murmured, "You tell me."

My hands slid around her throat and up into her hair. So strong was the need to choke her senseless. So demanding was that inner voice insisting she needed to be punished for everything that she was that I wasn't.

It made me hate her more than I already did and it made me hate myself.

I knew how to beat this. But I also knew it would change everything. No matter how this all went down, we would leave here different than we'd been when we arrived.

With an aggravated shake of my head, I clenched my teeth and gave a frustrated cry. The words came unbidden, and I almost choked myself in an attempt to swallow them back down. I didn't want to do it. Didn't want to feel it. And I sure as shit didn't want to make this any more real than it already was.

Although I might have been Alexa's bitch, I was not Envy's. Forced to choose between a devil and the woman who'd turned my entire life upside down, it should have been easy.

Nothing about this was easy.

"I need you," I blurted, cringing as the words left my lips. "I want you. I desire you. But I can't love you, and it fucking kills me because part of me wishes that I could."

There. Done. My existence as I knew it was officially over. I'd just cut my own balls off and gift wrapped them for this damn woman.

CHAPTER TWENTY-FOUR
SHAZ

Surrounded by demons on every side, I watched as the love of my life bled from wounds inflicted by a man I'd known she couldn't trust. Helpless to do anything but watch, it hurt me to see her willing to bear such pain for him. He'd gotten too close. I knew that Alexa wanted him there, but I would never understand why.

"Did you really think it would be that easy?" Envy all but laughed in Falon's face. "You think you've figured it out. But we've only just started."

From somewhere behind me, I heard Arys mutter something about tearing the wings off that godforsaken angel. Maybe I would help with that, but right now I agreed with Alexa. We had to stay united.

Next to me Sloth literally twiddled his thumbs, waiting for something. I got the feeling a guy like him did a lot of waiting and not so much doing. Every now and then he slid me a sidelong glance, gauging my reaction to the spectacle before us. Hands stuffed in my pockets, I did all I could to mask my feelings.

"Why stop there?" Envy continued. "Let's work our way through your companions, shall we? Tell me, Falon, which of them do you envy most? The vampire who made her? The werewolf who speaks to her heart? Perhaps the guardian who will always hold a special place of honor like none you'll ever know again. Show them. Show them all exactly what you'd like to do to them."

Falon's unwelcome confession had somehow grounded him. So Envy did all he could to rip that rug out from beneath him. And it worked.

Hands wrapped around Alexa's throat, Falon bashed her head against the board behind it. Fumbling about blindly, he snatched up a jagged knife from the table and ran it over the gash in the side of her neck. When he cut without hesitation, I was done being patient.

"Make this stop," I spat at Sloth who took several long seconds to acknowledge me. "Now. Whatever it takes. I don't care. I'll do it."

A slow grin spread across the demon's face. "You might want to find out what the stakes are before you make that claim."

On Envy's altar, Falon dragged the jagged blade down Alexa's chest.

She screamed.

That sound reverberated in my ears. The wolf within cared for nothing but the pain of its mate. Nothing else mattered.

"Name the fucking stakes then," I shouted in the demon's face, fists clenched, ready to smash his jaw in.

Sloth put two fingers to his lips and whistled, a shrill, ear-splitting noise that cut through the din. Raising a hand, he gestured at Envy who grabbed Falon by a shoulder and spun him away from Alexa.

"The wolf has decided he'd like to get involved," Sloth announced, sounding as bored as he looked. "He's willing to do… anything." Giggling to himself like a teenage stoner, Sloth waved a hand.

A man emerged from the crowd. Dressed in an expensive suit, hair short and styled, he carried himself like a man who knew great success. But he stank of fear.

"Kill him," Sloth said, still smiling although not kidding. "Not just kill. Rip his throat out. With your teeth."

"What? Why?" Truth be told, I'd expected worse. However, it quickly became clear that it wasn't about the difficulty of the task. It was about what it would take to complete it.

A cold-blooded kill. Without remorse. A stranger in exchange for the woman I loved walking free of further torment. That kind of person, someone who could easily make such a trade for selfish reasons, I'd never been that guy.

Until now.

"Because I told you to. Everyone has a price. This is mine." Sparing an uninterested glance at the man, Sloth shrugged. "Do my dirty work."

My gaze darted from the man in the suit to Lex who vigorously shook her head. It wasn't often that I ignored her opinion, but this time

I had to. She'd stand there and let Falon beat her senseless in order to keep me from crossing this line.

It wouldn't be the first time I'd killed in cold blood inside this building. Lex had to stop clinging to this false ideal of what she wanted for me. I was in this with them, all the way.

She saw it in my eyes because her head shake grew more desperate. In a hoarse voice she shouted, "Shaz, no. Don't do it."

Would it be two losses if I did as Sloth demanded? So many stares were upon me, awaiting my decision. The scent of my mate's blood on the air, I knew I'd kill for her. Still, I turned to Arys who struggled against the demons who held him back.

Our eyes met and he simply nodded. Just once.

It was all the encouragement I needed. There was no point asking Sloth why he wanted the man dead. No point to knowing anything about him at all.

"Five seconds, wolf," Sloth said in his slow drawl. "Then the fallen angel carves his name in your girl."

The wolf took over. It had no problem killing to protect its own. No second thought or hesitation. With fangs bared, I lunged at the man Sloth wanted dead. All the wolf knew was that he stood in the way of Alexa's safety. So he had to go.

The guy tried to fight, throwing up his arms and pummeling any part of me he could hit. I felt nothing. I grabbed him by both arms and threw him against the staircase that led up to the altar. In seconds I'd slammed his head back and sank four large wolf fangs deep into his esophagus.

A savage snarl erupted from me as I tore away flesh and muscle. Blood poured like a river, and I shoved away to avoid the flood. Spitting a chunk of meat on the floor at Sloth's feet, I growled steadily, unable to calm the beast.

I couldn't tell if this meant I'd won. Somehow, it felt like a loss. Like we were screwed either way.

Sloth had accused me of not knowing how far I'd be willing to go for those I loved. Now we both knew.

CHAPTER TWENTY-FIVE

Everything was a blur. From the moment Shaz leapt on the man and ripped his throat out to when Arys rushed the altar. He shouted something at Envy, but all I could focus on was the blood that spilled down my neck and chest.

Falon did that to me.

My hands suddenly came free, my ankles next, and I collapsed into Arys's waiting arms. He snarled at Falon who dared to venture closer. I tried but failed to form words. Despite being under the demon's influence, Falon had held back. I'd seen it. The cuts that marked me were much shallower than they would have been, only because of how hard he'd fought.

"It's really not so bad," Arys assured me, inspecting the wounds closely. The warmth of his healing energy touched me then as he addressed the uglier gashes.

Throat raw from the crushing grip of my fallen angel, I coughed a few times. "Don't blame Falon. He fought hard. He didn't want to do this."

Pushing bloodstained blonde locks back from my face and neck, Arys didn't acknowledge either Falon or my statement. "I say we fuck this game and bring the whole building down. Just destroy everything Harley had left and walk away while we can."

"If only you could do that," Pride said from the top step where he stood watching Arys comfort me. "You made an agreement to face seven challenges. You've done four. Having only one win certainly does not put the odds in your favor. However, you still have one more chance to turn this thing around for yourselves."

My ass we did. The entire challenge was nothing but a charade. Pride had orchestrated it right from the start so that we couldn't win. Gabriel's unexpected victory had been a delightful surprise to Pride who appeared to be having a crapload of fun at our expense.

"Lust." I flung the word at Pride as Arys helped to steady me on my feet. "I want to face Lust now."

The worst part of Falon's torture had not been the physical pain by any means. It had been the terror of watching him struggle against such sinister urges and knowing they lived somewhere inside him. It had been hearing him tell me that he wished he could love me. Nothing he'd done to my body could ever compare to what that had done to a deeper part of me.

Automatically my hand went to the silver feather on my neck, feeling for the knife wound there, but it was now gone. And the mark remained. For reasons I didn't want to explore, it filled me with relief.

"I'm a fair man," Pride said with a laugh, like it was some inside joke we were all in on. "If you want to face Lust next, then so be it. Let's move to the theatre."

Sure it was suspicious that Pride gave in so easily, but he seemed to be enjoying the game. I didn't think he was ready for it to end just yet. If giving me what I wanted would keep us in the game a little longer, then he saw no real risk in allowing it.

He descended the steps and joined Loric who seemed more uncomfortable every time I looked at him. He knew he was just a puppet to these demons, that he had no control here. He'd never really been the threat. Merely a catalyst of sorts.

"I'm fine." I assured Arys with a gentle kiss on the corner of his mouth.

He didn't seem to buy it. Shooting a warning glare at Falon, he took my hand and led me from the platform.

Over my shoulder, I glanced back to find my fallen angel standing on the platform staring at the crossed beams. Something haunted and morose stole over his beautiful face. I recognized it as something I'd seen during some of our more emotionally charged encounters. What had just transpired between us had cut him deeper than he'd cut me, and I knew it would leave scars behind.

The second my foot hit the bottom step, I launched myself into Shaz's arms. I didn't ask if he was okay or worry over his mental state. I knew who he was now. A man more capable of doing whatever it takes than maybe any of the rest of us. I simply hugged him tight and nuzzled my face against his.

Did I wish he'd held back and let Falon torture me instead of killing in cold blood to stop him? A thousand times yes. We'd all done things we felt were necessary in the heat of the moment. The wolf's need to protect its mate knew no right and wrong, only survival. This is what we were.

Pride led the way as we were ushered along to the theatre with a sulking Loric following behind. There was no way to prepare for this. Rolling Lust as a group would exceed any power play I'd ever attempted before.

What if I couldn't control the flow? What if we just turned the entire place into a powerhouse orgy and rolled ourselves in the process? There were plenty of risks, especially among the vampires.

"Shaz, I'll need you to help keep me focused. To remind me of the goal if I start to lose myself in here." The doors to the theatre were held open. Just stepping back into the melee of fleshly delights tested my will. "You and Falon together have to keep the rest of us from losing control."

On my other side Arys nodded his agreement. "There's no way of knowing how this will go down, but if anyone stands a chance at staying clearheaded enough to steer this ship, it will be the two of you."

Arys turned to look for Falon who ambled along behind us, hands shoved into his pockets, his face expressionless. Falon gave one short nod to acknowledge that he'd heard.

Not a single one of us was in the right headspace for what we were about to do, and that would have to change quickly. We were again greeted by dozens of people engaged in carnal activity, and my dark side rushed to surface.

We could do this. We had to do this.

From his place at center stage, Lust sat on his throne, laughing his gorgeous ass off. Who could blame him? He'd failed to keep me only to have me return of my own free will. But he didn't know that I'd come to win this. Driven by three losses, I was willing to go out of my comfort zone to kick some demon ass, and I wasn't the only one.

Pride went ahead to speak with Lust privately, giving us one last chance to change our minds or brace ourselves for the show we were about to put on. Still clutching Shaz's arm, I turned to survey each of the guys in turn, lingering longest on Willow.

"You don't have to do this," I said, trying to shut out the distracting sounds and sights. "Anyone who's uncomfortable with what we're about to do can sit this one out."

They glanced about at each other, weighing the option. Most of them straight up shook their heads that they weren't leaving. Even Willow. The only one who showed reluctance was Falon, because Lust didn't affect him the same way.

I tried to catch his eye, and he purposely dodged my direct gaze. What the hell? Unfortunately, I couldn't take him aside for a private moment. After what just went down between us, all I wanted was a minute of quiet to check in with him.

"Falon?" Saying his name finally dragged his gaze to mine. I remembered what I'd said to him back in the bathroom of our suite at Caesars. *I need you, Falon. You're the only one I trust.*

From the misery in his silver eyes I knew he was thinking about what he'd just said to me. *I need you. I want you. I desire you. But I can't love you, and it fucking kills me because part of me wishes that I could.* It had played on repeat in my head while he dragged a blade through my flesh. Of the many times Falon had said or done something that blew my mind, nothing came close to tonight.

"No worries, your highness. I'm not going anywhere." Falon held my gaze, letting me see the pieces of him broken open by Envy's torment. Because that's who the torment had really been meant for all along. Not the one receiving but the one inflicting.

His simple declaration meant more than I wanted anyone else to know right then, so I turned back toward the stage and led the way. No sense in prolonging the inevitable.

"Succubus." Lust rose from his throne and greeted me with a dramatic bow, long red locks tumbling about his robe-clad shoulders. "I cannot begin to tell you how thrilled I am to see you again. And so soon."

"Spare us the song and dance," I said, ready to fight fire with fire. "You know why we're here. Let's not waste time."

Lust slid a grin Pride's way. "I love this woman. It's a shame I can't keep her. Can I?" When Pride merely snickered, Lust waved a heavily jeweled hand, gesturing behind the throne. "I believe this will suit your group. And what a fine group it is."

Behind the throne was a large, round bed with a curved headboard. It could easily sleep six or more. Plenty of room for me to entertain six men. The first pang of insecurity struck. Had I lost my mind? Six men?

I looked to Arys for reassurance. He stuck close, never more than a few inches from my side. It would take the two of us to reach the pinnacle of our power and turn this thing around. Still, it was rather daunting to be the one woman amid the six of them. Daunting as hell and yet exciting too.

"So what are the stakes?" I addressed both Lust and Pride. "Isn't that something we establish before anything gets underway?"

On the chaises surrounding the throne, humans, vampires, and demons engaged in acts so down and dirty that it embarrassed me to watch. Yet, it was damn hard not to. My skin prickled from the sexual energy running rampant through the theatre.

"You learn quickly. Good for you." Pride didn't seem to realize or care that he spoke to me like an obedient pet that just learned a new trick. He grinned right through my scowl. "Face Lust's test and resist. You know the drill."

Pride was an annoying asshole who severely tested my patience. So I ignored him and waited on Lust's command. This was his challenge after all.

"Get on the bed with your men, my lovely. If you can resist them while under my influence, which we both know you cannot, then you will be victorious. Succumb to the pleasure and forfeit." With a snap of his fingers, Lust's chair rotated, so he could face the huge bed.

We'd waltzed in here knowing we'd never be able to take on Lust and win under his rules. No, we'd seize control of Lust's whole operation here and force him to submit to us. Impossible? No. Unlikely? Definitely. We weren't exactly on a winning streak here.

The bed itself was tucked away, near the back of the stage, giving it the illusion of privacy. The red velvet sheets were clean and inviting, I went and sat in the center without hesitation. My black skirt flowed out around me. Following Arys's lead the guys spread themselves out at the edge of the bed, standing rather than climbing in just yet.

Propped against a few pillows, I sat there with my heart thudding in my ears. I could really use a pep talk right now.

Sensing my nerves, Arys leaned down to slide a hand around the back of my neck, rubbing gently. "You questioned our willingness, my love, but what about yours? Are you sure you want to do this?"

Arys was always up for anything, but he respected the boundaries of his lovers. That was one thing I didn't question concerning any of them. They respected me. I'd formed a unique bond with each of them. That's why I could do this.

"Yeah," I said with a nod, "I do. Game plan?"

Lust eyed us from his throne, giving us a few moments to anticipate the coming assault. If he knew we were up to something, he didn't show it. Although I felt certain that Pride suspected something and was all for taking us out in a real battle. Overconfident ass.

"There's no planning for this," Willow muttered, bitter from experience. "Don't try to predict anything with demons. They'll surprise you every time."

Confident in the face of pure evil, Arys slid me a mischievous grin. "Well we've got a surprise for him too. For all of them. In the meantime, Alexa sets the pace. She's in control. Until she isn't, in which case we take this and run all the way with it."

"Yeah, I'm sure it will be that simple." My tone dripped sarcasm. My stomach turned at the way Lust leered at us, that lecherous glint in his eyes.

We had no time left to strategize. In a blink he was just there, standing at the foot of the bed. "What's wrong, succubus? Surely six lovers does not intimidate you. You were amazing with one. I can't wait to see what you do here."

Yeah, that made two of us. I didn't bother with a reply, and I didn't think that Lust expected one. He walked a slow circle around the bed, assessing each one of the men in turn. Pausing behind Willow, the demon smirked to himself. Seeing the way he treasured that victory over my guardian made me that much more determined to beat him at his own nasty game.

To my relief, Lust continued to move around the circle. Next he stopped at Gabriel who stood next to Arys near the foot of the bed. "You were here last night. You exude new power. Youth at its finest. Let's start with you. Join your queen."

Gabriel's dark gaze flicked to mine. I sat tense against the pillows piled behind me. It didn't matter who Lust chose to go first.

Nothing about starting this off was going to be easy. And by the time it did feel easy, I feared I wouldn't be able to do what I'd come for.

I gave Gabriel the slightest nod, permission to do as he'd been told. Although my permission didn't mean shit once Lust snapped his fingers next to Gabriel's head. Just like that, the glint in his eyes hardened. Incubus hunger blazed as he crawled onto the bed.

I knew that I had to resist if only to convince Lust that's what I'd come to prove. All too soon I would have to take control of this freak show, which meant becoming everything that the succubus within me longed for.

I'd hoped we'd all be able to maintain some semblance of control, but that had been wishful thinking. Gabriel fell victim to Lust just as he had last night. Grasping my ankle, he slipped a hand up the inside of my leg as he crawled closer to me on the bed. It tickled, sending a pleasurable jolt toward my groin. I tried not to react, not to move a muscle. But he could sense my arousal.

It was impossible not to vibe off everything around us. Factoring our heady power into that equation, this was about to turn downright explosive. For Sin City's sake, I hoped some of their dealers could still shuffle by hand because the electric grid was about to be sorely tested.

I held my breath when Gabriel paused to shove my long skirt up, baring a thigh. Pressing his lips to the curve of my knee, he tensed, trying to resist the demon's manipulations of his inner desires. Nice try, but he didn't really need to resist so much as I did. Clenching my teeth, I laced my fingers together, hoping it would keep me from touching him as he drew closer.

Beside me, Gabriel brushed a few strands of hair away from my face, his gaze dropping to my mouth. Somehow he'd managed to stop himself at my knee. His resistance was impressive, but we both knew it would be short lived. He kissed me with a firmness that was new and exciting to me still. Every touch thrilled in our new relationship.

His tongue slipped between my lips, and I kissed him back with a growing fervor that I couldn't deny. So tightly I crushed my interlaced fingers to keep from touching him. Even the discomfort of my bones grinding on one another wasn't enough.

Just when I was about to give in and grab hungrily for him, Lust chuckled. He made his way around to Jenner. Just a tap on his shoulder was all it took, and Jenner blinked through besotted desire.

"Let's turn this up a notch." Lust raised a dark brow in devilish delight. "Join them."

Jenner climbed on the bed in a heartbeat. Despite his immaculate control in such situations, he very much enjoyed his incubus nature to the fullest. His bright blues sparkled with primal need as he joined me on my other side.

While Gabriel kissed a warm path down the side of my neck, Jenner claimed my lips. Sparks went off inside me. So badly I wanted to touch both of them. And I would, but Lust needed to see me put up a fight while the power built.

Gently, Jenner held my face as he devoured my mouth in a drowning kiss. Gabriel kissed and nipped playfully at my neck and shoulder, pressing his straining erection against my leg.

I'd like to think I have reasonable self-control, despite certain past incidents that might suggest otherwise. However, sitting on that giant bed between two vampires struggling to keep from touching either one of them, the few shreds of control I had left began to slip away from me fast.

I clenched both hands into weak fists. I didn't want to resist with Lust around. His mere presence made it hard to focus on anything but floating away on a sea of bliss at the hands of the men surrounding me.

Clenching my fists tighter, I used the tip of a claw to gouge the inside of my palm. The pain helped to clear my head briefly. Much too briefly. Jenner's mouth moved to the swell of my cleavage. The wet heat of his tongue traced an erratic path as he licked my skin, stained bloody from Falon's assault. A groan threatened and I bit it back.

Lust again paced the circle of men who watched and waited. They each wore varying expressions of arousal and intrigue. Even Falon, who still wouldn't meet my gaze when it landed on him.

Leaning in close enough to Willow that their faces almost touched, Lust mocked him with a laugh. "Would you like to help get her started, angel? Or would you prefer to finish her off?"

"There's nothing you can do to me that's any worse than what you've already done." Unaffected by the demon's unnerving proximity, Willow gave Lust nothing.

Lust didn't appreciate that reaction. With a flick of his wrist, he took Willow under his spell. My men could play many roles here tonight, some of them more intimate than others. Willow wouldn't have to go to the places he went last night if he didn't want to. I would do my best to make sure of it.

Gabriel kissed and sucked at my collarbone, a hand trailing over my breast. Both of my thighs were now exposed since Jenner had hiked my skirt up to reveal the black panties I wore. Willow paid no mind to either of them when he joined us. His captivating stare was all for me.

From the very foot of the bed he crept toward me. Prowling like the hunter he was now, Willow moved with an ethereal grace.

Anticipation gripped me. Watching him advance closer, my stomach fluttered. Pressing my lips tight together, I felt like I was about to burst with the effort it took to keep my hands to myself. Among other things.

Willow started where he knelt. Like the gentleman he was, he carefully untied my boots and slipped my feet free. One hand encircled an ankle and I sucked in a breath. He held my gaze the entire time. His mindful observation struck deeper than the hands and lips of the others.

A look could be a powerful thing.

I especially loved Willow's commitment to doing things his own way. To Lust it might appear as if he gave in, but I saw the true strength within him. "Relax." One word, smooth as silk. Fangs flashed from beneath Willow's lip. No matter whether he had wings, fangs, or fur, he could never be anything less than beautiful.

A nervous laugh bubbled up. "Doing my best." My hands shook where I held them stiffly at my sides.

Gabriel wrapped a warm hand around one of mine and gently pried my fingers loose.

The hand on my ankle slid higher, but unlike Gabriel, Willow didn't stop at my knee. With both hands he caressed up my thighs until his fingertips reached the waist of my panties.

I couldn't hold off any longer. No way. Even without Lust's ridiculous pull amping up the many sensations bringing my body alive, I'd never have been able to resist the three of them touching me like this.

Aware of the others watching, I found Arys blazing with ravening anticipation. Not even Jenner's presence on the bed kept him from enjoying this. Shaz watched as if he wanted to look away but couldn't bring himself to do so. I suspected it was because he liked it just as much as Arys did. And he simply didn't want to.

With arms crossed, his face molded into a stony mask, Falon forced the disinterested front that he wanted me to see. Yet even in my intoxicated state, I could see right through him. He did not want to share me with the others like this.

But he couldn't stop himself from reacting anyway. Because it was me that drove him. Me that got beneath his skin and made him remember what it was like to feel alive. Falon might have watched because he had to, might have felt uncomfortable, but he didn't hate it.

Lust stepped back, giving himself space to really take in his handiwork. He seemed satisfied, allowing this seduction to take its natural progression before interfering again.

The gentle scrape of fangs along my neck made me shudder. Jenner loosened the ties on my dress so he could grab a handful of my breast. Rolling my nipple into a taut point between his thumb and finger, he nipped at my cleavage.

With one hand I pulled Gabriel's face back to mine, needing to taste him. My other hand grazed the side of Jenner's face in a soft caress. A tug on my underwear was the only warning I received before Willow whisked it down my legs.

I gave in and welcomed their advances.

Pretty sure this was the point where we officially lost.

But Lust had no interest in stopping us when he could glean a boost from the power we called. Instead he accepted his victory in silence and continued to pull the strings.

Willow's palm rubbed against my core. He kissed my abdomen, then my thigh, and finally between my legs. An aching throb began as my body responded with a flood of natural moisture. I moaned softly into Gabriel's mouth. The vampire in turn guided my hand to the hard-on bulging in his pants. Jenner sucked my nipple into his mouth while I rubbed Gabriel through his jeans. Between my legs came the welcome touch of Willow's tongue as he flicked it over my clit. Lightly his fingers teased me, playing about in the wetness at my entrance.

That tease drove me crazy.

Deep in the recesses of my mind where my conscious thought had been temporarily caged, I knew that Willow and I would need to talk when we got home. He'd barely said a thing to me since we left this theatre last night, and here he was between my legs once again. I didn't doubt that Willow could handle the emotional repercussions that came with this territory, but I refused to let our friendship pay the price. I could accept a lot of relational fallout with a lot of people, but Willow wasn't one of them. I wouldn't compromise our friendship despite the way it had been changed. I hoped he wouldn't either.

On the large circular bed, under the watchful gaze of Lust and the three men closest to me, I writhed beneath the attention of my three incubus vampires. Throwing my head back, I sank into the fluffy pillows and gave myself over to them completely.

After Willow brought me to a moaning climax, Lust took several slow steps back toward his throne. He waved a hand at the rest of his temporary subjects. "Make her howl. I want to see magic happen."

CHAPTER TWENTY-SIX

Bodies shifted as Shaz slid onto the bed beside me. Willow moved from between my legs to recline against the headboard next to the pillows propping me. His eyes were wolf and heavily dilated as both monsters ran amok within him. Scrubbing a hand over his faintly stubbled jaw, he swore softly to himself. Gabriel adjusted so he sat above my head on the other side, allowing Shaz to take the place beside me where he'd just been.

I expected Arys to take up the space between my legs which Willow had abandoned. He knelt on the edge of the bed instead and glanced back at Falon.

The fallen angel wasn't affected by Lust as they were, but he'd said he would be here, that he wanted to fight. Still his eyes narrowed and he glowered at Arys. "Why are you looking at me like that?"

Rather than answer him, Arys's midnight gaze swung to me. "Do you want him, my wolf? Do you want your fallen lover inside you?"

A wickedly seductive grin played about my face. It echoed the one that Arys wore. Peering past him to where Falon lingered, I beckoned my angel with a finger.

"Always," I purred, the word slipping forth to touch Falon like an unseen hand.

It shook him, delving past his guard to the inner parts I should never have been able to access. With an irritated, "Fuck," Falon stripped off his jacket and let it hit the floor.

"Don't stop there." Twirling a finger, I motioned for him to continue disrobing. "I want all of you." I extended my finger twirl to include the rest of them, but my eyes remained locked on Falon. When he hesitated, I clutched a handful of the soft black fabric he had clothed me in, then drew the material aside to expose myself fully to him.

Falon's silver gaze smoldered. He wanted me, and he didn't need Lust's influence or even my own to drive him.

Holding his attention, I touched myself. I held them all captive in that moment, but it was Falon's need I sought.

"Goddammit, woman, you'll be my undoing." Peeling his shirt off, Falon cursed me several times.

I didn't care. Being able to ogle that fine physique was worth his annoyance.

While Shaz and Jenner paid special attention to my neck and breasts, I continued to stroke Gabriel with a hand raised above my head. Once his naked shaft filled my hand, he succumbed, a groaning mess of desire.

Falon shoved his pants off, got on the bed, and roughly grabbed my hips. To my surprise, he addressed Arys. "This is what you want? To finally watch me fuck her?"

Still sitting on the sidelines, Arys allowed himself a glance at Falon's impressive cock. He raised a brow playfully. "Alexa's pleasure is my pleasure."

If Falon wanted a better answer, he wasn't going to get one. With my free hand I touched one of his. He gripped me tight, fingers biting into my flesh. Drawing his gaze back to me, I nibbled my bottom lip with a fang tip.

"Yeah, you'll definitely be my undoing." Falon gave me no warning, but then again, he never did. Holding my hips, he thrust inside me as if he needed this to be over right this moment.

What he and I shared, we hid. From the entire world other than the two of us. Could we do this without going to that place we went together? Without showing it to the rest of them? I hoped so.

A sharp pain in my breast made me yelp. Shaz had bit me in his frenzy, marking me. Shaz had never been a fan of Falon or my tie to him. His wolf was acting out in the only way it knew.

Arys chuckled softly. He watched with growing arousal as Falon drove into me. Prowling around to where Shaz lay next to me, my dark vampire grabbed a handful of platinum hair and jerked our white wolf's head away from the wound. Then he kissed Shaz, tasting my blood on him before leaning in to put his mouth to the bite in my breast.

I stroked Gabriel to climax and reached for Jenner, giving him the same pleasure. The heady energies crashing through us made every sensation stronger. It took only a few solid strokes to bring him to his peak as well.

When I reached for Willow, he stiffened but didn't reject my touch. With a hand on his arm I drew him near. Jenner and Gabriel pulled back against the headboard while the others moved in closer to me.

Shaz and Arys were occupied with touching and kissing both my body and each other. Nestled between my thighs, my fallen angel used his grip on my hips to turn me slightly, angling me partially on my side facing Willow. Guess he could be a team player after all.

Using both hands, I freed Willow's thick erection from his pants. Rolling my eyes up to see his face, I found him watching me with unrepentant yearning. He hadn't let me pleasure him last night. I paused, giving him the opportunity to say no. When he just kept looking at me like a man who'd spent far too long denying himself, I had my answer.

Holding his gold and green gaze, I dragged my tongue slowly along his shaft. When I reached the head, Willow shuddered and moaned. He needed this probably more than any of us.

A few light tongue flicks and then I took him full into my mouth. The sound he made set off fireworks in my brain, creating a delicious sensation that traveled to my loins where Falon filled me.

Shaz's hand groped my breasts, but Arys had lost himself in our white wolf. The two of them lay on the bed beside me, kissing and murmuring filthy nothings. Their carefree expression spurred me higher.

I craved more.

More of all of them. More power. More pleasure.

Sucking Willow deeper into my mouth, I made a small squeak when Falon slapped my ass.

"It's getting a little tough to hold off here, wolf." Falon leaned close to snarl into my ear. "If you're taking my blood, you better do it now."

Shit, that's right. To take my power to the max, I needed Falon's blood. Caught up in them all as I was, I'd fallen in too deep.

I wasn't stopping until Willow came. Every one of them had to. I needed the intoxicating swell of their individual climax, the power in it. Letting my heady succubus energy roll over my guardian angel, I used both my hand and mouth to coax more than a satisfied groan from him. When the salty taste of Willow coated my tongue, I drew on the overflow of lusty vibes that poured from him in excess.

Before moving away, Willow leaned down to kiss my nose first, then my lips. A gentle brush of his on mine. Then he slid from the bed, leaving me to the three men who'd come to be the closest to me. The three I couldn't imagine myself without, each for very different reasons.

Pulling Falon closer, I slid my arms around him and whispered, "I want on top."

He ducked his head to kiss the feather on my neck and chuckled, low and sexy in my ear. "And I want to fuck you on all fours from behind in front of every person here. We can't always get what we want."

The picture he painted gave me a thrill as I considered it. Next to me Shaz had Arys pinned to the bed, dragging vicious wolf fangs along his exposed throat. Arys plunged a hand into my hair, his expression tortured in the best way. "Let us see you two together."

That request hung between the four of us. I hadn't anticipated it. Shaz lifted his head to glance between Arys and me. Falon's pace faltered and slowed. Before he could withdraw I wrapped my legs around his waist to stop him.

When Shaz inclined his head to agree with Arys's statement, I looked to Falon. What we had was just ours and I liked that. However, there never would be another time when our inhibitions were so low, when doing what felt natural came so easy.

Falon tipped my head back to trace a finger over the feather on my neck. It was easy to forget that he'd just dragged a blade over my flesh.

But not what he'd said. I'd never forget that.

As soon as he saw the softness creep into my eyes, Falon tilted his head to offer me his neck. "Have your way with me, succubus. Make it fast because I'm finishing with you on your knees."

If we'd been alone, he'd have spewed something dirtier. I didn't need the encouragement though. Baring my fangs, I jerked him close. He held perfectly still inside me as I bit him.

Immortal blood hit my tongue, and I shut my eyes in bliss. Due to his immediate healing, I had to bite him more than once. Falon held himself rigid over me as I basked in his power, making it my own. A bright light exploded behind my eyes, and I gasped. My fingertips tingled and burned.

"All right, you're cut off." Falon pulled away and used his hold on my hips to guide me onto my knees. "Can't have your fool head exploding now, can we?"

A drunken giggle spilled out. Somehow I had to contain Falon's power until I needed it most. Easier said than done.

When his hand on the back of my neck suddenly forced me down against the pillows with my ass in the air, my laughter stopped. I quivered with anticipation, and the bastard made me wait for it. He rubbed his cock over me several times before sliding inside. Clutching the pillows beneath me, I licked the remnants of angel blood from my lips and teeth.

How much Falon got off on his power position gave me more of a boost than his blood ever could. It got inside me in a different way. I delighted in it.

But seeing the reaction of my two loves took this exchange to an unprecedented level. As I expected, Arys watched with the keen interest of someone who'd been waiting for this visual. And he liked what he saw. He took us in from head to toe, a long, slow appraisal.

Shaz tied Arys and me together and made us work. So I met his gaze nervously to see what expression he wore.

His desire shocked me.

Eyes pure wolf, fangs slightly bared, Shaz wasn't looking at my face. He sat propped on an elbow, taking in the whole sight. And because he now wore only boxer shorts, I could see that he was hard as a rock. When he managed to drag his gaze to mine, I saw the desire flicker over his face. The raw response to his mate's pleasure. It must have matched the expression on my face when I'd walked in on Arys and him.

Shaz might have hated Falon, but he enjoyed what the fallen angel did to me. Limits were being tested tonight. For all of us.

Falon thrust hard and deep, forcing cries from me. Because he wasn't always an asshole, he reached down to rub my clit as he chased his orgasm within my body. He waited for me to clench him tight as I came before releasing inside me.

With a rustle of feathers he withdrew and pulled away. I reached back to grab his hand, whispering, "Stay close."

We had to bring this to a conclusion, and we had to do it swiftly. I needed to beat Lust at his own game. He sat there on his throne while two women and a man pleasured him and each other, basking in all this power we'd cooked up for him.

Or so he believed.

Falon moved to my unoccupied side, giving us space but staying within reach. Without missing a beat, Arys gently but firmly put me on my back. He caught Shaz's arm and pulled him in for a deep kiss before giving the wolf a playful shove.

Only once Shaz had positioned himself next to my head and I had taken him into my mouth did Arys enter me. Hooking my legs over his arms to lift my hips, he slid deep in one stroke. A visible spark lit up the bed. Being between the two of them felt comfortable even in such an overexposed setting. And yet, I still found myself reaching back with a hand for Falon to pull him closer. He obliged, letting me fist his still hard cock. Had to love that immortal stamina.

With Arys inside me the circuit felt complete. Stronger. We could snatch all the wild, sex-charged energy in the theatre and rip it away from Lust. Of this, I was certain.

No slow start for my dark vampire. He'd watched long enough to jump right to the heart of why we were here. Pumping steadily, he angled himself just so, to rub against my g-spot with each entry. I could feel his watchful stare as I sucked Shaz into my mouth over and over again.

Falon stretched out beside me, his lips grazing my shoulder. His breath came hot and fast against my skin as I slid my hand along his shaft, teasing the head with my fingers.

"Touch her, Falon." Arys's command was husky and hurried. He was tapped into all three of us, just as I was to all three of them. The cycle of energy grew, spiraling towards culmination.

Both my body and mind struggled to keep up with the onslaught of sensations. Maybe the three of them at one time was more than I could handle. It was definitely a challenge I'd be up for conquering again, provided they were all on board.

Falon's hand traveled down my ribs and over my abdomen. Despite their rocky relationship, he obeyed Arys without pause. We were all chasing the same goal. Victory.

A delicate but firm touch on my clit had me moaning around Shaz in my mouth. While Arys fucked me like a man on a mission, Falon teased the most sensitive part of me. I writhed between the three of them. It felt like I was falling. Through the bed, the floor, down into nothing.

The abyss waited, stretching its jaws open.

No power high I'd ever experienced compared with this. Based on the sounds the three of them made, I wasn't the only one.

I felt Shaz's climax before it touched my lips. His aura hummed with a palpable vibration. The taste of his pleasure brought my own, and I tumbled over the edge for the third time. Moving in unison both Falon and Shaz pulled away.

Arys dropped down over me, aligning his body firm against mine. Darkness lurked in his eyes. Holding my hip so he could thrust hard and fast, he waited for the first orgasmic waves to hit. On a ragged groan, he whispered, "Show Lust who he's fucked with, my queen."

Metaphysically I reached out for the massive swell of lust and desire that drenched the entire place and every person in it. Falon's power raged through me, allowing me to grab hold of it all. Now to channel it through me, guided by everything Arys and I together commanded here with our companions.

I grabbed everything I could, flavored it with my allure and threw it right at Lust. Arys sat up, pulling me with him, holding my hand to help guide the flow. Meeting the demon's scarlet gaze, I watched his eyes widen as realization struck.

But it was too late for him.

So much primal force overwhelmed Lust. As I'd learned from my time here, these demons only had the power that their victims gave them. And I took it all for myself.

Lust underestimated me. He didn't know what I was capable of. Sometimes, neither did I.

This time I knew.

Confidence curled my lips into a sensual smile. Holding Lust's attention was easy enough. All of that erotic energy flavored with my touch, driven by my command, I fed the force into him, drowning him in it. I willed it to take him. Luring him in and under my thrall.

The demon's fingers clutched the arms of his chair as he fought the urge to come to me.

I didn't move a muscle, just kept that heady force flowing, pounding him like a torrential downpour.

And it worked. Lust pushed away the people who'd been servicing him without so much as a glance. He couldn't tear his gaze from me. Tucking his robe around him, the demon glided toward the bed.

My heart flipped as I steeled myself. Lust wouldn't be the first demon I'd seduced. There was no room for nerves or second guessing.

Lust stopped before the bed, and for a moment I thought he'd resist. Then he ever so slowly slithered onto the mattress next to me and cupped the side of my face in a hand.

I crushed Arys's fingers between mine, hoping that he'd stop this at just the right time. We had to make our point, but I wasn't screwing Lust to do it. My harem was as big as I intended it to get. For that matter each had been carefully chosen: Only those I trusted. Only those I loved, in one way or another.

Lust deserved to get played at his own game. I was going to enjoy this.

In a swift motion I never had time to prepare for, Lust crushed his lips to mine. A forked tongue delved into my mouth. I braced against the unexpected invasion. The demon's hand crept to my throat, and Falon's mark grew warm in response to the unspoken threat.

Willow's voice came from behind me. "Call it, Pride. He forfeits."

"I'm not sure about that," came Pride's smooth reply. "It appears to be a mutual exchange to me."

"That's bullshit," Willow argued, ire in his voice. "He's completely under her thrall. This challenge is over. Alexa is the clear winner. Now fucking call it, asshole."

Pride's silence concerned me. So I grabbed Lust by the jaw and shoved his face away. "On the floor. On your knees."

The moment of truth.

Now we'd all discover if Lust was just a dirtbag using any excuse to cop a feel or if he'd really fallen victim to my supercharged thrall. I'd taken command of the theatre, bent all the power to my will. Now I would bend him too.

A soft laugh fell from Lust's lips. He shoved away from me like he couldn't refuse the command. Sliding from the bed and going to his knees on the floor beside it, the demon obeyed.

"Well played, succubus," Lust said with a nod of defeat. "You are a queen worthy of the title. I don't suppose you intend to finish what you started." He tipped his head in the direction of his robe-clad erection.

Without bothering to answer, I tugged my dress back into place. It would be nothing short of a miracle if I could walk on these wobbly legs now.

"All right," Pride finally agreed. "Well done. I have to say it was nothing short of entertaining."

You'd never have guessed the guy had just watched a succubus and her lovers roll a Lust demon. If Pride himself wasn't involved, it didn't seem to affect him. Whereas poor Loric had dissolved into a puddle of desire and ended up in an orgy with several others. Maybe he wouldn't be such an uptight dick afterward.

"Clean yourselves up," Pride quipped, spinning on the heel of an expensive shoe. He spared a derogatory glare for Lust who still knelt on the floor. "One of you faces Wrath next."

CHAPTER TWENTY-SEVEN

Twenty minutes later we stood in front of Wrath and his fight cage. Our success with Lust had inspired a renewed confidence in all of us. We'd found our stride, and now we had to take this all the way to the end.

My entire body trembled under the onslaught of power that ran wild through me, demanding release. My fingertips kept bursting into silver flames with unfamiliar whirls of color, everything I'd stolen in the theatre. Falon covered my hands with his, quelling the fire.

Power crashed about inside me. Primed from everything I'd taken in Lust's theatre, I had become a weapon that knew only destruction.

Tapping Falon's power had given me the boost that made it almost easy to topple Lust, but I would still need it to break us out of here. I could feel it. Meanwhile I commanded a force created for an immortal, not for a hybrid who'd once been human. I wouldn't be able to hold this long.

Arys stuck close on one side to help me manage the overload. On my other side, Falon kept the top of my head from blowing off. For now.

"Let me fight Wrath." Nobody expected Willow to make that demand. Like the rest of my vampires, he buzzed with the aftereffects of the high in the theatre. It seemed to have filled him with pep and vigor.

Pride frowned. We'd been entertaining to him until now. After turning the tables on Lust, he didn't seem as fond of us. "You haven't even heard the stakes."

"Yeah, don't care." Willow turned to Wrath who leaned on the cage of the ring, looking bored. "You want this, don't you?"

Wrath considered this, eyeing our group with slight interest. "Sure, why not?"

Pride huffed in annoyance. "You know what? Fine, have it your way. When he makes a mess of you in there, don't ask for a do-over."

"What are you doing, Willow?" I touched his arm.

"I'm challenging Wrath." He turned an uncharacteristically vicious grin my way, like fighting a Sins demon was no big deal. Despite wolf eyes, the intoxication of so much vampy excess pushed his limits. He had a jovial but dangerous glint in his eyes. I'd seen it before, usually preceding his involvement in a bar brawl. "Once I finish with him, we can deal with this asshole and go home." He jerked his thumb toward Pride.

As an angel Willow could lay a beating on a demon and brush his hands off after, no problem. I worried that he was forgetting his new limitations.

"Do you really think that's the best way? Shouldn't beating Wrath require a more peaceful approach?" Beating Wrath by giving in to wrathful urges seemed counterintuitive. And most importantly, I didn't want Willow to get hurt.

"All that matters is that I beat him." Willow shrugged and tucked a lock of disheveled hair behind my ear. "Trust me. I know what I'm doing."

He turned to enter the ring. Not one of my companions seemed to find Willow's choice to be as solid of a plan as he did. We all watched in silence as he took his place in one corner. Falon, however, seemed relieved that it wasn't him in the cage this time.

When they met in the center, Wrath's massive antlers and thick body gave the illusion that he towered over Willow. Nothing about this felt good to me.

"If he gets his ass kicked, we intervene," I informed Falon, aware that he might be the only one who could fight an immortal like Wrath.

"Breaking all the rules tonight, are you?" Pride mused. "Trust me, I hope your man wins. I want my turn to make all of you regret intervening in my business."

Loric, having recovered somewhat from the orgy next door, flung a hand in Pride's face. "How can you let them get away with this? You saw what they did in the theatre. You said they'd never get this far."

Did he now? Yeah, I didn't doubt that. Pride couldn't fathom for a second that we might actually be a threat to him and his demonic playground.

"I say a lot of things," Pride agreed with a nod meant to placate the irate vampire. "But have I ever steered you wrong?" So confident in that statement.

Loric faltered. The poor bastard didn't know what the hell was going on. Pride had him second-guessing his own good judgment.

A bell signaled the start of the first round.

Willow darted forward like a savage beast that knew no bounds. He rushed Wrath, slamming a fist into the demon's jaw hard enough to cause blood and spittle to fly. Willow pulled back to avoid a defensive hit and launched a shot of amped-up energy that ran dark and hot.

Naturally, Wrath's immediate reply was a spinning psi ball he slammed at Willow.

He expected no less. Holding both hands out, he pushed back before the psi ball could hit, deflecting it back at Wrath. It struck him in the wing just above his shoulder. An audible pop and Wrath unleashed a pained shriek. Though the target had appeared random to me, Willow had exploited a known weak point in the wing structure.

The demon reacted with nothing but the wrath of his kind. Being pegged so early on in this fight understandably pissed him off. However, nothing about Wrath could compare to all that Willow had once been or even all that he was now. His own worst enemy, the angrier Wrath grew, the more he drew the same emotion from Willow.

And Willow had the control to use that to his advantage.

The fight went well until a slap of power nailed him in the middle, doubling him over. When Willow went down with blood pouring from his nose, I gasped and took an involuntary step forward.

It left him open for another attack, which Wrath didn't hesitate to take.

Falon caught me by the wrist and whispered, barely enough for me to hear, "Wait. He's baiting him."

Sure enough, when Wrath surged close with a dagger mysteriously in hand, Willow met him with both hands outstretched. The force that burst from him threw the demon off his feet. Wrath slammed against the cage and dropped hard to the mat.

I expected him to get right back up, but he flailed about and clawed at his throat. Blood stained his lips and spilled from his nose.

Willow jumped Wrath in a blink. He slammed the demon's head against the mat. At point-blank range he fed the metaphysical attack. Wrath had left his guard down after underestimating the guardian angel-turned-hybrid. Perhaps Willow's power was no longer angelic, but his heart always would be.

Besides, he had the knowhow to kick some demon ass.

They should never have expected less.

As I watched Willow unleash his fists all over Wrath, it became evident that he had a fuck ton of steam to let off. This was therapy for him. Wrath tried to fight back, but the sulfur-tainted blood pouring from every orifice in his head made that difficult.

When Brook had come to confront Willow after his turn to vampire, he'd promptly had his ass handed to him in a similar fashion. He hadn't stood a chance. A demon of higher standing, Wrath proved able to withstand more abuse than Brook.

In my excitement my fingertips again burst into flames. Falon quickly subdued the immortal charge. "If you can't keep this under wraps, I'm going to have to siphon it off you. Calm down before it gets away from you."

"Are you okay, Lex? Your eyes are flashing silver." The concern in Shaz's tone didn't match the rigid way he held himself, eyes all wolf and senses on high alert.

"Yeah, no worries. I'm not hearing thoughts this time." And thank God for that. In my pre-vampire days a dose of Falon's power had left me setting things on fire at random and hearing the freely given thoughts of every being around me. I hadn't been strong enough then to block it out.

Standing stiff, as far from Falon as he would let me stretch, I flinched when Wrath lashed out with a wild, frantic attack. Willow tumbled and rolled ass over end. Blood streaked his face, but I couldn't tell who it came from.

The demon shoved to his feet, but he was weak and injured. Willow had not been fucking around. I was starting to think that none of us knew who he really was.

Wrath must have come to this conclusion too because he didn't waste a second calling forth a searing shock of red lightning. It lit up his hands as he advanced on Willow. I pulled against Falon, but he held tight and bitched about my idiotic impulsiveness.

However, Willow anticipated Wrath's desperate attack. He knew if it landed it would be brutal. Possibly even fatal. So he never let it land.

On his feet by the time the demon threw the lightning bolt, Willow didn't defend or block. He surprised us all by extending a hand, palm open, and catching the bolt. He tamed Wrath's magic and bent it to his will. Then he threw it right back in the demon's face.

Wrath went down twitching and grunting. His face smacked off the mat, antlers clattering, twisting his head at a forced angle. Before he could recover Willow was on top of him, swinging a hand tipped with fierce claws. He punched those razor-sharp points into Wrath's chest. The demon screamed, a shrill sound that drew the attention of nearly every person in the place.

Willow tore the demon's heart free and dropped it to the mat before crushing it with a heel. That effectively put an end to Wrath's activities here tonight. Forced back to the other side, the demon vanished, leaving only a crimson smear behind.

So that answered the question regarding whether or not demons could be banished while the wards were in place.

"Well, what do you know," Falon muttered, half in wonder, half annoyed. "You can change a tiger's stripes, but he'll still be a tiger."

His ridiculous observation didn't really make sense, but I was too busy gaping at Willow in awe to think about it. Pride also watched Willow, and he looked pissed.

When Willow exited the cage rubbing his knuckles and returned to where we waited, Pride snapped something in the language of the immortals.

It sounded like a threat. Falon, Willow, and Gabriel all reacted, taking defensive stances that made me nervous.

"Care to repeat that for the rest of us?" Arys oozed menace.

Pride's glare tossed daggers, though Arys was unflinching since he himself was simply too arrogant. "Any further rule breaking or game changing from any of you will be met with the immediate death of one or more of your party."

A murmur of angry mutters and expletives moved through our group. If Pride was threatening our lives, he must be worried. Our last challenge would be his.

"Cut the crap and get on with the show," Falon snarled. "Let's be done with this already."

He had yet to let go of my hand, and it was a damn good thing too. I felt like I was about to burst. A steady, knife-like throb began in each of my temples. Not a good sign.

"Oh, we are most certainly getting on with it." Through clenched teeth, Pride struggled to keep up his cool-as-a-cucumber front. "You will all regret coming here."

"Trust me, we already do," I said, every word taking more effort than it should. All of my strength was being used to hold back the force from the theatre. That self-generated barrier wouldn't hold much longer.

Pride's mood had changed significantly enough that I knew he'd finished having fun with us. And I knew before he laid out his challenge he would choose Arys. Still, it came with a twist that threw me.

"The only way to beat the sin of pride is to lay down your own." A mask of malice stole over Pride's handsome face. "And I know from our very little time together that two of you simply can't do that. It's such a shame when brothers fight, isn't it?"

Arys and Jenner exchanged a look. Son of a bitch. Pride was a clever bastard. He knew it too.

When nobody responded to his purposely dramatic remark, Pride ran a hand over his lapel and chuckled. "Brothers often want what the other has. A city. A woman. Power of every kind. There are only two ways for such rivalry to end. Death. Or humility. Either one of you submits or you destroy each other. Best of luck to you both."

"Wait, what?" Alarmed enough to make the air around me crackle and pop, I blinked in confusion. Did I really hear that?

"Why so befuddled, succubus? Surely they've fought over you before. Though I can't imagine why." Pride caught a black lock of my hair between his thumb and forefinger, twisting it. His devilish gaze raked over me, and he frowned. "These things happen. It's only a matter of time really. I'm just helping the natural course along."

I slapped his hand away and recoiled.

With a simple question, the demon brought Jenner and Arys under his influence. "What is the one thing you can never forgive the other for?"

Was this guy freakin' kidding me right now? The one thing I'd been telling Arys and Jenner they needed to get over was what Pride would use to pit them against each other.

I questioned Pride's tactic when neither vampire reacted… at first. Next to me Arys stiffened, his hands clenched into loose fists. When I reached to touch his arm, Falon snatched my hand back with a vigorous headshake.

Jenner broke first. He let out a harsh breath and gave a mirthless laugh. "You know what you did, Arys. I wish I could forgive you for it, but it's hard when you're not fucking sorry. I want to be the bigger man here, but every time I look at your smug face, I relive the night I caught you with her."

"Oh, for fuck's sake," I hissed beneath my breath. Pride had compelled them to lay it all out there, and it was happening.

"Your problem, Jenner," Arys fired back, all hot under the collar, "is that you never let anything go. You never learned to share. Whether it be Harley's affections, this nightclub, the city, the women—who, by the way, make their own decisions, past and present. You fucked my wolf in your hotel room. Trust me, you'll never be the bigger man."

The absurdity of it all had me doing a literal face palm. Confidence suited Arys, but ego didn't look good on anybody. Arys always had been a cocky guy who ran too high and hard at times. Still he'd humbled himself to both Shaz and me. I knew him to be capable of laying down his pride for another.

But for Jenner? I couldn't be too sure. Pride had chosen well for Arys's challenge.

"Never learned to share?" Temper flaring, Jenner's brows snapped together. "Maybe because I spent decades getting your cast offs and hand me downs. Everything and everyone had to be yours first, and you needed me to know it. Just like you flaunt Alexa. *Your* wolf."

"Hey, Alexa isn't some trophy to be won," Shaz protested.

I shook my head to quiet him. We couldn't argue here. This wasn't our fight and Jenner wasn't wrong.

Arys sure thought he was though. "Alexa being my wolf is just a fact. Clearly, I don't make her decisions for her, or you'd never have gotten close enough to do more than grovel at her feet. You came to me for help this time, Jenner. Have you forgotten that?"

Surely there had to be a way to bring their feuding to an end although I couldn't see it. I glanced at Gabriel but he shrugged. He knew nothing.

"You know what?" Throwing his hands in the air, Jenner launched into motion. Everyone tensed, but he just headed for the elevator. "I don't want the club anymore. I'm done with this city. Done with all of this shit. Let me the fuck out of here." Anger guiding his stride, Jenner stalked away.

We all knew that Pride had no intention of letting us leave here as anything but defeated. He would never give up his hold on this place. That meant that Jenner had to. That was the real test, wasn't it? The twist so to speak. Either Pride didn't expect us to catch onto it, or he didn't realize that he'd left that loophole.

So why didn't it feel like we'd won?

Arys followed hot on Jenner's heels. Grabbing the other vampire by the shoulder, he whirled him around. "Don't you dare walk away from me," Arys seethed through bared fangs. "The only reason we're even in this mess right now is because of you and your sick attachment to this hellhole. You don't get to just leave."

Jenner shoved Arys's hand away. "Don't fucking touch me."

Here we go. I couldn't count how many bar fights I'd seen start this way. So tightly I clutched Falon's hand, it made my muscles cramp and bones ache. Yet it was nothing compared to the mass of power that swelled inside me, threatening to force its way out.

"Falon," I said for his ears only, "I can't hold it any longer." I peered up at him, an unvoiced question flitting through my eyes.

He merely nodded. "Trust your timing."

Jenner threw the first punch. Pretty sure we all saw it coming, including Arys who held up a hand to invite a second one. His head snapped to the side, and he rubbed his jaw with a devious glint in his eyes.

"You're fucking crazy, you know that?" Jenner lifted his chin, a silent invitation for retaliation.

Arys slammed a fist into Jenner's face. "Oh, yeah, I know."

The fight was on as the two vampires beat each other bloody. Broken noses and split lips were just the tip of the iceberg. The fight grew deadlier with each swing.

"Lex, we have to stop them." Rocking on the balls of his feet, Shaz was ready to jump in to split the vamps up.

"Wait," I said through clenched teeth as the pain in my head grew stronger. More demanding.

Arys threw the first power shot. The tug on our bond rippled through me, and I toppled to my knees as the energy surged to my limits. Silver fire filled my hands but didn't burn my flesh. I marveled at it in wonder, amazed by the colorful, oily sheen of the power. How the hell could I control such a force?

Both Shaz and Falon moved to help me up, but I waved them off. On my knees with my skirt pooled around me, I held out palms filled with flames. I knew what I had to do. It was the only way to truly end this.

As my two vampires fought, I felt their internal tug of war, the never-ending battle between them. Somehow they would have to begin again, start over with each other. There would be no winner here tonight. Pride had made sure of it.

However, I planned to make sure that he too lost something.

The demon's attention was occupied by the sheer hurt the two vampire brothers inflicted on each other. Presuming we fought by his rules, he had no idea what was coming. Both Pride and Loric watched as shots were taken and insults hurled.

They had this in the bag.

Until they didn't.

Refusing to play this game any longer, I gave in to the tsunami-like force and let it spill out, using my body as its vessel. Flames poured from my fingertips. I directed the flow like a sea of molten titanium that engulfed Pride and Loric.

The demon recovered fast, quelling the flames that ravaged his suit and singed his hair. Loric suffered greater damage as he fled in a panic. I let the fire pour out, needing to purge myself of everything I'd stolen. Quickly the flames spread, igniting patches of carpet, Gluttony's altar, and a large tapestry on the wall behind the fight ring.

People panicked, fleeing for the various exits. The spells of the Sins demons shattered as the humans' base need to survive overruled all outside influence. Pandemonium broke out. Everything Pride and his crew had built began to crumble around them.

In the face of defeat, Pride's ego proved fragile. Watching the flames spread fast from altar to altar, climbing the walls to the main floor, he lifted a dismissive hand. "This was merely one of many such establishments I occupy. Your stunt is little more than a minor inconvenience. Do you think they'll feel the same way?"

Pride inclined his head to where Arys and Jenner had Loric cornered near the elevator. The latter was no longer in flames, but he crouched on the floor, burnt hands raised in surrender. The demon didn't wait for a reply. He vanished, as they often do, leaving me with the choice I'd just made.

"Come on, we have to get out of here." Shaz pulled me to my feet.

My hands were soot stained, but the flames had stopped. No matter how much I wanted to let my wolf drag me along to the nearest exit, I couldn't leave anyone behind.

"You go," I told him, shoving him gently. "I'll be right behind you."

Shaz was the only one who'd die from smoke inhalation. Lung damage would hurt like a bitch, but it wouldn't kill me. I waved a hand at Willow and Gabriel to go with him. They didn't hesitate.

The heat grew immensely as the fire spread. Flames now engulfed the theatre. We had to hurry before the building collapsed.

"What is with you and fires in this city?" Falon shook his head.

Together we waited while Arys pinned Loric in place. Jenner snapped the leg off a chair and shoved it through Loric's heart. I watched them united in this small act of vengeance. When Loric was just ash on the blackening floor, the four of us ran for the exit behind the fight ring with Falon bringing up the rear.

Up a flight of wrought iron stairs and out in the night, we were greeted by the sound of sirens. Although when wasn't there the sound of sirens in this city?

I coughed and spit as my lungs rejected the trauma I'd just subjected them to. My chest ached but my head felt clear.

"Jenner," I said when I could suck in a lungful of fresh air. "I'm sorry. About your nightclub."

We stood in the alley behind The Wicked Kiss Las Vegas, listening to the approach of emergency vehicles. I did feel bad, but it was just a building. Jenner needed to know that it didn't define him or what he had in this world.

"No worries, Alexa." Turning his soot-covered face away before I could read the emotion in his ice-blue eyes, Jenner massaged the back of his neck. "It was just another hand-me-down anyway. I'm done with that shit." He trudged down the dark alley, leaving us to watch the last piece of Harley Kayson's legacy burn.

He'd clung to his maker's memory as long as he could, but now he walked free. Whether he liked it or not.

CHAPTER TWENTY-EIGHT

Our bags were packed. I was more than ready to leave the city that had never been mine. Dropping my bags near the door of the suite, I ventured down the small hall toward the room Willow, Gabriel, and Jenner shared.

Jenner had disappeared after the fire. Just before sunrise he'd returned to the hotel. He really had nowhere else to go. He had spent the day in this room not wanting to speak with anyone, especially Arys or me. But our flight was leaving soon. Right after sundown. And I needed to know if he planned to be on it with us or not.

As far as what the news reported, the fire appeared to be an unfortunate accident. Most likely a story spun by the local FPA to keep anyone from looking too closely. Nobody was killed, although some were trampled as people rampaged their way out of the building. By the time the fire department had the blaze under control, nothing remained worth saving. Not that there ever had been.

The Wicked Kiss Las Vegas would be a complete tear down.

The door to the room opened, and Gabriel stepped out with a small suitcase in hand.

"Has he said anything about coming home with us?" I asked in a hushed tone.

"Not really. Willow asked him about it, and he seemed kind of on the fence. He doesn't think Arys wants him there. I'm not sure he's too keen on being there either." Gabriel flashed me an understanding smile. "I get it. I've been the one on the outside looking in. But personally, he's better off with you than without you. Maybe you can make him see that while I take your things down."

"Hey, Gabriel," I called after him.

He paused and glanced back.

"I'm sorry. For believing what Hurst said about you." I wished that I could give him more than that, but it seemed to be enough.

He gifted me with his soft smile. "It's cool, Alexa. I'd have believed it too."

Willow, Arys, and Shaz had gone down to the lobby already. I didn't doubt that they'd found their way to the roulette table while they waited for the rest of us to get our shit together. Knowing that Jenner was alone in the room, I went to the door and knocked without hesitation.

"Jenner?" Slowly, I nudged the door open to find him sitting on the sofa staring out the window at the city below. "Can we talk for a minute?"

"Don't you have a plane to catch? Wouldn't want to miss that." Jenner never glanced my way. With his knees drawn up in front of him, arms clasping his legs, a boyishness clung to him that caused me to stop in the doorway.

Not that long ago I'd tried to encourage him to leave my city. Now I was going to encourage him to come back and stay. I took a steadying breath.

"I don't want you to miss it either," I replied. Assaulted by his morose vibes, I waited there in the doorway, wary of venturing too close unless invited.

Jenner continued to face away, speaking to me without looking in my direction. "I thought I'd be staying," he said softly. "It never really occurred to me that it might not work out that way. I feel like an idiot."

"Jenner, no, you're not. Of course you're not. Anyone in your position would have thought the same. But I want you to know that you'll always have a place with us in Edmonton. There's so much more to you than this city. Maybe it's time to let it go." When he whirled to face me, I expected anger.

Instead his shoulders slumped. A dull cast dimmed his usually brilliant eyes. "You're kidding yourself if you think Arys would be okay with that."

My blonde and black ponytail bounced as I shook my head. "I don't give a crap what Arys thinks. I want you there. Maybe I'm wrong, but I kind of think you want to be there too. Unless you hate me for burning your nightclub down, in which case I totally understand."

It was a shit poor attempt at humor. Jenner and I didn't know each other well enough for me to recognize how to bridge this gap. Just because he and Arys had their issues didn't mean that he and I had to. I hoped we could get past this. It had just started to feel like we were getting somewhere.

A tight, pinched smile marred his features in a way that looked painful. "I know it was probably for the best. And I know I should probably stay here and figure out my next move. But honestly, I'd rather be with you. All of you. Your cold-ass city, your demon insanity. Even Arys, that shit-sucking motherfucker."

"Then what's stopping you?" I gestured to the T-shirt flung over the back of the couch and his obviously not packed suitcase.

Jenner glanced back out the window, and the longing expression he wore made my heart ache. This was the only home he'd known for so long. It had been ripped away from him, and starting new could be so damn terrifying.

"Fear, I guess," he admitted with a sheepish grin. "Of change. And you. Maybe myself."

There was my invitation. Not spoken in so many words but I recognized it just the same. I crossed the room to the couch and sat beside him. "Please don't be afraid of me. That's the last thing I want any of you to feel. Hate me if you need to but don't fear me."

Pressing his lips into a tight, thin line, Jenner mulled this over. His gaze darted to mine for a brief second before flicking away again. "All right, so maybe it's not you so much as it's me and the way I'm starting to feel toward you. Not to mention my rotten history with Arys."

I tensed, unprepared for this part of the conversation. Knowing when to keep my big mouth shut, I said nothing and let him put the words together on his own.

"I don't know why I said that. It's not like that. I mean, it is but not the way it came out." Making a noise of frustration, Jenner punched the couch cushion. "Don't worry, Alexa, I'm not in love with you or anything like that. But I like being around you. I like having a relationship with a woman that isn't just blood and sex. You're different. You actually give a damn and I like that."

His words meant a lot to me. My connection with each of them had been weighing heavily on me lately. To have him acknowledge me as something other than a mad queen made me feel like I was doing something right.

"Thank you, Jenner." I picked at a loose thread on the seam of the couch. "It's been a difficult adjustment for all of us. I don't want anyone to feel like they don't matter. I'd like us to be close, in whatever way feels safe to you. And I hope that includes coming home with us."

Unfurling from his curled position, Jenner swung his legs down and turned to put us shoulder to shoulder. Then he stretched like every guy in a teen movie ever and slid his arm around me. "You are definitely the better half. Arys does not deserve you." Resting the side of his head against mine, Jenner released a long sigh filled with decades of exasperation.

Patting his leg, I chuckled. "I know."

He seemed to just need to sit there in the quiet hotel room before making his final departure from Las Vegas. So I sat with him until we couldn't stay any longer.

Gently taking his chin in my hand, I pressed a kiss to the edge of his mouth. Then another directly on his lips. "We have to go. Need a hand packing?"

Jenner lingered, prolonging the small intimacy. "No, I'm good. It'll only take a few minutes to throw my stuff in my bag. I'll meet you guys down there."

With a nod, I gave his leg a warm squeeze and got up to leave.

As I passed through the door, Jenner called, "Thanks for trying, Alexa. We didn't exactly get off on the right foot with each other, but I feel good about where we are now."

"Me too." I did feel good about it. Incredible really.

The rocky relationships I'd had with both Jenner and Gabriel were evolving into genuine friendships. It brought me nothing but relief. As long as Willow and I were still all right after everything that had transpired here, I could rest easy.

I left the suite and ventured downstairs where I found Shaz and Gabriel waiting in the lobby with the small mountain of everybody's bags. Shaz jerked a thumb toward the casino, indicating where the other two had disappeared. Just as I'd thought.

Unable to quell my eagerness to leave, I glanced out the front doors of the lobby, watching people get in and out of taxis. I just wanted to be home. Texts from Jez had informed me that all was well. But when she asked if I'd spoken to Falon today, I knew something was up.

Aware we were flying home right after dark, Falon hadn't shown here. I expected to see him back at home. Apparently he was supposed to have told me something. When I pressed Jez further, she claimed to be busy, told me to have a safe flight, and said we'd catch up later.

I'd be annoyed at the two of them later, when I was safely back on the ground in my own city.

* * * *

I never understood why people rave about hotel beds. Finally back in my own bed after three nights of mayhem and fuckery, I'd never felt anything better. After what we'd endured in Vegas, I was treating myself to a solid twenty-four hours in bed with Netflix.

"Totally saw that coming," Shaz said, munching loudly on barbecue potato chips. He waved a hand at the TV across from the bed. "I never trusted that guy."

I scoffed and fluffed the pillows behind me. "Gotta call bullshit. You had no idea. Unless you watched ahead without me, and you would never do that would you, Shaz?" Turning my best threatening glower on him, I held it until he laughed first.

"No, never. That would be a gross betrayal of trust."

"Damn rights." I settled back in against the pillows, ready for another episode of *Ozark*.

Shaz surprised me by pausing it. A serious expression stole over his face. His jade-green gaze strayed toward the bathroom door. The sound of the shower came muffled from within.

"Do you really think it was a good idea to bring Jenner back with us?" he asked, voice low. "I mean, there's a lot of history there. Bad history."

Certain that Arys couldn't hear us and not giving a damn if he could, I shook my head. "Then it's time for them both to grow the hell up and get over it. Make new history, so to speak. How this all plays out is up to Arys and Jenner. For the most part, we need to stay out of it."

Shaz stared at the closed bathroom door for a moment longer. "Yeah, you're probably right. With everything that's going on right now, I just hope they can work together when it matters most."

"Arys is an instigator. I don't think he can help it." With an eyeroll in the direction of the bathroom, I puffed a loose strand of hair out of my face. "But I know deep down they love each other. Otherwise they'd have killed each other by now."

His soft laugh lightly shook the bed beside me. "Good point. I can definitely relate to that."

I rolled my head to the side to better take him in. Since we'd been home a mere twelve hours, we hadn't spoken much of Vegas or anything that occurred there. The three of us had dropped our bags and lounged in bed for some much-needed chill time.

"So... Vegas." It wasn't the smoothest start and I chuckled awkwardly. "Are you cool with everything that went down there? Is there anything we should talk about?"

Shaz propped himself on an arm facing me. He pretended to think hard about it, furrowing his brow and pursing his lips. "Well, the group scenario was interesting to say the least. I'll admit I enjoyed parts of it more than I expected. However, I could do without the demon audience and surrounding orgy next time."

"Next time?" Surprised, my brows shot up. He had to be joking.

Shaz's expression turned flirtatious and playful. A teasing smile tugged at his mouth. "Knowing you and Arys, there's bound to be a next time. And I'm up for that. Although I think I'll always prefer a smaller group."

"Too many swords for you?" I teased, wiggling both brows.

"Yeah, I'm still getting used to just having an extra one around—I think that's my limit personally—but whatever you want, I'm on board." He leaned in to press his lips to mine. "Even Falon. I hate him but he does something to you. It's almost therapeutic."

You have no idea.

It felt good that, of everything Shaz had taken from that strange encounter, he'd gained an understanding of Falon as someone of substance.

"Yeah, he does." I nodded, my cheek rubbing against the soft cotton pillowcase. "Thank you for noticing. Really. I mean that." What a weird friggin' thing to thank him for.

He seemed to think so too because we both burst into simultaneous laughter. "It was hot though," he added. "I have to admit it."

"You know what was hot?" I countered with a naughty smirk. "Arys and you, together in that room. It was like opening the door to a fantasy I didn't know I had until then."

As I'd hoped, Shaz's pulse ticked up a notch. A pink tinge painted his cheeks. "Oh yeah?"

"Yeah. It was sexy as fuck." I bared fangs and bit the air, coaxing a laugh from him. "So I take it you've discovered what you want from Arys?"

Shaz gently rubbed a leg against mine, nudging his knee between my thighs. "I feel good about what went down between us in Las Vegas. Maybe it will go further one day, maybe it won't. I like where we are right now."

"Good. I'm glad. So, um, serious question. I imagine a man would know how to please another man quite well, having personal knowledge of the parts and all." I broke off, my own facing growing hot as I stumbled over what I wanted to ask him.

"Yeah, that wasn't a question, Lex." Shaz poked me in the ribs, nailing the spot that tickled.

The bathroom door swung open, and Arys strode out bare-ass naked, rubbing his hair with a towel. "There's no clever way to ask someone how good a blowjob was, my queen. Although I wouldn't mind an answer to the question you never really asked."

"Let's put it this way. If there is such a thing as a bad blowjob, I haven't had the misfortune of experiencing it." Shaz slid a sly glance in Arys's direction. "But nobody holds a candle to you, Lex."

Arys's devious chuckle made my skin break out in goosebumps. "Playing it safe, wolf. Smart man. Also, not wrong."

I stared at the two of them wondering how and when we'd entered the twilight zone. There wasn't anything about it that I didn't love, and yet it still kind of threw me for a loop. Seeing them so easy-going with one another. Cracking jokes with ease while Arys strutted about the bedroom without a stitch of clothing. There'd been a time when that would've caused major tension. Although there'd also been a time when I never imagined Shaz would ever allow Arys to get so close.

"You guys are both idiots," I declared, snatching the remote from Shaz and hitting play on *Ozark*. "Now you know the rule. No talking. And take it easy on the chip crunching."

As a result of my playful commands, the two of them tackled me. I squealed and wrestled to squirm away, but they caught me between them. Suddenly I didn't want to escape anymore.

CHAPTER TWENTY-NINE

It was nothing short of a relief to find my nightclub still standing. For obvious reasons I'd expected somebody to cause shit in my absence. It happened the last time I left. Walking inside gave me a sense of safety that I never felt in Las Vegas. This place was mine, and I would protect it from anyone who dared to threaten it for those who called it a sanctuary.

Shaz had gone to Doghead. His pack needed him, and I didn't want to monopolize all of his time. Arys had gone with him, claiming he needed a casual night of shooting pool before the inevitable shit storm began. And I'd come here, to The Wicked Kiss, to check up on my establishment and those who played within its walls.

I nodded to Justin on my way through the lobby. He beamed a brilliant smile at me and then went right back to flirting with a middle-aged lady dressed in fetish wear. This place drew all kinds. Most especially those you'd never expect. Everyday types like soccer moms and frat boys, doctors and lawyers. People whose daily lives hid their dark streak well.

Jenner and Willow were both in the building. Right away I could feel them. If Falon knew what was good for him, he'd make an appearance at some point. I wouldn't be staying long, but he could find me anywhere so he had no excuse.

After three days with six men, I needed some girl time. Jez and Smudge were watching a building on the other side of town. Something about a man with a suspicious mark, possibly ritualistic in nature. I planned to go meet them just for shits and giggles as soon as I knew everything was as it should be here.

First I slowly walked the perimeter along the wall. It gave me a good vantage point to take in everybody inside, feeling out the multiple energies for anything amiss. Many of the people, human and otherwise, were regulars that I saw frequently.

There were always new faces though, and I scrutinized each one. Anybody in here could be a spy for Lilah. Anyone could be working for her.

The thought crept under my skin and dug inside my mind. I didn't want to let her get inside my head, but out of every demon I'd faced in Las Vegas, not one of them came close to what those two twin flame demons could do together.

None of the Sins demons intimidated or frightened me.

Lilah and Salem did.

They were everything I could never be. Immortal, for one. Power that came from the deepest recesses of the abyss. How could I stand up against that? Arys and I were something unique, and we could do many things nobody should ever be able to do.

But I wasn't sure that defeating Lilah and Salem was one of them.

Falon had already placed a ward on the building to alert him to any demonic presence. Knowing that, I felt secure enough to seek out Willow. We needed to talk. I felt compelled to touch base with him more than anyone. Our friendship had severely been tested. But had it survived?

On my way toward the back hall, I passed Jenner who lounged on the red couch in the corner, flirting shamelessly with two women. Anything for the bite and tickle. Momentarily, our eyes met, and he raised his hand in a small wave. I gave him a small nod and a wink. He was such a player.

The back hall with the private rooms oozed comfy, warm desire. Yet nowhere near the amount that Lust had stirred up in the theatre. And for that I was grateful.

I hesitated outside Willow's door, Kale's old room. Only his energy seeped from the room, so he was alone. I knocked before I could chicken out and put it off for another night.

The door opened, and Willow greeted me with a friendly smile. His aura buzzed with the telltale vibe of a recent feed. Some lucky lady had just left. But I knew she hadn't gotten much more than the bite he'd sought. They never did.

"I'm going to head out to meet Jez in a bit, but I just wanted to grab a few minutes to talk to you if you're not busy." Why the hell did I have to feel so awkward? Willow was a close friend. Someone I respected and admired for who he was more than just about anybody else I knew. And yet I found myself fearing that he would look at me with dread now.

He stepped back and waved me into the room before closing the door.

Feeling uncertain standing in the middle of the room, I took a seat at the small bistro table.

"Alexa, don't feel like you have to explain yourself or apologize for anything. I know you, and I know you're probably feeling guilty as hell. Nothing that happened is your fault." Willow pulled out the seat across from me at the tiny table and sat down. He didn't look comfortable though.

"I know that," I said, even though he'd nailed the part about feeling guilty. I crossed my legs first one way then the other, unable to get comfortable myself. "I just wanted to check in with you. Make sure that everything is okay with us."

Willow erupted into reassurance. "Nothing will ever change our friendship. You know that, right? We were both victims that night."

I stared at my lap for a moment, picking at an imaginary hangnail. Once it was out there, I couldn't take it back. "I know and I'm sorry that happened to us. I'm sorry it happened to you. But what about the night after? When we made our own choice."

"We did what we had to do." Willow swallowed hard and scrubbed a hand through his dirty blond hair. Pinching the bridge of his nose, he muttered, "Fuck. That's not entirely true. I wanted to do it. Both nights. Lust may have forced me to face it, but he didn't force the rest. That was real."

I'd known that, of course, but I had needed to hear him say it. We couldn't go forward as friends, lovers, or anything at all if we didn't know where we stood with each other. "And the craving you have for me? It's more than blood." It wasn't a question.

"Yes," Willow said on a sigh, having an incredibly tough time looking me in the eyes. "Being with you made me feel more like myself than I have in a long time."

Hearing this was bittersweet. I didn't want the vampires linked to me to suffer.

Except for Briggs. He posed a problem. A problem I would have to think long and hard on how best to solve.

"Anything you need from me is yours." Steeling myself with a slow breath in, I reached across the small table to touch the back of his hand.

Willow stared at my hand on his for so long, I felt like I should snatch it back. But he got up suddenly, saving me from making the choice. "It's been so long since I've touched anyone like that. Physical intimacy isn't my strong suit. I've always been afraid of crossing the line. It seemed safer to abstain than to engage and get in over my head. I don't think I've felt as alive as I did with you that night."

I understood why he wrestled with it. I'd been his charge, the one he'd been appointed to protect. Getting involved with me would clearly be wrong if he were still in that angelic position. But he wasn't. Things changed and so did we.

"It was wrong of Lust to force us into that situation, but it wasn't wrong that we wanted it to happen. It's not wrong that we enjoyed it." Remaining seated, I met his worried gaze, seeing his need for reassurance. "It's not wrong if you want to have a physical relationship with me, Willow."

He blinked in disbelief, like he couldn't wrap his mind around the concept.

Just in case I was reading this all wrong, I added, "It's also totally cool if you don't. No matter what, you'll always be one of the best friends I'll ever have."

Willow's tension made the tiny hairs on my arms prickle and stand on end. Clutching the back of the chair he'd just vacated, something like relief overtook his handsome face. "You're not obligated to meet my needs, Alexa."

A brief flash in my mind, a memory of Willow holding me against him, shielding me the best he could as we writhed together on that chaise lounge. Even as Lust's bitch, he'd made the entire sordid thing somehow beautiful despite the circumstances. Remembering how he felt inside me brought a flush of heat to both my face and my groin.

Banishing the memory before it could coax me down a path I wasn't sure Willow was entirely ready to follow yet, I rose from my seat. "I know that I don't have to. I want to."

His knuckles strained beneath his skin. So tightly he held to the back of the chair. I expected it to break apart in his hands.

I went to him and put a hand atop his. Gently, I peeled a few of his fingers from the chair before he released it. Touching a hand to his face, I went to kiss his cheek. A friendly peck meant to bridge the awkward gap between us. He turned his head so I got his lips instead.

The kiss was soft and tender, filled with genuine affection. And that was all, because that's all either of us needed it to be right then. It felt new and strange to kiss him. I liked it though.

I turned to go but paused near the door. "I want to thank you, Willow. The respect you showed me that night when it was just the two of us, it meant a lot to me. Don't ever worry about turning into a filthy dog like the others. It'll never happen."

He cracked a grin at my teasing reference to the other guys. But he had treated me differently from them with his old school code of honor. I knew the others respected me as well, but there was a deep yearning in Willow that came out in the way he'd made love to me. The way he handled me with such care.

I wasn't sure I could fulfill that yearning, but I was willing to try.

CHAPTER THIRTY
SHAZ

The loud crack of pool balls smashing together broke through the classic rock music that blasted from the house speakers. Being back at the Doghead clubhouse felt like stepping into a corner bar after the demon insanity of Sin City. Even with the occasional brawl breaking out and the smash of dropped beer bottles, it felt peaceful.

Nearly fifty werewolves spread out around the modest-sized building. Most of them occupied the pool tables lining the back wall.

Arys and I played on the table closest to the front door. We were expecting somebody.

Since the incident with Rylan Chow being turned against his will and going on the run, I'd made it a mission to scope out the city streets and track down any werewolves without a pack. The loners and the new shifters often didn't know they were missing out on the family bond of a tight pack. I couldn't make anyone join us, but I always extended the invitation.

Slowly our pack was regaining size. The FPA had wiped out a good number of our wolves, but like the agents, there would always be more of us too.

And we all needed a place to belong.

"You son of a bitch," I swore when Arys tapped the end of my pool cue right as I took my shot. The shot rolled wide, nudging one of my own pool balls into the pocket. "I should have known you were going to do that. Dammit."

"And yet you left yourself wide open." Standing to take his shot, Arys made his way around the table. As he went by he passed especially close. Almost close enough to touch. The simplest of actions but it still caused the back of my neck to tingle.

Las Vegas had been a hell of an experience to say the least. I knew I wasn't the only one that came away from the city changed. Boundaries had been challenged and crossed for many of us.

Lex had seemed a little worried. Like she was afraid I would feel resentful once we got home. I had no regrets.

Except possibly for allowing Arys to convince me to call Falon here tonight for a little private talk. Ever since that angel mark was put on Alexa's neck, Arys had been more hotheaded and uptight than usual. I suspected he felt threatened by Falon. He was an immortal after all.

But that was the reason that I didn't feel threatened by him. Long after the rest of us had met our end, no matter at what point that happened, Falon would remain. He couldn't hold onto Alexa forever. Not any more than the rest of us could.

The thing that currently bothered me the most about the fallen angel was not his feelings toward Alexa, however fucked up they were, but the danger he put her in. Which was why I'd agreed to this meeting. Also, I figured I should be here to referee.

I don't know why I expected Falon to use the front door. When he appeared right beside me, I almost crapped my pants. Turning the pool cue on him like a weapon I snarled, "I can't help but wonder why a guy like you doesn't have a lot of friends."

Falon gave me a long, lingering assessment before he decided I wasn't worth more than a scowl. Turning to Arys, he leaned on the edge of the pool table with both hands and a raised brow. "Care to tell me why you're wasting my time?"

Arys chalked the end of his cue. Moving around the table, he evaluated each possible shot and decided on which exact one he wanted to take. He bent over and lined it up. Only after he'd successfully sunk three of my balls did he acknowledge Falon.

"Care to tell me why you really marked my wolf?" The pool cue rested loose in his grip, but I knew Arys. The tension showed through the hard shine in his eyes and the rigid set to his shoulders. Easy signs to miss for a casual observer.

"Here it comes." The fallen angel had the audacity to laugh like Arys's question was a big fucking joke. "I've been expecting this conversation, but I'm surprised it took you so long."

"Answer the question. Everything you wanted to hide all came out anyway. You're willing to go full dark for Alexa, and I want to know why." Arys twirled the cue lightly between his fingers. The illusion of cool and composed but for how long?

All three of us stood on a different side of the table. Arys stood directly across from me lengthwise, and I knew if he lunged at Falon I'd never reach him in time. Although I hadn't yet decided if I wanted to.

Falon wasn't going to tell us anything. Not the full truth anyway. Somehow, it factored into his twisted feelings for Alexa.

He looked from Arys to me. "Are you kidding me right now? The two of you are teaming up to pull some jealous boyfriend bullshit? The mark is to protect her. The second any demon so much as touches a hair on her head, I will know it. I might be responsible for one demon's interest in her, but in case you've forgotten, there's a powerhouse duo coming our way that makes Bane look like a raging Chihuahua. Might I suggest that the two of you get your heads out of each other's asses and pay the fuck attention?"

Even I couldn't adequately argue with that, aside from the whole heads in asses bit. So I tried to be the voice of reason. "Look, Falon, this isn't about jealousy. It's about how dangerously close you've gotten to Alexa. Close enough that your problems are following her. We just want to make sure that you really have her safety in mind. Nothing wrong with making sure we're all the same page with that. Right?"

The caustic scowl Falon turned on me was almost laughable. "Ri-i-ight." He dragged that word out in a sarcastic drawl. "Well, if we all want to make sure that no demon can get to her without someone knowing it, then I'd say we're all on the same page about the mark. Now, is there anything else you'd like to discuss, or can I be on my way?"

I tried to catch Arys's eye. His jaw twitched, the only sign of his temper climbing. It wasn't worth the fight. Alexa had been right when she said we needed to stay united right now. I backed her on that completely. Even now that we were home.

"She trusts you," Arys snarled, flashing fangs in a manner meant to be threatening. I found myself captivated. "Maybe you have some twisted affection for her, but I don't trust you. I don't trust what you do to her."

That was crossing into a harsher zone than I preferred. Alexa's safety had to be a priority for all three of us. Making it personal didn't keep the focus on her. When the focus shifted, it became too easy to let personal feelings cloud rationale.

Falon managed to sneer in a way that was both offended and disgusted. He crossed his arms and shifted his weight to one foot, appraising Arys like he was a bug he couldn't identify. One he considered crushing. "I have gone over and above to protect both you and Alexa during the last several months." The words hissed through Falon's clenched teeth. "Maybe you don't owe me shit, Arys, but I don't owe you shit either. Least of all answers to anything involving Alexa and me. Anything you have to say about it, you can say to her or to the both of us. I can't help but notice she's conveniently not here. Seems to me that you're missing Kale Sinclair being here to take the brunt of your jealous crap. Don't make the mistake of trying to put me in his place."

I held up a hand. When neither of them looked at me, I banged the pool cue on the edge of the table. "This isn't supposed to be an ambush or an accusation. We all want the same thing here. Falon, I'm sure you must understand on some level how we feel."

"Oh, I most definitely understand how threatened you both feel by my ability to fuck the woman you both love into a state of frenzy so powerful she forgets both your names. I also understand that neither of you would feel this way if you didn't worry that her attachment to me was more than succubus hunger and unfortunate timing." Silver wings flared wide behind him, a small but clear reminder that he was not someone to be messed with. "I never forced either myself or my mark on Alexa. The woman knows what she wants, and she knows how to get it. I suggest you take it up with her if you have a problem."

He vanished before Arys could spew whatever threat he'd been concocting as his jaw twitched and his eyes dilated dangerously.

I chuckled and reached for the chalk. "Well, that went pretty much exactly how I expected it to."

While Arys stood there fuming, I did my best to steer his mood in a better direction. When the game ended I moved around the table, collecting the balls to rack them for another round.

I paused to touch his arm. Such a small insignificant action really, but it felt big. When his immediate reaction was to grasp my hand in his, it stirred something inside me.

We'd all formed relationships that we hadn't expected. I might not like Falon and Alexa's link, but I knew that I had to respect it. Arys's connection to her made him a possessive, stubborn pain in the ass. The thought of her developing an attachment to anybody but the two of us drove him crazy despite his willingness to share her as a lover. The vampire was a puzzle.

I pressed my face to Arys's in a wolfish nuzzle which he turned into a partial kiss. A bare touch of lips before he pulled away and left me wanting.

"Your turn to break first," I said. "Care to make this interesting?"

Just the tease of a flirtatious bet and Falon was temporarily forgotten. Arys lifted a dark brow. His deep-blue gaze slid down the length of me. "What did you have in mind, pup?"

CHAPTER THIRTY-ONE

After leaving Willow's room, I took a short jaunt down the hall to check in on my office. Of course I never made the mistake of leaving anything especially valuable in there. Pausing on my way past the room that Briggs usually occupied, I poked my head in the door and glanced about.

Empty. No sign that he'd been here recently. I could only assume that meant he'd spent the last few days keeping an eye on my sister, like I told him to.

I would never trust Agent Briggs. He would never be considered a friend or family. Our unfortunate tie to one another made dealing with him all that much more difficult. Though not as difficult as his tie to my sister. I didn't want to hurt her, but seeing as my choice might come down to either killing her man or taking him to my bed to keep him from eventually losing his mind, I knew which I'd prefer.

I would rather kill Briggs than fuck him. A harsh truth but a truth nonetheless. And I was pretty sure that he felt the same. I could only hope something would occur to take the decision out of my hands. I didn't want to hurt my sister that way.

Continuing to my office, I shoved the door open and glanced about. Nobody had been in here since I left. Still I wandered over to the desk where my computer sat. My phone vibrated in my pocket, and I pulled it out to find a message from Jez telling me to hurry my ass up and to bring her some snacks.

Before I could type out a reply, the air moved behind me. Falon grabbed hold of me as I turned, causing my phone to tumble to the floor. With a hand on the back of my neck, he pressed me up against the wall beside the desk.

His breath came hot against my ear when he spoke in a harsh whisper. "Did you send your boys to interrogate me, Alexa? Doesn't quite seem like your style. Still I have to wonder." Falon held tight to the back of my neck, threatening to shove my face against the wall.

With my hands in front of me, I braced myself so that my face wouldn't get flattened. I couldn't decide if I was pissed off or turned on. A little of both.

I had absolutely no idea what he was talking about. No matter what he referred to, I knew without a doubt that Arys was the mastermind behind it. "Do you really have to ask me that? I thought we knew each other better than that by now."

"Do we?" he hissed in my ear, grinding against my ass. "You need to tell them to stand down, Alexa. They're overstepping their bounds."

Part of me was furious with Arys for whatever shit he'd done now. But it was hard to tap into that with Falon's body trapping me.

"Tell me what happened," I said, making no effort to escape.

"Your vampire's ego happened. He and your wolf called me for a little meeting in which they hassled me about this mark. Somehow Arys got it into his head that it means more than my intent to protect you from Bane." His voice came in a vicious snarl that sent a tremble through me.

Falon's hand crept up the back of my neck into my hair. He fisted a handful and pulled just tight enough to make his intent clear. The hum of his aura was strong and hot; his energy excitable with both anger and passion.

Taking every opportunity that I could to needle him, I laughed wickedly. "Arys also watched you shout in my face that you can never love me but you wish you could. Can you blame him for being blindsided by that? Because he wasn't the only one."

Saying it gave me a jolt of adrenaline. I had replayed those words so many times since he'd said them. Leaving it in Las Vegas had not been an option. An inner truth had been exposed, and it couldn't simply be swept under the rug.

"So that's where you want to take this," he responded with a sinister laugh of his own. Using the fist in my hair, he turned me slowly to face him but kept me trapped against the wall. With the other hand, he grabbed my jaw and forced my gaze to his. "You really want to tear this open and dig around in the ugly insides? All right, let's do it then. Tell me exactly how it made you feel when I said that. The truth."

Oh, fuck me. There was no looking away. No getting away. He quite literally had me exactly where he wanted me.

"Scared," I admitted honestly. "I don't understand this thing between us. I don't know how we got here. So why don't you enlighten me? It was your confession after all."

Murderous intentions flitted through his silver eyes. Seeing it gave me this little jolt of satisfaction. Falon merely tilted his head in the direction of the door, and it slammed shut. Anticipation met uncertainty in a tight coil in my belly.

Without a word Falon held my gaze, unflinching and with total command. Using the hand tightly woven into my hair, he slowly guided me to my knees before him. "You've got to give in order to get, wolf."

A strange lull settled over the room. I recognized it as the calm before the storm. So Falon needed a little encouragement to open up, did he? Our experience with Envy had left us with plenty to purge. Some of which we never would fully shed.

I moved fast but without hurry, freeing his shaft from his ridiculously overpriced pants. My hand gripped the base tight, and he groaned. I stole a moment to observe him as he watched me twirl my tongue around the delicate head. The dark desire that I'd come to know well overtook his face. He stared at me with utter contempt and yet... possession.

It wasn't really me that he hated in this moment. It was himself.

Falon meant it when he said that I was his. He believed it. And he was willing to protect that.

Breaking eye contact, I turned my full attention to forcing the right response from him. I wanted more than his pleasure. I wanted his truth. Like the night he'd broken open before me so completely.

I devoured him with my mouth, taking him as deep as I could. Firmly holding his shaft, I didn't play around with the tease or a slow build. I wanted Falon gasping my name, and I wanted it now.

"You said that you need me," I murmured, my lips moving against his sensitive flesh.

Falon quivered, and his wings flared behind him. "I need you to give me a little less talk and a lot more sucking my cock." As an afterthought, he added, "Your highness."

Freezing midmotion, I contemplated the many ways I could respond to that snarky crap. I opted to take the route that was most fun. For me. "Have you considered the care I must take with fangs in my mouth? A little slip and you could lose an inch."

"Very funny." Despite his sarcastic tone, Falon decided not to tempt the beast.

Grabbing me by my upper arms, he lifted me to my feet like I weighed nothing. He kissed me hard, crushing his lips to mine. Then he spun me around and bent me over the desk. An excited thrill swept through me from the soles of my feet to the top of my head, leaving me slightly giddy.

When he tugged my pants and underwear down in one swift motion, I clutched the edge of the desk in anticipation. I hadn't realized how much I needed this myself, but when he stroked a finger along my entrance, I was ravenous for it.

The lightest of touches teased me. Before I could enjoy it, his fingers disappeared only to be replaced by the familiar sensation of his cock at my entrance. I bit down on my lip. Falon slid deep inside me in one slow, agonizing thrust.

I gasped. "You said that it fucking kills you that you can't love me."

As expected, he slammed into me harder. "It wasn't enough for you to hear it once, was it?" he growled. "You have to throw it in my face too."

The more vulnerable Falon felt, the nastier he got. It's how I knew I was getting to him. Holding onto the desk to brace myself, I took the impact of his furious thrusts. My smile was just for me. "Why do you wish you could love me?"

He shocked me then. Suddenly he withdrew. Grabbing me around the waist, he all but flung me down on the couch flat on my back. "What I really wish is that you'd shut the fuck up. Your voice is making my dick soft." That was a blatant and obvious lie.

Falon stripped us both of the pants bunched around our ankles. Then he pinned me beneath him on the couch in my office and fucked me with a passionate fury. The way he took me with such frantic abandon had me moaning beneath him.

Forcing me into a vulnerable, intimate position was his attempt at controlling this encounter. Physically perhaps, but there were strings and I had to pull them.

"You are my queen," Falon groaned in a breathy whisper. "You are the most annoying, frustrating, pain in the ass I've ever known. I envy you. I despise you. I want to throttle you every fucking time I look at you. But you are my queen."

Catching my face in his hand, he pressed an angry kiss to my lips. We didn't do words and emotions. Not the warm and squishy kind. Everything Envy made him say was as close as it would ever get.

Kissing him back, I dipped my tongue into his mouth before pulling back to say, "Fuck me harder, you pussy."

Couldn't let it get too intimate now, could I? Because that's where the danger dwelled. I opened myself up to him, embracing the forceful way he claimed my body. Envy had exposed the broken parts of Falon that Winter had left behind. Put them on display for everyone to see. Worse than that, he'd exposed Falon's true feelings for me, and they were a complicated mess.

Falon's thrusts grew deep and punishing. This was what he needed. What we both needed. To take the angst and emotion Envy had caused and fuck it out of our systems.

We hadn't needed the demon to paint so clearly for us the intricacies of our strange relationship. On some level we had known. Since the night in the hotel room when Falon begged me on his knees, we had known.

So here we were, dealing with it the only way we knew how.

Just before I reached orgasm, Falon pressed his forehead to mine. "Everything I said on Envy's altar was true."

A small shriek spilled forth as he continued in his delicious ravaging of my body. Caught up in the dizzying spiral of pleasure, I clutched him tight with claw-tipped fingers. "I know."

"What am I to you?" Falon's question came ragged and rushed. Holding himself over me, he searched my eyes, knowing that with him inside me, I couldn't lie.

He hadn't been the only one to spill truth on Envy's altar. *I never wanted to be whatever it is I am to you. Just like I never wanted you to be what you are to me.* I had said that to him.

It wasn't something I let myself think about. And yet, the words spilled out. "A kindred spirit. Both light and dark. You think that you don't walk in both worlds, but you're wrong. Nobody knows my pain the way you do."

A slight wince creased his brow. Anguish burned in Falon's silver gaze, there for a second and then gone. He silenced me with a frantic, drowning kiss that echoed the frantic thrusts that quickly brought us both over the edge.

After the initial bliss moment faded, Falon promptly shoved away from me. Without so much as a glance in my direction, he went about getting dressed. It wasn't a classic Falon move. Rather, it seemed to be a page taken out of my playbook.

"That's it?" Sitting up on the couch, I watched him slip his pants on. A flicker of irritation chased away the afterglow. "You come in here to bitch at me, fuck me, and then leave?"

"Are you new here?" he asked with sarcasm so thick I could've walked on it. "It's what we do, isn't it? You're usually the one in a rush to take off. What do you care?"

Swallowing back my rising temper, I had to remind myself that this was merely self-preservation for Falon. A layer of his armor had been stripped away. Naturally he felt defensive.

"I don't care. You made me late for meeting Jez." Implying that I'd had better things to do wasn't the most mature response, but it sure beat slashing claws across his throat like I wanted. "Who, by the way, mentioned that you were supposed to tell me something while I was in Vegas."

Falon shrugged, in full asshole mode at the drop of a climax. "It's not a big deal. We found more ritual evidence. Looked like one of Lilah's people may have been trying to locate Shya."

"What?" I was off the couch and tugging my pants into place in record time. "When? Why didn't you tell me?"

Now I was angry. Anything to do with either Lilah or Shya was immediate need-to-know information, and he damn well knew that.

"I'm telling you now." Looking especially bored, he scrolled through his phone, most likely checking for messages from Veil members. He didn't seem to use it for much else. Angels didn't generally possess the interest in technology that the rest of us did.

"Falon, you know how important it is for me to know that. I trusted you to keep me informed of anything going on here." My voice wavered as I tried not to shout at him. It was his attitude about it that pissed me off more than anything.

Dragging his annoyed gaze to my furious one, Falon gifted me with one of those snarky asshole eyerolls I loathed so much. "I figured it could wait. You had your hands full in Vegas. Along with a few other select parts."

The way he said it took my temper from a soft boil to a raging inferno. This nasty insinuation, like I'd spent my Sin City visit indulging like a tourist on vacation. Like I should feel wrong about what happened there. What he himself had participated in willingly.

Intense, blinding rage held me captive. Speechless. Motionless. Until the first prick of angry tears stung the back of my eyes. Launching into motion, my hand flew and I slapped him hard across the face.

Gold and blue jolts of power crept up my arms. All I knew was that I needed to separate myself from him before I gave in to the violent urges.

I darted for the attached bathroom, slammed the door, and locked it. A futile effort really when dealing with someone who could easily bypass doors and walls. Leaning on the door, I fumed at the ceiling and willed myself to calm.

Falon knew how to piss me off. He pretty much dedicated himself to finding new ways to do it.

My hand stung. I hoped his face stung more.

I figured if I waited long enough he would just leave. After fifteen minutes of silence, I opened the door to find him sitting on the end of my desk.

"Alexa, I'm sorry. You didn't deserve that. Do you want to get in another one?" Turning his face, Falon offered me the cheek opposite the one I'd slapped. That apology had not been expected.

"Yes," I said honestly. "But you steal the joy from it when you offer."

"Fair enough." He dipped his head, contemplating. "How about you take a free shot any time you like? Really catch me off guard with it. I'll never see it coming." So earnest he was, willing to offer me some random abuse to show his remorse.

It did something to me. It moved me, touching me in a place I'd promised myself would forever be off limits to Falon.

Our connection often felt like feeling my way through a minefield blindfolded.

"I'll consider it," I said, teasing now. No longer could I find any rhyme or reason to this thing Falon and I had going.

A knock at the door interrupted.

I opened it to find Willow, his face etched in concern, with Justin lingering in the hallway behind him. "A courier just delivered a package for you, Alexa. I think it's from Lilah."

EPILOGUE

I rushed out of the room after Willow with panic chasing me. Any gift from a demon was no gift at all. This wouldn't be the first time Lilah had dared to send me a disturbing package right out of *Seven*. Falon followed right behind me.

Justin led us back to the front entry where he had another guy watching the package in question. One perfectly sized for a severed head. "I didn't want to bring it all the way inside without knowing what it was," he explained.

"No worries. Did anyone see who left it? If they're still in the area, we need to find them now." Seeing as the wards hadn't been triggered, she had to have used a human or vampire to send it.

"I'm on it." Justin turned to bark orders at another staff member and disappeared into the parking lot.

Turning to the inconspicuously plain box sitting near the coat check counter, I was afraid to look inside. Remembering I had found a severed head the last time.

Willow didn't hesitate to grab it. "Let's get this out of here." He didn't wait, just started moving.

So I wasn't the only one who thought there might be spies among us.

Falon nudged me to go with him and said, "I'll be right back."

I had no choice but to keep up with Willow while trying to appear calm and unaffected. I dreaded what or who I might find in the box. The bitch thought she was clever, throwing a blast from the past at me.

Well I wasn't that person anymore. I was ready to protect what was mine.

Sure she scared me. But I scared me too.

The small commotion drew Jenner's attention. Moments after we disappeared into Willow's room with the box, he entered. "What's with the mystery package and the seriously tense expressions?"

Pointing at the box Willow had placed on the bistro table, I said, "A gift from She Who Shall Not Be Named."

Jenner blinked a few times as he realized what that meant. He'd never met Lilah, so he didn't know what he'd been missing out on. He was about to find out. "Oh, I see. Well, fuck. That can't be good."

"No, it was definitely very far from good the last time she sent me a box this size." Because I'd opened it to find the head of a pack member. I still owed Zak some payback for that one.

Lilah would get hers.

Leaning over the box, my nose easily picked up the scent of blood. A scent that I knew well. Because it belonged to my favorite playmate, Ebyn Tyler.

I ripped open the box, needing to see the contents and end the agony of wondering. Like last time, I fully expected to find his severed head. But I didn't.

The box held some clothing, but it had been weighted with a few stones to make it feel heavier than it was. The only other thing inside was a small yellow envelope with bloodstains and a handwritten note.

Falon returned as I drew out the envelope first. "Found a UPS guy down the block. Pretty sure she sent him. He didn't remember anything though."

With a nod of thanks, I opened the envelope and looked inside. A chunk of fur matted with blood. No, not just fur, as I soon discovered. It was the tip of Ebyn's ear. The blood was still fresh.

"Fucking bitch," I seethed but a chill stole through me.

Lilah had come back into my city, learned about the new people in my life, and gone after one of them. From what I knew about her, this was only the beginning.

Reaching for the note, I held it out for them to read as well: *Your wolf for Shya. An easy trade. For every night it takes, I'll send you another piece of him.* She'd never been a woman of many words. Not until she was spewing vitriol at me about the curse of the twin flame bond.

Crushing the note in my fist, I shook with rage.

"Don't let her get under your skin, Alexa." Gently, Willow pried the note from my grasp. "She's not worth it. We'll find Ebyn."

I accepted his friendly reassurance with a nod, patting his arm. To Falon, I asked, "Can you make sure there are wards on my sister's apartment, Briggs's house, and the FPA building? Doghead too."

Juliet popped first into my head. She'd been the one to drive my dagger through Lilah, sending her back to the cage Salem had made for her. The demon queen wasn't so forgiving as to overlook that.

"Of course." He nodded, and a tendril of silver hair fell over his forehead. "Anywhere you want. I'll take care of it."

Falon and I shared a look. He held my gaze, encouraging me without saying a word. So much would have to be done. Protection for our homes and establishments. Nobody getting caught alone.

Dammit, I had to inform everyone who needed to know, and I had to do it fast. We had no time to waste.

Unable to keep still, I paced across the small room. When the walls began to close in on me, I had to get out. Flinging open the door, I went back to my office for my phone. I had to call Jez.

"I guess now we know for sure who was trying to locate Shya." Falon caught my elbow as I rose from picking up my phone from the floor where it had fallen. "Hey, wolf, don't let her get to you. She didn't send his head. I'm taking that as a good sign. She wants Shya bad and she's willing to negotiate."

The promise in Lilah's note echoed in my mind. "She's going to keep hurting Ebyn unless we give Shya to her. And we cannot fucking do that." My voice rose a few octaves, and I choked on my effort to breathe evenly.

Falon took me by the shoulders and forced me to meet his imploring gaze. "Don't you dare let that vile woman inside your head. Not for a second. You are the Queen of Light and Dark, remember? She is a queen of only dark." His hand was warm on my face as he touched my chin.

Thinking about Ebyn at Lilah's mercy while she did God only knew what to him brought on this overwhelming anxiety. Falon's touch steadied me, helping to clear my head and ground me.

"She's an immortal. And she isn't alone." I panicked at the thought of facing both Lilah and Salem together.

"And you were created for exactly this. To kick some demon bitch ass." Falon lightly touched the feather marking my neck. "I'll have your back. We'll do this together. All of us."

The fact that he still said that after whatever nonsense Arys pulled on him earlier spoke volumes. I knew in that moment more than any other, even after what he'd done to me on Envy's altar, that I trusted him implicitly.

Several seasons of growth and change had shaped me, bringing me to this point. My relationships were solid or getting there. Rocky starts with some of the men in my circle had been overcome. Bonds had been formed.

Arys and I had faced our worst enemy and greatest weakness, each other. And we'd survived.

We could face Lilah and Salem too. We had to.

I put my hand over Falon's. "Thank you. For everything." I wanted to offer him more, but he didn't need it.

Lightly his thumb traced the outline of my mouth before he captured my lips in a kiss that said more than either of us ever would. "Always happy to serve, my queen."

He was gone before I could fire off a snappy remark. His departure left me uneasy. I wanted all of us together right now.

I fired off a fast text to Jez, giving her a heads up and a warning to stay safe. To stay with Smudge. Then I texted Briggs. He would be more likely to respond than my sister. She was still pissed about Arys going after her.

Leaving my office, I strode down the hall with purpose in my step. It was time to gather everyone. Anger and upheaval over the past would have to be set aside by any and every one carrying a grudge.

None of that mattered now. Lilah had thrown down the gauntlet, and I wasn't backing down without a fight.

In my mind, I reached out to my dark half. Arys and Shaz needed to know. 'Bad news, babe. The bitch is back.'

ALSO BY TRINA M. LEE

Rebel Heart Series

Angel blood runs through her veins.

Half human and half angel, Spike is a rare female nephilim. Like all nephilim, she's caught in the middle of the war between angels and demons. The light and the dark.

All Spike really wants to do is chase a rock star dream with her band. She's got a best friend who's a werewolf, a penchant for partying and a problem with commitment. So she's doing her best to avoid choosing a side.

Until she meets the foxy Rowen and sly devil Arrow. Nephilim like her, they're the only pair of siblings to exist among their kind. And for some reason, the dark is hellbent on claiming them both.

These two brothers, as different as night and day, challenge Spike to discover where she belongs in this battle. They're about to turn her world upside down.

ABOUT THE AUTHOR

Trina writes urban fantasy that is dark and gritty with a twist of romance and horror but which is ultimately about people in dark places discovering who they are and what they're made of.

A lover of rock music, vampires and muscle cars, Trina is a dreamer who always secretly wanted to be a rockstar. She lives in Alberta, Canada with her bass player husband, ukulele playing daughter and small herd of cats.

Trina loves to hear from readers so don't hesitate to drop her a line on social media or via email. Find her info at trinamlee.net.

Printed in Great Britain
by Amazon